THE KING'S REDRESS

The Bewildering Adventures
of King Bewilliam
Book Three

DEVORAH FOX

Mike Byrnes and Associates, Inc.
355 Keewaydin Lane
Port Aransas, Texas 78373

Also in *The Bewildering Adventures of King Bewilliam* series:
The Lost King, Book One
The King's Ransom, Book Two

Also by Devorah Fox
Naked Came the Sharks with Jed Donellie

http://devorahfox.com
ISBN: 0-9778245-5-1
ISBN-13: 978-0-9778245-5-7

DEDICATION

to my parents, who taught me to read and always thought I'd write a novel

and to everyone who read *The Lost King* and *The King's Ransom* and asked for more.

AUTHOR'S NOTE

This is a work of fiction. Therefore, names, characters, places, and incidents are the product of my imagination or used fictitiously. Any resemblance to actual events, places, or persons living or dead is purely coincidental.

THANKS TO

Barbara Sanchez and Alice Marks, for encouragement on call.
Beta readers Mike Green, my secret weapon all these long years, and Samantha LaFantasie. The book is better because of you.
Ian Ridout and John Rojas, for having faith in me.
My Street Team: Chip Cooper, Alan White, Ellie Killian, Joyce Walters, Theresa Guettler, Orville Ballard, and Andrea Dobson. You rock.
The members of the Rockport Writers Group, the South Texas Scribes, and The Addicted to Heroines Blog Tour, all astounding writers in their own right.
Kenneth Scott, John Howell, the Parrot Heads of Port Aransas, and Mike Daigle

and Mike Byrnes, always.

CHAPTER ONE

Meeyoo had been missing for days, and King Bewilliam found it difficult to get through the day without her.

The king's dilemma would likely surprise anyone else. Meeyoo was an ordinary stray cat possessing no magical powers or exotic pedigree.

To King Bewilliam, however, she was special. She had befriended him when she was just a kitten and he was at his life's lowest point. He had not been king then, just Robin, a penniless vagabond estranged from his kingdom. At the end of a grueling day of hard labor just to keep body and soul together, he would at last bed down for the night. Meeyoo would curl up on his chest and give him comfort.

Now restored to his throne, King Bewilliam held court with Meeyoo by his side. She had her own "throne," a quarter of a barrel lined with a cushion and placed discreetly behind his grand seat on the king's dais. Although no one said as much, some might consider it inappropriate or even disturbing that a cat rather than a queen sat next to the king.

There *had* been a queen. No one spoke of her, not King Bewilliam or his sons or his knights or subjects, her betrayal had been that profound.

A queen had once warmed King Bewilliam's bed, too. These days, Robin indulged in the occasional dalliance, but if it weren't for Meeyoo he would sleep alone. A king's pampered pet, Meeyoo had grown big and heavy. While she no longer slept curled up on his chest, but instead on the pillow beside his head, Robin found it difficult to fall asleep without her purred lullaby.

Where was Meeyoo? These last few days holding court Robin would cast a hopeful sideways glance only to see her little throne vacant. *Had some harm befallen her?* Robin could not imagine what that could be. Bell Castle was a strong fortress, a solid defense against predators both animal and human. Certainly no one here meant her ill. Everyone liked Meeyoo, especially the carpenter who had crafted her throne and the baker who made special treats for her.

Meeyoo must have been enjoying those treats more than usual lately because when Robin had last seen her she looked especially fat and sassy.

He hoped that she had crept into the bedchamber during the night. He called her name but she didn't answer which was odd. She was a vocal cat. When just a kitten she had spoken to him, told him that they were destined to be companions. "Me. You," she said. "Me. You." So he had named her Meeyoo.

Maybe the stubborn feline was playing a game, hiding under the bed. Robin lit a candle to brighten the predawn-dark bedchamber and was disappointed not to find Meeyoo under the commodious bed or snuggled in the fluffy wool blankets heaped at its foot. The extra coverings were an unnecessary precautionary measure. On a winter's night, a sudden blast from the north could indeed sweep across the Chalklands and make a cold night even colder. However, the windows' sturdy shutters and bed's heavy drapes kept all but the strongest drafts at bay.

Meeyoo wasn't in his ornately carved clothes chest where she liked to burrow if he left the lid open, or on his desk, although if he were there she usually was too. *What was it about a cat and documents?* It seemed to Robin that the very scroll or parchment on which he worked or book he read was the one on which Meeyoo wanted to sit. Nor was she in his chair. Normally he needed to vacate it only for a minute to find her furry bulk filling the seat on his return.

She wasn't nosing around the breakfast tray either. Along with the king's food, the cook always prepared a dish of morsels for Meeyoo: small chunks of fowl or beef, sometimes bits of cheese or fish. As it had the last few mornings, Meeyoo's meal sat untouched.

Robin nibbled at his own repast, a little smoked fish and some watered wine that was just enough food to stave off hunger throughout a busy morning and keep him sated until dinner. He caught himself eating mindlessly and chided himself. It wasn't that long ago when vagabond Robin's morning meal consisted of water and a dried crust of trencher.

Breakfast eaten, he returned to the matter of the errant cat. Meeyoo had to be somewhere in Bell Castle. No more worrying and hoping she'd show up. Today, he would make a concerted effort to find her, conduct a thorough search. The sooner he started looking, the sooner he'd locate her.

Robin rinsed his face and hair but avoided his reflection in the polished brass mirror for fear of finding a new wrinkle near his eye, more gray in his red hair. Yes, maybe he was getting older. Well, of course he was aging but it was beginning to show in his face. Odd. He didn't feel old; he was as strong and quick-witted as he had ever been. Perhaps a bit portly these days but it behooved a king to look well fed. It spoke reassuringly to the subjects of the kingdom's prosperity. True, some mornings his joints ached on rising and after a long day of sitting on the throne. After exertion his breathing was a bit belabored. Alright, he reluctantly admitted, he was getting older.

He bid his waiting page to enter, and went about the business of getting dressed. The page shaved Robin's stubbly cheeks, helped with his many layers of clothing, and adjusted the ermine-trimmed red velvet cloak so that it would drape just right and show the heraldic crest embroidered on the back to its best advantage. Robin was fussy about that. There was a time not so long ago that he had to keep his royal blood a secret. He had removed the ermine trim and stitch by painful stitch plucked out the barry waves, the red shield of the warrior, the orange chevron of ambition, the white bull, and the falcon, transforming what had been a king's robe into a simple cloak.

Robin began a room-by-room search of Bell Castle's keep. Once the main defensive structure, the keep now housed royal bedchambers, a private dining hall, storerooms, and below ground, the dungeon.

He started with his sons' bedchambers. His inspection of his eldest son's room was cursory. For the most part the room remained closed off since Conrad no longer slept here. Having taken a vow of poverty he eschewed the luxury of royal accommodations and slept on a humble pallet in Bell Castle's house of worship.

Robin shook his head. *Where did young people get these notions?* When he was a prince he had no such inclinations. Instead he considered it his highest priority to attain the knowledge and master the skills that would serve him when he took the crown. He had taken eagerly to lessons in martial arts, in diplomacy and negotiation, in military strategy.

Conrad, now Brother Thaddeus, spoke of a desire to serve people. Why couldn't he see how much good he could do and the multitude of people that he could serve as Prince and ultimately as King of the Chalklands?

Just as problematic was Conrad's vow of chastity.

Robin sighed, closed the door, and moved on to the bedchamber of Conrad's younger brother, Zachary. Meeyoo was primarily Robin's pet but she had taken a liking to Zachary. She sometimes kept him company.

The door stood slightly ajar and Robin could see that the bed was occupied. Flung across the foot of the bed was a handsome gown, yesterday's garb of the day. The dawn light fell across Zachary's fair complexion and cast shadows on his cheekbones under dark lashes. Long strands of mahogany hair curled around Zachary's face. The shading along his jaw could be a trick of the light or whiskers that Robin knew his son would go to great pains to remove before leaving his bedchamber. In the dim illumination, Zachary presented an optical illusion. Was the figure in the bed a young man with delicate features or a tall and robust young woman?

Robin felt a pang and ground his teeth in frustration. Zachary's insistence on living as a female, on being called Princess Dale, caused Robin pain that never quite subsided. His advisors told him in as gentle and respectful terms as possible that Prince Zachary was becoming a laughingstock.

As a child, Zachary had shown a predilection for play-acting. No one took it seriously and everyone assumed he would grow out of it. Now not only did the adult Zachary pretend to be someone else, he asserted that he wasn't acting and that Princess Dale was his true self.

Like any parent, Robin wanted to see his children happy, their wishes fulfilled, but he couldn't believe that this fantasy of Zachary's was genuine. Like his brother Conrad, Zachary's personal goals removed him from the line of succession. Robin fervently hoped that Zachary could be brought to adopt the role of Prince of the Chalklands with as much enthusiasm as he embraced the part of Princess Dale. Perhaps in the light of Conrad's ecclesiastical mission, Zachary saw himself slated to inherit the throne. Maybe he found the prospect intimidating and thought to avoid the responsibilities by assuming another identity. Robin would have to show the young man that he could and probably would someday be king. He would be best served by preparing to rule rather than trying to avoid it.

Not finding Meeyoo anywhere else in the keep, Robin started down the stair tower steps. The lightening winter sky was a dull white. Against the background of unbroken cloud cover flew a single bird so huge it had to be an eagle or perhaps a vulture. It circled over the bailey and then flew off to the woods beyond the castle walls.

Robin descended the keep's motte and crossed the moat to the bailey. To his right, appetizing aromas and warmth radiated from the kitchen. He fully expected to find Meeyoo there but the kitchen staff said that she hadn't been seen that morning. "We haven't seen her for several days, Sire," said the baker. His furrowed brow spoke of his concern. "We thought that she was with you, was perhaps ill and under your care."

Robin reassured him that Meeyoo was probably fine, just hiding in a new secret place.

Robin set out for the barracks. He doubted that he would find Meeyoo there; the soldiers' quarters were noisy and busy and not a place that Meeyoo typically frequented. His gaze scoured the leafless winter shrubbery and trees for anything brown, fluffy, and frisky but all he saw was the occasional crow or sparrow taking flight. He scanned the wall walks and parapets. Guards in numbers representative of a peacetime defense paraded along the top of the curtain walls but no cats accompanied them.

As Robin crossed the bailey, the frost-covered grass crunching under his boots, he noticed the light glowing behind the expensive glass windows in Bell Castle's house of worship. It had once been a simple wooden chapel, small and drafty with dreary unpainted walls. Robin had sometimes wondered if the intent was to make the preacher's words all the more interesting by contrast.

Brother Thaddeus had enlarged the building and brightened the interior with pale yellow paint, pots of flowering plants in season, and pleasantly scented herbs which even in winter gave the room a warm and inviting ambience. Despite the morning's chill, the door stood ajar. That was another of Brother Thaddeus's innovations. "We don't want anyone to hesitate to enter because of a closed door," he had said. "We want everyone to know that they can come in any time."

Robin suspected that Brother Thaddeus would appreciate the monarch stopping by this morning, or any morning for that matter. If Robin attended church at all it had nothing to do with duty to God and everything to do with Brother Thaddeus. Under the pretense of worship, Robin would take the measure of Conrad's involvement with this inconvenient new vocation, hoping for the day when his son would come to his senses. Robin had yet to see signs of Conrad's commitment waning and was running out of patience waiting for the young man to behave like the prince he was.

Robin would be the first to admit he lacked devotion to God and he wouldn't apologize for it, either. His support of enlarging Bell Castle's chapel was not owed to religious fervor. Rather it was to satisfy a pledge he had made to entice Conrad away from Mathus Abbey, bring him back to Bell Castle and, Robin hoped, into the royal fold. The latter half of that plan had hit a snag but Robin hadn't given up on it. It was just going to take more time and time was on his side.

Conrad had no particular affection for Meeyoo but she liked the warmth of the church and could sometimes be found there. Robin slipped into the chapel. Under the guise of being engaged in prayer he looked for the cat to no avail. He headed for the door and had just about made his escape when he heard "Good morning, Your Majesty. How wonderful that you would start your day here in God's house."

Robin sighed and turned to face Brother Thaddeus or, as Robin preferred to think of him, Prince Conrad, firstborn son and successor to the throne.

Conrad made a quick and economical bow. He smiled and his normally impassive face was alight with excitement. "We are so glad to see you, Sire. We have exciting news."

"And we are delighted to hear it." Robin looked about. Did the "good news" have to do with yet another improvement that Conrad—Brother Thaddeus—had made to the church building?

Robin would be proud of the enhancements which Brother Thaddeus had made with efficiency and frugality were it not for their implications. Every sprig of lavender, every new plank in the floor, every fresh coat of varnish on the settles signified Conrad's mounting involvement with the church and his growing distance from fulfilling his destiny as heir to the throne. Conrad had spoken of his intention to abdicate his position in the line of succession in order to pursue his vocation. Robin hadn't taken it seriously, chalking it up to youthful rebelliousness and the young man's desire to express his individuality before shouldering the responsibilities of serving a kingdom. Robin was certain that with time Conrad would lose interest in a career with the church and reconcile himself to a future at the head of the kingdom of the Chalklands.

"Before we hear of your news, we have a question," Robin said.

"Yes, Sire?" Conrad was almost breathless with excitement, anticipating perhaps that the king meant to inquire about a spiritual matter.

"Have you seen Meeyoo?"

Conrad was for a moment taken aback. He composed his expression and said, "Not in several days."

"Nor have we. As we make our rounds today we are also looking for her. If you see her, please bring her to us or at least send word of her whereabouts."

Conrad nodded.

"Now, your news?"

CHAPTER TWO

The young monk's face brightened again. "We have been accepted by the order of the Guardian Angels."

Now it was Robin's turn to be at a loss for words. The Guardian Angels? This was dreadful. The Guardian Angels were monks who like Brother Thaddeus had taken vows of chastity, poverty, and obedience but they added a fourth vow. They pledged to protect pilgrims journeying to the Holy Land. Those travelers often found themselves victimized by nonbelievers who saw the pilgrims as invaders and they retaliated, often with deadly brutality. The Guardian Angels was a military order. As a member, Conrad would be traveling far from the Chalklands and exposing himself to mortal danger.

"We thought you were already a member of an order," Robin stammered.

"Yes, of Mathus Abbey, of course."

"And you have accomplished much." With a sweep of his arm, Robin included the refurbished chapel. "How can you think of leaving? What about your work here, the people that you serve, the scholarly work that you have done?"

Conrad nodded. "You do not need to be concerned about that, Sire. Your Majesty can choose another brother to take my place. The abbot of Mathus Abbey would be happy to recommend someone. Many of them can more than adequately fulfill the pastoral duties and quite a few of them are skilled scribes as well. In fact we have the abbot's full support. The abbey has made a generous donation to the Guardian Angels in honor of our acceptance.

"The order is a perfect calling for us and we are perfect for it," said Conrad. "As a Guardian Angel, not only can we continue to do a monk's work, we can make good use of all the training in the martial arts and sciences that we received as a prince. For that we have you to thank, Sire. Had we known then how valuable that knowledge and skill would prove to be we would have been a better student." Conrad chuckled.

That training had been to equip Conrad as a ruler, not a soldier in some foreign legion, Robin thought. Anger and frustration took their place alongside the deep dismay that he felt.

"There are many who wish to serve in the order but few who have as much to give as we do," Conrad continued. "In addition, when we joined Mathus Abbey, we relinquished all our worldly goods. However if there is anything of material value to which we can still lay claim, we can donate it to the Guardian Angels to fund its works."

Anything of material value? Like the entire kingdom of the Chalklands which Conrad stood in line to inherit? The king felt lightheaded as he saw the land and possessions which he had fought so hard to reclaim and maintain sold off to fill the Guardian Angels' coffers. The end of a dynasty.

Robin opened his mouth to tell Conrad "no," that he was forbidden to leave, and paused. His efforts to get Conrad to leave Mathus Abbey had been met with outright refusal. Robin had managed to get his son to leave the monastery only by convincing him that he could fulfill his vows by serving at the Bell Castle chapel. It had been Robin's hope that once he had Conrad back in a royal setting he would remember that he was a prince, someday to be king. It hadn't happened yet but while Conrad continued to renounce that role he hadn't formally abdicated. Further pressure might cause him to do just that.

On the pretext of walking to the altar to adjust an arrangement of dried rosemary Robin paced off his mounting dread. "When do you start?" *In other words, how much time is left to talk you out of this rash, foolish, and deadly mission?*

"We leave tomorrow."

"What?" Suddenly time had run out. "No," said Robin.

A line formed between Conrad's brows, the suggestion of a frown. "No?"

"No, you may not go. It's too dangerous. We forbid it."

Conrad's usual benign smile faded. His lips pinched, his eyes narrowed, and his nostrils flared. "You can't forbid us, Sire."

"We can and we have. We're your father. We're your king. You will stay here. In fact, not only will you stay here but you will dispense with your priestly charade. You are not Brother Thaddeus, you are Prince Conrad and you will behave as such. Perform your royal duties, prepare one day to inherit the throne and rule the kingdom of the Chalklands."

"We cannot do that, Sire," Conrad said. His words were measured but his tone was as unyielding as hammered steel. "We took a vow, in God's name, to serve as Brother Thaddeus however we are called. At Mathus Abbey, at Bell Castle, or in the Holy Land as a Guardian Angel."

"A vow you should never have taken, should never have been allowed to make. You were born Prince Conrad with decisions already made for you, your future already determined."

Conrad snorted. "Nevertheless, we did swear. Would Your Majesty have us break our sacred oath?"

What broke was Robin's patience and the vase of rosemary when he threw it against the wall. "We have spoken. It is decided."

He stomped from the church and headed for the barracks, his blood boiling and head ready to explode. *We'll see what Conrad thinks is more important, an oath taken in a moment of weakness or his legacy as a ruler over the Chalklands.*

Robin could barely breathe. *What if Conrad defied him and went with the Guardian Angels in spite of the king's command? What if he didn't come back?* That left only one option: Conrad's younger brother. Zachary had shown no more inclination toward his royal duties than had Conrad. Even if he did, the decisions that he had made for himself doomed him to failure as a king. Robin didn't know which would be harder, trying to make a king out of Conrad or Zachary. Somehow Robin would have to prevail or the kingdom of the Chalklands would die with him.

There was the further risk that it would die sooner. Between Conrad's defection to the Church and Zachary's bizarre behavior it was already rumored that the line of succession was in question. Were Conrad to leave the kingdom and Zachary to continue in his masquerade as Princess Dale, the Chalklands would become a target for conquest. The peace and prosperity that the king and his subjects now enjoyed would be destroyed.

Robin shook his head and took some deep breaths to slow his pounding pulse. There was a solution to this dilemma and he would find it. He would put things in order, beginning with locating Meeyoo. To anyone else it might seem that the king was making a major crisis out of a missing cat, but Meeyoo was no ordinary feline. Loyal, she had stuck with him through thick and thin, and some of that "thin" had been so meager as to be nearly transparent. She had even saved his life. What if now she needed him?

He headed for the barracks. Typically a noisy place with men running in and out at all hours of the day and night, it was busy this morning with soldiers sharpening weapons, mending gear, polishing armor, and practicing maneuvers. Robin pulled one man aside and asked about the cat. The soldier regretted that he hadn't seen Meeyoo which didn't surprise Robin.

At the gatehouse, Robin managed to combine the business of the kingdom with his more personal agenda. He and the gatekeeper reviewed the list of guests expected to call on Bell Castle today for an audience with the king. Robin explained that a more urgent task would delay the opening of court. He instructed that the arrivals should be brought to the king's dining room in the keep and offered refreshments while they waited to be called to the great hall. Unless a banquet was being held, the hall offered minimal seating. When holding court Robin found it served to keep proceedings short if the only one who was comfortable was the king.

Meeyoo, however, was nowhere in the gatehouse.

Robin fought off looming feelings of despair. She was highly unlikely to be in the armory, foundry, or stables. The armory was cold and dark, the foundry noisy and smoky, and the stables were filled with large heavy-footed animals that Meeyoo avoided.

He walked slowly from the gatehouse trying to see the castle grounds from a cat's eye view. What structure would be so attractive to Meeyoo that she would stay there for days and not even report to the kitchen to seek out food? Not that she couldn't hunt her own game; she was an effective huntress. There had been more than one occasion when she had snagged a bird which she had offered to him—

"I said, 'are you all right, Sire?'"

"Huh?" Robin started out of his reverie to find a stable boy had come up beside him. A reedy lad just coming into his maturity, his face was pocked from some pox that he had barely survived.

The lad bowed. "I had bid Your Majesty a good morning and got no reply. I was just wondering if you are all right, Sire."

"Yes, we're fine. Please forgive our rudeness. We're simply distracted."

"Oh, no doubt, Sire. Concerns of the realm, I'm sure. They must occupy Your Majesty's mind day and night. Sire, is there anything that I can do?"

Robin considered. Would asking about Meeyoo lead the boy to think his king had nothing more pressing to think about than a missing cat? Would it make the business of running a kingdom appear to be petty and inconsequential? "As a matter of fact, we have been inventorying our livestock. And we seem to be missing ... a cat."

"A cat, Sire?"

"A cat, from the castle. About so long—" Robin held his hands about twelve inches apart. "Not quite as tall. Gray, and white, and tawny, very fluffy. Fat, one would even say."

"You mean Meeyoo, Sire?"

"Yes," Robin replied, uncertain as to whether it was a good thing that the stable boy knew of the king's cat, not to mention its name.

"She's not missing, Sire. She's in the stables. Was your Majesty not aware? I would fetch her but it would probably be better to take Your Majesty to her."

CHAPTER THREE

"Is she ill?" Robin asked as he followed the boy across the bailey.

"No, Sire, she appears to be fine."

The stable boy led the way towards the stall that housed Thief, an old chestnut nag. Thief was too swaybacked and feeble to be of any practical use. Robin kept him just the same and had given the stable hands instructions to feed, water, and exercise the horse and do whatever was necessary to see that Thief was comfortable. It was the least that Robin could do to repay an animal who had given him good faithful service in a time of need.

Thief stood in his stall, half dozing. In a corner, Meeyoo lay on top of the straw, surrounded by mewling little balls of fur.

"Kittens?" Robin said. "She had kittens?"

"Yes, Sire," said the stable boy. "We didn't know Your Majesty was unaware or we would have sent word."

Robin felt almost lightheaded with relief. He hadn't known Meeyoo was pregnant but of course that explained everything: her recent weight gain, her disappearance from her usual haunts. She had made a nest in a place where she felt safe. Ordinarily it might be curious that she chose the stables. Horses and cats were not the best of friends. However, when King Bewilliam was simply Robin, Meeyoo and Thief had traveled many long miles together with him and shared a stall on more than one occasion. Of all the places on the castle grounds, Thief's stall probably boasted the least traffic.

Meeyoo looked up at him, her eyes wide, her expression sober as if to say "Look at me, I am different now. I am changed. I am a mother. I have children."

Robin understood. He recalled his own transformation when his first son, Conrad, was born.

The birth of a king's son held far-reaching ramifications. The royal line had been extended. With the arrival of a prince, an entire new volume in the history of the Chalklands' monarchy was written instantly. The line of kings would continue for another generation. In Conrad, a previously indeterminate future had form and substance.

As important as that was to the kingdom and its subjects, Conrad's birth redefined Robin personally. He became a father. He had a son. From that point on, every decision that Robin made would take his offspring into account.

Even more amazing was the miracle of this new being. More than just a wailing lump of skin, muscle, and bone, here was a whole new person that hadn't existed before. Nothing that could happen would change the fact that Conrad had been born.

So it was with Meeyoo's kittens. Not much bigger than his palm, each was a brand new individual. If Meeyoo was a bit stunned Robin could certainly understand why.

"Would you like us to move her, Sire?" the stable boy asked. "We could collect her and the kittens, bring them to the keep or wherever you desire."

"No," said Robin. It didn't seem possible that the tiny almost hairless things, their eyes squeezed closed, could be handled without being crushed. "She looks comfortable here. Just keep an eye on her. See that she has food and water. Keep her warm. Get her a blanket, perhaps." The horses and donkeys radiated heat but it seemed to Robin that the air in the stables was chilly.

"A sheet, lad. Get her a sheet."

Robin turned and faced the stable master. The man bowed. "A sheet's better than a blanket, Sire. Kittens' claws can easily get snared in the weave of a blanket and they can get tangled up."

"A sheet, then," Robin said. "Thank you."

He bent to pat the new mother on her head. As he neared, she moved to put herself between his hand and the kittens. Robin straightened. "That's all right, Meeyoo. I understand. Protecting your children."

The mystery of Meeyoo's whereabouts solved, Robin left the stables feeling relieved yet strangely forlorn. Meeyoo had gained a new family but Robin felt as though he had lost an old friend.

Having spent the entire morning searching for the cat, he hastened to the great hall in the middle of the bailey. He never tired of climbing the hall's short flight of stairs and seeing the officers at arms respond to his approach by flinging wide the massive oak doors.

The entrance opened onto a foyer where new arrivals invariably paused, stunned by the vista before them. Ablaze with the light shed by golden candelabras and lanterns, the great hall was designed to impress the viewer with the grandeur and power of the kingdom of the Chalklands. Finely woven tapestries in vivid colors hung on the high walls against which stood heavy, ornately carved tables displaying the many gold, silver, and bejeweled gifts bestowed upon the king. A vaulted ceiling and arched windows drew eyes upward and channeled gazes toward the king's throne directly opposite the entrance.

Robin told the officers at arms that as soon as he had settled on his throne, the petitioners could be brought from their staging area in the keep.

Robin kept his cloak about his shoulders. Despite the braziers that had glowed all morning, the large room was cool. He glanced at Meeyoo's seat to the right and slightly behind his throne. Empty. He squeezed his eyes closed and pictured her contentedly nursing her kittens. Pushing thoughts of her to the back of his mind, he opened his eyes and readied himself for a long afternoon.

Robin enjoyed the work of being king, the challenge of decision making even though it was exhausting. He had to listen not only to what the petitioners said but had to hear what they really meant which wasn't always the same thing.

He heard a commotion at the hall's entrance. A figure burst into the room, skidded across the polished marble floor, and came to a sudden stop at the foot of the dais. He popped to his feet, a lean young man who had not left boyhood far behind. A broadening chest and shoulders and muscular arms hinted at the robust man he would become when the rest of his body caught up with his sprouting height. He bowed, straightened, ran a hand through his spiky dark hair, and straightened his tabard. "Sire," he said breathlessly.

"Sir Maxwell," Robin said, trying not to chuckle. Despite his youth, the young man had earned the honor when barely a squire by saving his king from certain peril. Still, having not served the usual seven years as a page or an additional seven years as a squire, even Maxwell acknowledged that there was much knowledge and skill left for him to acquire before he could consider himself worthy of the title. Not only did he need to perfect his fighting abilities, he was expected to observe courtly etiquette and be learned in dancing and music-making.

"I have been looking for Your Majesty all morning," Maxwell said. "I knew Your Majesty would be holding court today and I reported here but the hall was empty. Thinking Your Majesty had overslept—uh, been detained—I went to the keep." Maxwell described his efforts to locate the king, just missing him at every stop of Robin's tour of the castle grounds. "I didn't mean to leave Your Majesty unattended."

"You're a knight now, Maxwell, not a squire. Constant attendance is not your responsibility. We have pages, squires, and guards to see to our needs and our protection. Your time is better spent at your studies and training. Are you finding them to be more than you can handle?"

The knights charged with Maxwell's education reported the youth to be clever and quick to learn but impatient to move on to the next exercise and reluctant to practice the assignment at hand to perfection.

"No, Sire. I wish there were more hours in the day, that I didn't have to sleep or eat so that I could more quickly become the best knight Bell Castle has ever had."

"A worthy goal," Robin said, wondering how he and Maxwell's teachers could temper the youth's restlessness without damping his enthusiasm.

"I was just concerned about Your Majesty's welfare," Maxwell said.

"For which we are grateful." Not that he owed the boy an explanation but Robin nevertheless found himself saying, "We were looking for Meeyoo who has been absent from her usual haunts which caused us concern."

"She has been in the stables. She made a little nest for herself there in Thief's stall and gave birth to a litter of kittens."

"So we discovered," Robin said. *Had everyone but him known about Meeyoo's condition?*

"If only I had known that Your Majesty wasn't aware. I could have spared You Majesty any worry." Maxwell lifted his chin and squared his shoulders. "I will keep an eye on her, Sire, and report any developments. And Sire, might I be permitted to adopt one of the kittens? After they've been weaned, of course."

"We don't see why not," Robin replied.

Maxwell cut a quick bow, straightened, and breathless, his eyes bright with excitement, said, "Sire, I have made the most amazing discovery—"

Please, let Sir Maxwell not tell me that he too has joined the Guardian Angels.

Before Sir Maxwell could elaborate the officers at arms released the day's petitioners. They burst from the foyer into the great hall and rushed toward the dais as fast as possible without causing an actual stampede, each bent on being the first in line.

"You'll have to tell us about it later, Sir Maxwell. Today's session must be brought to order."

"Yes, Sire, thank you." With a bow, Sir Maxwell backed down the dais and withdrew into the crowd.

Robin surveyed the people arrayed before him and was surprised to see four knights standing at quiet attention behind the crowd. None of the men had official duty at the castle this day and had in fact traveled some distance from their manors. Robin wondered what their interest was. Did they bring bad news?

A scribe stood by to record the proceedings for the year book. Not a servant or even a member of the castle's staff, the scribe was an independent reporter who had Robin's leave to attend court and make notes, as long as a copy would be provided to the king. Other copies would be sold to lawyers who would add the decisions to their canon of precedents and to universities of law as reference material in the study and advancement of the legal profession. Robin would hear no petty disputes; those matters would be taken up in manorial courts. Only the most serious of offenses such as murder, treason, rape, and burglary were brought for the king's judgment. Those found guilty at the king's bench could be sentenced to death therefore only the most serious of crimes were judged here.

Robin heard a complicated case in which the warden of the king's forest brought in a boy charged with taking deadwood to use as fuel without paying the wood-penny tax for the right to do so. The boy was very young and pleaded that as an orphan he had to provide for himself. Pilfering sticks and twigs may have seemed to some as a minor civil crime and the boy's plight deserving of sympathy. However, poaching was stealing from the monarch himself and therefore a grave offense.

Robin found himself recalling a time in the not too distant past when he himself had been challenged to scrape together enough kindling to get a small fire going. He could empathize with the desperation the boy felt. Robin ruled that the offender be given a sentence of service to be performed at Bell Castle. Some familiarity with what transpired behind the castle walls might give the boy respect for the monarchy. It would also give Robin a chance to provide the little orphan with some food and shelter, thereby disguising an act of charity as punishment for a grievous crime.

One man accused his neighbor's pig of theft, stating that the animal had squeezed under a fence, come onto his property, and carried off a fallen apple, a petty crime that in Robin's opinion should have been brought to a manor court if it was to be brought at all. The aggrieved party maintained that the offense was akin to burglary, a charge worthy of being addressed in royal court, and demanded to be heard.

The respondent's owner brought the alleged offender to court so that he could speak up in his own defense. Just in case the pig had trouble making himself understood, the owner brought an attorney as well. Robin assumed the lawyer was being well paid as compensation for embarrassing himself by being associated with such a silly matter. On the other hand, Robin found himself impressed with the legist who comported himself well. In all seriousness he made a compelling argument that since the plaintiff had not secured the apple, the pig made a reasonable assumption that it was fair for gleaning.

The plaintiff argued just as persuasively that just because his possessions weren't locked up, that didn't give others permission to steal them.

In the end, Robin decided that to keep the relationship between the two neighbors friendly he needed to find the pig liable of something. He declared the porker guilty of trespassing, a lesser charge than theft, and ruled the payment of a fine equivalent to the value of the apple rather than corporal punishment of the defendant.

The parties left the great hall together and Robin hoped this meant that peace had been restored. He spied the attorney in conversation with a merchant and concluded that by virtue of the lawyer's performance he had obtained a new client, which may have been the goal all along.

As Robin readied to hear the next case a disturbance at the door caught his eye. A tall woman wearing a crown and royal robes stood at the entrance. The herald raised his trumpet to announce her but she waved him off and strode into the hall.

CHAPTER FOUR

A servant hastened to find her a chair.

Prince Zachary was attending court as Princess Dale? Not only attending but seemingly taking notice of the proceedings which Robin found puzzling and disquieting. Born the second son, Zachary had shown only cursory interest in the kingdom's affairs. *What could be the reason for Dale's presence in court now?*

The better part of the day was taken up with challenging disputes that seemed to Robin to be petty and frivolous which he found baffling. After years of hard work, order and prosperity had been brought to the Chalklands. *Why couldn't people relax and enjoy their good fortune? Did the absence of challenges leave them so bored that they had to pick fights?*

Fights. Perhaps he could arrange some controlled contests, host a tournament. That would engage his subjects at all levels. Nobles would be engrossed in choosing the best knights to represent them. Pages and squires would have the additional tasks of preparing their knights' regalia for the tournament. Stable hands would give extra attention to the destriers, the handsome, well-muscled warhorses whose powerful hindquarters enabled them to easily coil and spring, to stop, spin, turn or sprint forward in the lists. Seamstresses would be engaged in constructing the tents and furnishings that would equip the pavilions, the temporary structures that would house the competitors. The knights would put in additional hours practicing with their weapons and training with the quintain, a shield, board, or even a mannequin on a pole that would serve as the same type of target presented by the real opponent. Merchants would stockpile additional inventory to sell to the spectators while purveyors of food and drink would plan to supply refreshments.

Yes, preparations for a tournament would keep all the subjects occupied productively. Bread and circuses. Robin chuckled. The Roman leaders of old had used the ploy to placate their restless citizens. Pleased with the solution, he thought to retire to his bedchamber and sketch out initial plans. Instead, his eyes met Princess Dale's. She curtsied, straightened, and met him halfway across the hall.

Robin regarded the face before him. The features were those of his youngest son, Prince Zachary, but the clothes, the mannerisms, were those of the persona that Zachary had adopted: Princess Dale. It was like approaching a mirage. From a distance Robin saw Princess Dale, a tall and somewhat broad-shouldered but handsome woman. As he drew closer, he saw Prince Zachary, a strapping lad who in his gown could be mistaken for a cleric or an academic. When they finally came face to face, Robin saw neither.

"You looked ... interested," Robin said, trying to keep the incredulity from his voice.

"Of course we're interested," said Dale. "One day we will be seated on that throne, making those judgments. We thought it behooved us to study how it's done. We consulted with the usher to see what petitions await to be heard and we arranged to be present so that we may learn from the proceedings. Lessons we missed when we were younger."

For a long moment, Robin was so flabbergasted as to be speechless. As Prince Zachary's father, Robin had certainly seen to it that the boy was schooled in the matters of running a kingdom, a subject in which young Zachary seemed to have little interest. Was this castigation a subtle stinging reminder of the vacuum left by Robin's long absence as Zachary came to manhood?

As for someday assuming the throne, this was the first inkling Robin had that Zachary had any such ambitions. *And how did he propose to do that?* What about this other identity, that of a woman? Zachary's adopting it had put Robin through hell. Had Zachary become bored with his "Princess Dale" persona? Did he intend to return to his true self, the younger son of King Bewilliam? Was this whole "Princess Dale" personification just a pretense, a game? Robin was reminded of his son's behavior as a child when he would pretend to be many different people.

"We didn't realize that you had those aspirations," Robin said slowly while he collected and composed his thoughts.

"Naturally I do. I am the next in line since Conrad—Brother Thaddeus—has dedicated himself to his vocation. We understand that he has accepted a commission with the Guardian Angels. "

How was it that Zachary knew about that when Robin had found out only hours ago? "But," Robin said, picking over his words as carefully as a kitchen maid sorted beans, "Princess Dale can't be King."

"Because I am a woman? I will be Queen, then."

"But a Queen isn't a ruler. She is the wife of a King. The wife, not the ruler herself."

Dale propped her hands on her hips and pouted. "Why not? Why couldn't a woman rule?"

"It's just not done, that's why. It's never been done."

"Why?"

Robin felt dizzy, as if he'd time-traveled back to when two-year-old Zachary's only words were "no" and "why?"

"I ask you, Sire. Why?"

Robin had no ready answer and in the face of his silence, Dale simply smiled. "You are king. If you rule that a princess can take the throne and rule, it will become law of the land."

"While that is true, that doesn't guarantee the response of the people. How would the subjects react to being governed by a woman? A woman might take the throne but if she does not have the people's respect she cannot secure their loyalty and their obedience. There could be so much dissension that the result would be chaos, perhaps even revolt or anarchy."

Dale studied her fingernails. "Queen Daya ruled quite capably in Your Majesty's absence."

Had she? Robin would be hard pressed to say if his former wife had made good decisions for the kingdom or good decisions for Daya. "To rule a kingdom you must be a king. Prince Zachary is always welcomed to attend court, not—" Robin finished his sentence with a dismissive wave of his hand. "You are excused."

In a low voice Dale said, "You are wrong, Your Majesty. We will show you how wrong." She turned on her heels, and stomped from the hall.

Furious, Robin marched toward the four knights who had stood quietly and patiently throughout the day's proceedings. Their meticulously maintained armor shined but they were unarmed. One did not come to the king's court brandishing a sword. At his approach they greeted him with bows.

"Gentlemen," said Robin. "While we are always pleased to see you, we wonder to what we owe the honor of this unannounced visit."

"We have been talking," began Sir Kenneth.

Sir Howell held up his hand. "Lest you think, Sire, that we have been conspiring against you that is simply not the case. Please, put aside any such thought. We have no higher priority than the welfare of the Chalklands and the continued successful reign of our king. We four share this concern. It came to light that we were all of a like mind about a matter. We decided we owed it to Your Majesty as faithful knights to bring it to Your Majesty's attention."

Glowering as only he could, Sir Alan nodded. He had piercing eyes whose gaze could bore through a man like the sharpest spear unless mitigated by a smile. This afternoon he was not smiling.

"Sir Albert?" Robin asked.

Sir Albert bowed slowly and deeply. He rose and said, "I am here, Sire. Therefore yes, I am in agreement with the other men." Worry lines surrounded his brown eyes.

"We will then hear of this matter that so concerns you all. Come, let us walk." It had already been a long day, the morning spent in the search for Meeyoo and the afternoon in court. The hour was late and the sun already waning. It would be cold outside but the heat generated by all the people who had filled the great hall and the smoke from the braziers had made the room stuffy. Robin felt in need of some fresh air to clear his head. With instructions to a servant to bring them all ale, he led his knights out to the bailey.

"We have seen justice prevail today, Your Majesty, and witnessed many examples of wrongs being righted. But there are crimes that have gone unpunished," said Sir Albert.

"Then the plaintiffs and advocates should bring these matters to the court," Robin replied.

"The plaintiff has not spoken for himself, so we are speaking up on his behalf," said Sir Alan.

"And who would this bashful plaintiff be?" Robin asked.

With a slight bow, Sir Howell said, "You, Sire. Crimes committed against Your Majesty have gone unpunished.

CHAPTER FIVE

"**We** are unaware of any crimes other than those such as the poaching that we addressed today."

"We speak of the offense committed by the King of the Palisades and his conspirator," said Sir Kenneth.

Despite the chilly air, Robin felt his face grow warm at the reminder of the very personal betrayal that had nearly cost him his kingdom. "That was dealt with, in a worthy and reputable court."

Sir Howell cleared his throat. "A church court, Sire. Which dealt with the moral aspect of it, the sin."

"And handed down a severe penalty," Robin said. King Ulric of the Palisades and his wife, Robin's own Queen Daya, had been found guilty of adultery. Robin's marriage was annulled, any and all of Daya's claims by reason of marriage invalidated. The sinners were excommunicated but Robin had an idea about where this conversation was headed. He felt his muscles tense with dread.

"Severe indeed and their eternal souls are doomed. Treachery is the ultimate sin, worse than pride. However the church court does not levy capital punishment," added Sir Alan.

Of which Robin was well aware and was precisely why he had chosen that route. A king's bench surely would have meted out the death penalty but Robin doubted then that he could execute Daya and was no better prepared to do so now.

"Sire, with all due respect, in fact, because we respect Your Majesty, we feel that justice has not been served," said Sir Kenneth.

"It's like striking a cymbal that doesn't ring," said Sir Alan.

Despite the seriousness of the matter, Robin had to smile at the musical analogy. Sir Alan was a fearless fighter and fault could not be found with his martial skills. Just as important to the man, however, were his musical talents.

"As well, we feel this reflects poorly on the king," Sir Albert said.

"King Ulric is a festering wound," said Sir Alan. "Like a limb with an ulcer it should be amputated before the infection can grow and spread and poison the entire body."

Robin's steps slowed as he weighed the remark. These four were his trusted knights who more than anyone knew the facts of the matter. If this was how they felt, how did the rest of the Chalklands' subjects? Did they regard their king as fool? Robin considered his recent judgments. Perhaps they should have been tougher.

"So, what would you have us do? Declare war on the offender?"

The knights didn't say yes but they didn't say no. Their silence spoke louder than words.

Robin shook his head. True knights, in fulfillment of their vows they sought to correct injustice wherever they found it. *Had the dearth of wrongs to rectify left them bloodthirsty and looking for a fight to pick? Very well then. A fight they would have.*

Without further delay Robin would announce a tournament. His subjects could pick their champions, busy themselves arguing over who were the best fighters, and leave him out of the fray, the better to attend to the more pressing issues of running the kingdom. Preparing for a tournament would have knights polishing their armor and honing their technique which would help to keep them in fighting trim. As for ennui, getting pounded in a melee or thwacked off a horse by a lance would knock some fight out of and some sense into his knights. They would remember the pain and fear of battle and be grateful that they no longer had to risk life and limb on the battlefield.

He dismissed the knights with a promise to take the matter of King Ulric under advisement. He told the herald that a tournament was in Bell Castles' future and a date for it would soon be set then headed for the forge. Among the subjects who would be tasked to prepare for the tournament, the blacksmiths would be kept the busiest. Of all the tradesmen they had borne the biggest burden of restoring Bell Castle, having to fashion tools so that others could perform their job. Added to that was the charge of creating an arsenal of weapons.

The mammoth duty back then had fallen to Robin's original lone smith. Aided by his young son, Gregory had worked day and night in spite of his debilitating gout. Robin owed much of Bell Castle's present day splendor to Gregory's faithful and determined efforts. Had Robin been able to award Gregory a knighthood he would have. Instead he compensated the man handsomely and knighted his son. It wasn't an honorary title; young Maxwell earned his knighthood on his own merits. Nevertheless, Robin was glad to have the chance to reward the young man and, by association, his father for their labors and loyalty.

Since those early days of reestablishing the kingdom, the production demands on the smiths had been steady but fairly routine. That was about to change. Equipping knights for a tournament would increase the workload. Robin thought it advisable to give the smiths plenty of notice.

Against the chill of the day, the heat radiating from the forge was inviting. Robin heard the clanging of tools and the shouted instructions and banter well before he opened the door.

At his entrance, the smiths laid down their tools and bowed. Gregory slid from the stool at his workbench where he sat sharpening blades, a skill that Robin had taught him since blacksmithing kept the older man on his stricken foot for too many hours. "Your Majesty," he said, and bowed.

"We have come to give you the earliest notice of an impending event whose success will depend on your efforts. Bell Castle will host a tournament. Our knights will have great need of equipment. Coronals, lots of them, for their lances, just to name one."

As if already exhausted from the effort of manufacturing massive quantities of the pronged steel tips, Gregory sank to his seat. Remembering that a monarch stood before him, he rose and balanced on one foot, holding the other just off the ground.

"Sit, please," said Robin. "Your foot is hurting."

"Thank you, Sire." Gregory retook his stool. "I'm fine. It's just been a long day and ... I wanted to start forming a plan for meeting those additional needs."

"Your gout bothers you more every day, doesn't it?"

Gregory gave a rueful smile. "Is it that obvious?"

"Don't worry. We're not here to chastise you for lack of productivity. We have no complaints. We're confident that you can keep our knights supplied." Robin looked about the forge. Not long ago, Maxwell would be driving the bellows and swinging a sledgehammer alongside his father, sullen but dutiful. Now the new knight's days and nights were spent making up for a deficit of years of training. "You miss the extra pair of hands that Maxwell supplied, don't you?" Robin asked. "He is applying himself diligently to his training but perhaps he is needed here, especially in light of the needs of the tournament. He can always resume his studies afterward."

"Thank you, Sire, but we'll manage. A tournament. That will be something to see. I wouldn't be surprised to learn that Maxwell—Sir Maxwell—will be eager to assist the knights who have helped with his training." Gregory's pride lit his tired and dingy face and softened the lines carved by stress and a life of hard work.

"Your son's achievements are your glory," Robin said. *Maybe it had been wrong of him to tempt Maxwell away from the forge, make possible a career path so divergent from what his father had hoped for him.* "Doubtless you thought he would grow to take your place, run the smithy, enlarge it perhaps."

"Or hoped that he would someday run a forge at a castle in direct service of a king?" Gregory smiled. "Yes, that would surpass any ambition I ever had for him, much less serve that king as a knight. His rise in status has exceeded anything I would have ever hoped for him. It's a father's dream that his children have greater success and a better life than their parents."

Indeed, Robin thought. He recalled his own delight and feeling of accomplishment and validation when Conrad would excel in his lessons or get a bull's-eye at archery. It gave Robin a foreshadowing of the king that Conrad would one day be. Robin's dreams were shattered when Conrad announced that he aspired to follow a different path. The life of a poor chaste monk was not at all what Robin had in mind for his firstborn and he was not by any means ready to concede defeat. Conrad would come to his senses and embrace his destiny despite this talk of Guardian Angels.

The door swung open and Sir Maxwell burst into the room. "Father, guess what I've heard?" He spotted the king, stopped short, and dropped to one knee.

"Sir Maxwell," Robin said.

Maxwell straightened. "Sire. I just heard. Is it true; Bell Castle is hosting a tournament?"

News travels fast, Robin thought. Clearly the herald was already at work announcing the prospective event. "Yes, Sir Maxwell, it's true. We've come to alert your father since there will be much work to do in support of it."

Sir Maxwell seemed as giddy as a child on his birthday. "I must go accelerate my training if I'm to compete." He paced in a tight circle. "I will practice day and night without ceasing. I will ..." He stopped and regarded his father and the king. "Much work, you said, Sire. Here, in the forge?"

"Indeed. As you can imagine, the knights will have long lists of equipment tailored specifically for the tourney. Lances, of course, fitted—"

"Not with sharp points but with coronals, pronged points better suited for jousting. After all, the object is not to run through the opponent, only to unhorse him. Am I correct, Your Majesty?"

"You are indeed."

Maxwell beamed.

"They will need maces, swords, daggers, and shields. The armor worn at a tournament differs from that worn into battle," Gregory said to Maxwell. "Armor for jousting has heavier protection on the side that faces the opponent. Some knights may want a special shield to place at the waist to repel a lance striking there. The helms are also customized for tournament use; they will have eye slits at the upper part so that the knight can see but the slits are narrow and slightly upturned to protect the man's eyes from splinters from shattered lances."

Sir Maxwell looked at his father with wide eyes and raised eyebrows. "You know all this, Father?'

Gregory gave a modest shrug. "Armor will be needed also for the horses. A lot of work, as you said, Sire."

Maxwell's face fell. "You will need my assistance, Father."

"Nonsense, Son. We can more readily find lads to drive the bellows and run the grind wheels than our king and his knights can find able seconds such as you. You should assist Bell Castle's fighting team. There will be much to learn and you will gain much valuable experience. Am I not right, Sire?" Gregory's eyes were pleading. "I assure you, Your Majesty, that you will have no complaints about the productivity here."

"We expect that we won't," Robin said.

CHAPTER SIX

Robin set out for the great hall across a chilly bailey. He drew his cloak closer. The past weeks had not brought warmer weather to the Chalklands. Now, what was he to decide today? Oh, right, Lord Quentin's request for a loan to underwrite the expenses of entering a squire in the preliminary tournament events.

"He is young but promising," Lord Quentin had explained. "He has the makings of a good knight. The tournament would afford him this opportunity to demonstrate his potential." As true as that might be, Robin didn't understand why he should bear the cost—

"Sire, Sire."

Robin looked up to see Sir Maxwell racing towards him.

The young knight bowed and straightened in one rapid movement. "Sire, I had promised to keep you informed about Meeyoo. Today I am pleased to report that Meeyoo's kittens have all been weaned and adopted," said Maxwell.

"And you? How are you and your new pet getting along?"

"He's a little scamp. He gets into everything. And for such a tiny thing he has very sharp claws." Maxwell pushed back a sleeve to show a forearm striped with long red scratches. "He got me good one morning and had me crying 'Yow, yow.' He repeated after me: 'Me. Yow. Yow.' So that's his name: Meeyowyow."

Robin chuckled. He remembered Meeyoo when she was just a kitten. Indeed, her claws had been needle sharp until she started exploring the outdoors and the rough ground had abraded them. "So she is done with mothering, at least until the next litter?"

"Yes, Sire. Thief has got his stall all to himself again."

Robin frowned. *If Meeyoo was no longer in the stables where was she? Out somewhere seeking a mate for her next litter? Wasn't it too soon?*

Throughout the court day Robin cast a furtive glance at Meeyoo's throne which remained distressingly vacant. At day's end, Robin made for the keep, detouring here and there to ask about the cat's whereabouts.

Weary, Robin trudged up the keep's staircase and lumbered to his bedchamber. Light from within outlined the door; servants had already lit lamps against the dark of winter night and fired braziers to warm the room. Guards and his page took their posts. Robin pushed open the door, unclasped his cloak, and was about to drape it over a chair when he heard a noise.

"Me. You."

He turned toward the sound and saw a dark shape sitting atop the blankets at the foot of his bed. "Meeyoo!"

Robin sat on the bed and pulled the cat to his chest. Her low purrs were comforting but her gauntness was disturbing. She had lost the weight that she had gained while pregnant and then some.

"The little ones took a lot out of you," Robin said, laying the cat on the blanket. "We'll have the cook bring you extra treats and we will have you fat and sassy and chasing mice again in no time." First thing in the morning he would begin a program of restoring her to her former robust self.

Despite eating the rich and generous meals that he arranged for her and getting lots of rest—it seemed that she did little but sleep—Meeyoo not only did not gain weight, she seemed to lose more. Scrawny, her shoulder bones and ribcage poked through coarse fur and thinning skin. She had none of her usual spunk and one morning as he dressed, Robin told his page, "We believe that Meeyoo is ill. She needs a physician. Summon the doctor."

"Now, Your Majesty?"

"Yes, now. Bring him here. We will wait."

Robin took a seat at his desk and tried to focus on documents that required his attention. He found himself reading the same lines two and three times without comprehension and realized it was no use. He couldn't concentrate. He stared out the window and came to his feet when he spied the page hurrying across the bailey toward the keep, a man in a long robe and floppy velvet hat at his heels. Moments later there was a knock at the door and Robin bade them enter.

The page and the doctor bowed. The page stepped to one side. Stretched out on the bed, Meeyoo submitted to the doctor's examination without protest. Robin stood and watched over the doctor's shoulder as he turned the cat this way and that, looked into her ears, her nose, and her mouth, and prodded her sides.

The doctor sighed. "I am sorry, Your Majesty. This little creature is gravely ill. I suspect an internal injury or infection."

Robin didn't like hearing the word "grave." Unable to breathe he said, "No, that can't be. She's young. She's only just had her first litter."

The doctor sighed. "That may be what caused her infirmities. Animals are strong, often stronger than we are in some respects, but childbirth is often no easier for female beasts than humans."

"Surely there is something you can do."

The doctor shook his head. "We can always pray."

"Pray," Robin echoed with no conviction. Asking for divine intervention seemed to him an admission of defeat. Leaving a matter in God's hands meant one considered his own hands powerless.

Clearly he needed a better physician. It wasn't that Bell Castle's doctor lacked talent. He had helped the stable boy who had been stricken with pox and healed many an injured knight and soldier. Perhaps the doctor was simply more knowledgeable about people than animals. Robin found himself thinking of a physician who had cured a donkey wounded by a dragon. The same doctor had even given a new lease on life to poor Thief whom Robin had found malnourished and abused. He had met that physician during his sojourn at Sea Gate Fortress, far too distant to be of help to Meeyoo. There had to be someone nearer.

"Yes, pray," said the doctor and then tapped his lips. "But that gives me an idea."

At the mere suggestion of hope Robin found himself once again able to breathe.

"There is a woman among your subjects," said the doctor. "In Windham Hill. She and her husband have a fondness for animals, there is no question about that. They are known by their neighbors for taking in all sorts of stray and injured creatures, to treat them and care for them. Some think the couple a little odd."

"Are they?" Robin asked.

The doctor shrugged his shoulders. "Perhaps a little. They are certainly godly people, some say especially gifted by Our Father in the treatment of small creatures. We can tell you this, Sire. They will try everything within their power to heal Meeyoo and will not stop until—"

The doctor no doubt intended to say "until there was no point in continuing" and Robin was grateful that the man left the words unspoken.

"We will send for them," Robin said.

"Nay, Sire, if I may be so bold. Take the patient to them. Over the years they have developed specialized equipment and remedies for the treatment of animals. We advise Your Majesty to go without delay. Time is of the essence."

"Thank you, Doctor." Robin turned to his page. "Go, speedily. Make preparations for us to take Meeyoo to Windham Hill."

The page bit his lip. "Sire, your audience later this morning with—"

Robin waved away the objection. Whatever it was would have to wait. "We leave immediately."

For speedy travel Robin directed the formation of a small party: a couple of soldiers to see to his protection, a page to see to his comfort. Witnessing the departure preparations, Sir Maxwell had wanted to come but they agreed it was best that he remain behind and attend to the care of the kitten Meeyowyow.

"And how is your little companion coming along?" Robin asked.

"He's so big, Sire."

"Cats don't spend much of their lives being kittens."

"Perhaps not, but Your Majesty, he has a voracious appetite. The bits and kibbles that I feed him no longer satisfy. He gets his own food now and he has snagged prey that surprises even me. Game worthy of a lion or an eagle."

"Indeed?"

"Birds, as Your Majesty might imagine, but I have seen him leap high and snatch one out of the air. He likes to be in high places."

"Cats do," said Robin. "Being high up is a good defensive position for them. It puts them above those animals that would attack them and they can easily scan their surroundings to make sure they're safe."

"Yes, Sire, that makes sense but it's how he gets there that's amazing. He doesn't climb, he leaps. He jumps and spreads his forelegs out, as if he thinks he's a bird that can fly. He alights most smartly on a limb and then I've seen him take a squirrel. And to come down, he doesn't inch along like I've seen other cats do. He'll launch himself to the ground. I wonder that he doesn't hurt himself when he lands."

"Cats are impressively spry and flexible," Robin said but he had to admit he had seen Meeyoo "take flight" like that only once and under the most exigent of circumstances.

"He's fast, too. I've seen him catch and eat a snake. And fish, Sire. I have seen him wade into a pond and snatch fish with his fore claws as if he were a bear. I didn't think cats liked water, Sire. He can use his front paws like hands and those claws are long and sharp as talons. And he has a dewclaw the likes of which I have never seen. It is like a fifth toe and it too has a big sharp claw. Sire, I have even seen him eat the remains of another animal's kill. I didn't think that cats ate carrion."

"He's still young, Sir Maxwell. Perhaps his appetite will change as he grows older."

"He doesn't know he's a kitten. I believe he thinks he's a big cat. When he's content he has a very deep purr but when he has brought down a particularly large animal he will let out a growl. And I've seen him stalk deer, wild boar, even a cow. I scold him and tell him that's poaching, sire. Those animals are reserved for the king."

Robin tried not to chuckle at Sir Maxwell's fanciful description. "Are you finding him too much to handle, Sir Maxwell?"

"Oh, not at all, Sire. He is an unusual animal and it gives me great pride and delight to see him curled up at the foot of my pallet, even if he is getting to be so big there's not much room left for me. The way he sticks so close to me and looks at me sometimes as if he thinks that I am special too ... well, Sire, I am most grateful to have him as a companion."

"It's the other way around, Sir Maxwell. As far as your cat is concerned, he is the king and you are here to serve him." He patted the young man on the shoulder. "We will leave you to his care."

Robin's seneschal hastened to prepare a carriage for the trip. Perched on four wheels rather than three and employing a springy suspension of Robin's own design, Bell Castle's vehicles gave a comfortable ride but Robin thought a carriage would slow their progress. He would travel on horseback, but how to transport his ailing cat? She was used to long journeys but her mode of travel had been nestled inside a rucksack that Robin wore on his back or hung from the pommel of a saddle. Thinking all the jouncing would add to Meeyoo's discomfort, he had a light cart outfitted with cushions to keep her comfortable, blankets to keep her warm, food and water.

The snow covering the trails impeded their progress and they had to slow almost to a stop every time they arrived at a particularly winding part of the track. The cart was difficult to steer around the tight curves. A thought flitted through Robin's mind to address the rigidity of the vehicle's fixed axles. Perhaps there was a way to make them pivot so that they could corner more easily. A task for another time; this day he was too preoccupied with Meeyoo's condition to pursue complex lines of thought.

The gray-and-white midwinter sky was a gloomy canvas marked only by the occasional huge bird. An eagle, hawk, or vulture perhaps. It flew too high for Robin to make out its features other than the massively broad wings and especially long and narrow tail feathers. It would soar above them then disappear into the trees only to reappear. It seemed to keep pace with them and while it never came anywhere near to being menacing, its persistent presence made Robin uneasy. Had it identified Meeyoo as vulnerable and potential prey?

The light waned and Robin's party was farther than he wanted to be from Windham Hill or any other settlement for that matter. "We think it would be ill advised to continue in the dark with the road so hard to traverse," he told his retinue. "We would hate to stumble on some unseen obstacle hidden under the snow and break an axle or injure one of the mounts."

"We could go very slowly," offered one of the soldiers. "We know Your Majesty is eager to get to Windham Hill."

"Thank you, but it's probably wiser to make camp and get started again at first light."

"As you wish, Sire." One soldier stood guard while the other set out to hunt some small game for their night's repast. Snagging a hare or wild bird on the king's land was a risk-free proposition when the king himself was a member of the party. The page set about securing the mounts, clearing ground, and building a fire.

The cold and darkness of a winter night fell quickly. Now wishing they had brought a carriage, Robin made room for himself in Meeyoo's cart. He slept fitfully, waking several times in the night to reassure himself that Meeyoo's silence was deep sleep and not the stillness of death. He had just managed to drift off when a crunching in the snow brought him to full alertness.

In the glow of the campfire's embers he saw the page and one of the soldiers sleeping huddled near the campfire while the other soldier stood alert and on guard. No movement there and he wondered what could have caused the noise. The sound came again and caught the soldier's attention. He looked about and he and Robin simultaneously directed their gaze to the pair of gleaming eyes at the edge of the small encampment. A wild animal had been attracted perhaps by the scent of the roasted meat on which they had dined or coveted the defenseless prey in the cart. Robin no sooner determined it was a wolf than he saw another pair of eyes and another. Not just one wolf, but an entire pack. Swift and sharp-toothed and desperate with hunger, there were more of them than there were of his party.

One hand on his sword, the soldier shook his comrade awake with the other and nudged the page with his foot. The soldier came to instant attention, sprang to his feet, and drew his sword. The page rubbed his eyes and when he saw the soldiers standing at the ready, struggled upright and patted his waist in search of his dagger.

The wolves were close enough now that Robin could hear their guttural growls. Their musky smell pervaded the crisp winter air. They stood bunched together, a formidable phalanx, teeth bared and muscles tensing, ready to charge. Robin directed his men to fan apart and make a wider target of themselves. He thought to inch towards the fire with the intent of snatching some bones from their supper and flinging them into the bushes behind the pack. Maybe one or two of the wolves would be distracted and chase the bait. Robin could then grab a smoldering brand, toss it into the pack. That might scare off another one or two more predators.

He was about to make his move when another sound froze the wolves as well as the humans where they stood.

CHAPTER SEVEN

Half roar, half-shriek, an utterance unlike any other Robin had ever heard, it raised the hairs on the back of his neck.

Had he and his men stumbled onto a dragon's lair? Robin had heard dragons bellow and this was nothing like that. The cry he heard was a throatier growl ending in a shrill screech.

His men's heads swiveled as they searched for the source of the unearthly sound.

The wolves' faces turned upward, scanning the trees above them. Ears twitching, shoulders hunched, the wolves drew close together and hunkered down. They made a nervous chattering and then turned tail and ran back into the depths of the wood. The crashing and whining noises of their retreat were drowned out by what sounded like the flapping of the wings of a very large bird. Robin squinted at the trees searching for an animal that could be connected with that noise but the sky was too dark and the trees' canopy was too dense.

From a distance came the wail of a wolf that had itself become prey and the mournful howling of the other members of its pack. The stillness that followed was profound in its completeness.

Robin caught the wide-eyed glances of his soldiers and the page and knew that like he, they wondered what winged creature had managed to carry off a wolf.

There were no further incidents that night but no one got any sleep. The page stirred up the fire and they all drew close to its warmth and illumination, weapons and firebrands close at hand. As soon as it was light enough to see, they broke camp and eagerly returned to the track.

The trees thinned as they neared Windham Hill. Once again, Robin spied the strange bird high above them. As if reluctant to enter the city, the ominous bird pointed its head upward and with a flapping of its wings that was so robust Robin thought that he could hear it, the bird flew higher until it wasn't even a speck in the sky.

It was not unusual for the king to tour the streets of Windham Hill. As much time as he spent in court on matters of the kingdom, Robin spent an equal amount traveling throughout his realm to see how his subjects fared. Nevertheless, the sudden appearance of the king was cause for concern. On such visits he could not only be made aware of problems that should be corrected, he could also discover unexplained wealth for which he had not collected his share or improvements for which franchises had not been obtained. With Robin's modest retinue it seemed unlikely that detailed scrutiny was intended although for all his subjects knew King Bewilliam could have some hidden agenda. So while some citizens rushed to greet him, pay him homage, and offer him food or drink, others ducked inside their shops, no doubt scrambling to hide any ill-gotten gains that they did not want discovered.

Robin didn't dwell on either activity, being single mindedly bent on locating the animal healer of whom his doctor had spoken. Robin's page ran ahead asking residents where the animal doctor might be found. At last Robin's party approached a wattle-and-daub house. Cats who lounged in the narrow strip of sunlight along the front wall scurried to hide under a small bush. Dogs of all shapes and sizes ran barking and yipping to meet him.

Robin's page went ahead to knock on the front door and call out the reputed healers while one of the soldiers sought to control the dogs eager to greet the new arrivals. Robin dismounted as the page emerged from the house. Robin expected to see a man in a robe wearing a cloth cap like Bell Castle's physician. Instead, the page was accompanied by a woman. Not a young woman, with her soft face, sweet smile, and small stature she looked more like someone's mother than a doctor. Her bright blue eyes, however, regarded him with alert and forthright scrutiny. Robin liked her immediately.

"Your Majesty," she said, and curtsied. "I am Alice."

Robin took her hand and inclined his head.

"Welcome. Windham Hill is all abuzz with Your Majesty's arrival. My husband and I are pleased to be favored with Your Majesty's presence. How may we be of service?"

Robin waved a hand at the cart bearing Meeyoo. "Our cat is very ill," he said, feeling as powerless and needy as a child. "We have been told that if anyone can help her it would be the animal healers in Windham Hill."

Alice drew aside the blankets covering the cat. "Oh, dear kitty," she said. "Look at you. Feeling poorly are you?" She reached in to chuck Meeyoo under her chin. Meeyoo burrowed deeply in the blankets.

"We're surprised that she didn't bite or scratch you," said Robin. "Maybe she likes you."

"That would be nice but I'm afraid it is more likely that she is too feeble to defend herself."

"Her name is Meeyoo," said the page. "She is our king's favorite."

"Meeyoo," Alice echoed. She bowed her head in Robin's direction. "We had heard that the king ruled with a cat by his side. We thought it would be delightful were it true but assumed it was just a rumor or a story to tell to children. Tell me, Sire, what made you think she was ill? How has she been behaving?"

Robin replied, "She was fine until recently. She is friendly and popular at Bell Castle. She is well fed and cared for, so much so that we feared that she would get fat and lazy except that she is active. A great huntress who keeps our quarters free of rodents," Robin said. "We became concerned when she put on weight but that was quickly explained by the fact that she was pregnant. She had a litter, her first. At first we thought that nursing the kittens caused her to lose weight."

"And that will," said Alice.

"But it's been weeks and instead of regaining her strength she has become only thinner and more listless."

Alice nodded. "Very likely she suffers from a complication of the delivery. Not common but we have seen it." To the page she said, "Please bring the king and his patient inside. It's cold enough out here for people and far too cold for a sick cat."

The page looked a question at Robin, who scooped up Meeyoo, blankets and all. Alice led the way inside the house, followed by several of the cats and dogs.

With a wave of her arm, Alice said, "This is our humble infirmary." Braziers kept the small room warm and lanterns provided bright light. The floor was neither pounded earth nor wood but costly glazed stone which shone as if freshly washed.

A standing screen walled off most of the entry-level floor except for a path to the staircase leading to the upper stories. Bowls of water and platters with food scraps lined the floor along the walls, and baskets large and small held a variety of animals, some of them with bandages wrapped around their legs or heads. Birds filled cages hanging from stands or the ceiling beams. In one corner stood an eight-foot tall pole tiered with small ledges at varying intervals, suggesting a tree with branches. A cat lounging on the topmost tier peered down at him. "Our recovery room," Alice said. "Some animals have a lengthy recuperation and it's better for them to be somewhat isolated from people and protected from predators."

The infirmary and recovery rooms left no living space for people. "Cats and dogs, rabbits and birds," said Robin. "It's a wonder that they don't attack each other."

"For the most part they are hampered by their pain or don't have the strength. All their energy is going into their healing. We provide food for them so there is no need for the larger animals to attack the smaller ones."

The menagerie was strangely silent and Robin remarked on it.

"Unlike people, injured animals tend not to moan. It would just draw attention to them, let predators know that they are feeble and defenseless. They prefer to hide until they feel better," Alice said. "Please, Your Majesty, bring Meeyoo over here."

Robin and his page followed Alice behind the screen. A stand held a basin, water pitcher, folded white sheets, towels, and rags. Alice spread a towel across the surface of a tall trestle table with a top of polished stone. "Please, Sire, place Meeyoo here," said Alice. "The stone is easy to clean and stays cool which helps with any fevers or festering wounds. The towel will help keep Meeyoo warm and comfortable.

"Excuse me just a moment," she said. "Let me get my daughters. They are learning the healing arts so that they may take after me, and I may need a bit of assistance with Meeyoo."

How curious that young women would be eager to learn how to work with sick and injured animals, Robin thought. He would have expected them to be interested in polishing the talents and skills that would enable them to find husbands. He found himself thinking suddenly of his sons. How thrilled he had been to be involved in their training, knowing that they would follow in his footsteps. Would that they had the loyalty and dedication that Alice's daughters apparently had.

Robin scanned the implements laid out on a nearby stand: shears, bandages, needles and thread, vials of potions and pots of unguents. He stroked Meeyoo's head. "You're going to be fine," he said, and he felt that indeed she would. The room had a certain comforting radiance about it and it wasn't just the glow of braziers and lamps.

Alice hastened towards the stairs. She returned with two young women. All three wore white aprons over their dresses and veils that covered their hair and kept it off their face. The fabrics hung stiffly with wax that had been applied as a protective coating. A simple white scarf draped their necks.

The two young women bowed politely. Alice introduced them to the king and the patient: Joy, the youngest, had her mother's fair complexion and light-colored eyes while Jewel had dark eyes and olive skin, no doubt features she shared with a father Robin had yet to meet.

Alice stroked Meeyoo's head. Robin saw the cat relax and from the way her eyes softly closed and her mouth stretched in the suggestion of a smile, it appeared that she was comfortable with the woman's ministrations. "Ah, she is quite warm. We believe she has an elevation of temperature, a sign of infection." Alice looked into Meeyoo's ears. "No problem here." She gently pried Meeyoo's mouth open. "Her teeth and gums look healthy." She prodded Meeyoo's belly which drew a small cry of complaint from Meeyoo. Alice pulled on white gloves and brought the scarf up over her nose and mouth.

"You needn't fear contagion," Robin said. "We have been in close quarters with her for days and have not become ill."

"Good to know, Your Majesty," said Alice. "Nevertheless, this could get smelly, and messy."

She proceeded to examine Meeyoo's rear end. "I suspect either she didn't discharge all the placental material or perhaps there's a fetus that didn't get expelled. In either case it's causing infection and will have to be removed."

"Can you do that?"

"It's complicated surgery because the structures are so small but we will have to try. There is little hope for her otherwise. Battling such a severe infection, she will not be able to get well." Alice pressed her lips together. "We will do our best but we cannot guarantee success. She may not survive. Does Your Majesty wish for us to proceed anyway?"

"You say it's her best chance."

Alice nodded. "We believe that the surgery, albeit risky, is justified by the risk to her life that the infection presents."

Robin swallowed hard and nodded. "We would like you to try then. May we be of assistance? Is there anything we can do?"

"Thank you, Sire, it would be best if you leave it to me and my daughters."

"We understand. We would probably just be in the way."

Alice gave him a polite smile.

"You may observe if you like, Sire, or if you would prefer, Your Majesty is certainly welcome to enjoy the comforts of our home upstairs."

Were there to be pain, and Robin suspected that there would be, would he be able to bear Meeyoo's cries? "Perhaps we could wait just outside the screen. If we are needed or could help ... or if she fails ...." Just the thought of Meeyoo dying caused Robin's throat to close and his eyes to sting.

"In that case, Your Majesty, let me make you comfortable." Alice hastened to shoo a cat from an armchair and brush fur from the seat." With a bow she said, "Your Majesty's prayers would be most welcome," and joined her daughters behind the screen.

CHAPTER EIGHT

"**Is** there anything that I can do for you, Sire?" asked the page.

Robin nodded. "An ale if you would, please."

The page bowed and hastened to fetch one. The soldiers took their posts just outside the door.

Too anxious to make even polite conversation, unable to think or even to breathe, Robin sat, sipped the ale he had been brought without tasting it, and gazed out the window. He tried to engage his mind with watching the people of Windham Hill as they went about their business, unaware of the battle for life taking place in Alice's infirmary but Alice's and her daughters' muffled comments kept snagging his attention and images of Meeyoo lying on the table suffering undoubtedly painful ministrations intruded. Every now and then he felt dizzy and had to remind himself to breathe. He dared not think about having to return to Bell Castle without Meeyoo and instead thought about her kittens. He smiled as he recalled how she had looked lying on the hay of Thief's stall surrounded by her wee offspring and her serious knowing expression. He chuckled thinking about the kitten that Sir Maxwell had taken for his own and named Meeyowyow for its vicious claws.

Pray, Robin thought. His doctor had suggested prayer and now so had Alice. Of course Robin wished with all his heart that Meeyoo would live. *Was that prayer?*

He closed his eyes and forced away the pictures of Meeyoo feeble and in pain and replaced them with his memories of her at the peak of health, scampering through a meadow chasing a bird or a mouse.

No, that probably wasn't prayer. He should ask God to intercede, to spare Meeyoo. That's what people did when someone they loved was endangered. Why, Robin wondered, should God care about a simple housecat? Perhaps it was part of a larger design. There was something that God wanted from Robin and it was Meeyoo's survival that was being held for ransom.

Yes, that must be it. Robin knew from the Bible that God was fond of bargaining. He struck covenants with people all throughout the Testaments.

What did God want from the king of the Chalklands?

Robin decided to ask and tried to picture God. Of course no one had ever seen God except perhaps for some mystics whose testimonies were so strange and incomprehensible that their witness could easily be taken for insanity.

Artists portrayed God in sculptures, tapestries, and paintings, usually as a grand old man with a white beard and hair and benign features. That could just as well be Robin's father and maybe it was the artists' intent that one was to think of God as a father figure: a provider, protector, teacher, taskmaster and, if need be, a disciplinarian.

Robin shook his head. The God who created the world and all that was in it was bigger than that. Immortal, omnipresent, omniscient. That could not be contained in a body with a head, fingers, and toes although people often made vows by swearing "by God's bones."

Robin sighed and took a sip of ale. His head throbbed with confusion. These questions about God were a problem to be addressed some other time. He went back to straining to hear Alice's instructions to her daughters, muted though they were by the screen and picturing Meeyoo finally curled up in her basket, beaming up at him as he sat on the throne.

At last Alice stepped out from behind the screen. Her white garments bore a few streaks of red. "We are pleased to report that the surgery was successful. We're sorry that you had to wait so long. We administered a soporific to Meeyoo and had to wait for it to have its effect before we could proceed."

"So she did not feel any pain? I expected to hear her cry out."

Alice shrugged. "We suspect that she did feel some discomfort but the soporific would have dulled it and her reactions to it. And of course I needed her to remain still so that we could operate on her. It will be a while before she is alert."

"May we see her?"

"Of course."

Stiff from sitting and clenching his muscles, Robin pried himself from the chair and followed Alice behind the screen. Covered loosely with a small blanket, Meeyoo lay sleeping on the table. Though she didn't move when he stroked her head he was reassured to see her ribcage expand and contract with her usual rapid breaths.

"Jewel will monitor her but perhaps, Sire, you would do with some refreshment. We will be partaking of our evening meal. Of course we had not anticipated that we would be entertaining royalty so it is simple fare, but we would be honored to share it."

Lightheaded, his mouth dry despite the ale, Robin thought that food sounded like a great idea. "We would be most appreciative."

He followed Joy and Alice upstairs where he met Alice's husband, Ferree, a woodcarver. The skin around his dark eyes was spider-webbed with wrinkles from years of squinting over the fine details of his constructions, Robin presumed, and his lips were slightly pursed, giving him a permanently thoughtful expression.

As Joy and Alice set the small table, Ferree ladled out portions of some dish and carried bowls downstairs for Jewel, Robin's soldiers, and page. He returned with the page at his heels, carrying the armchair. He bade Robin to sit. "Allow me to serve my king," Ferree said.

Robin invited the family to join him and they crowded around the small table. The page passed bowls of pottage.

Ferree bowed his head and clasped his hands and his wife and daughters followed suit. "Thank you, Lord, for giving us the opportunity to serve you today."

Robin was about to reply when he realized that he was not the lord to whom Ferree gave thanks. Usually hungry and eager to tuck into his food, it was Robin's practice simply to endure grace before a meal. It may have been the stresses of the day or possibly the intimacy of crowding around the family's small table canopied by a low ceiling because something about Ferree's words caught Robin's attention. Daily he was presented with decisions to make and tasks to complete, some of them frustrating and arduous. He took personal satisfaction when he had completed a task with a special degree of efficiency or finesse, congratulating himself on a job well done. He was a king, it was his duty, and he rarely attributed his work with any greater import. However Ferree had imbued his own labors with spiritual significance. Clearly he saw his efforts as part of a larger enterprise.

The meal concluded, Alice said, "I'll move Meeyoo after a while to a basket and keep her with us so that we can keep an eye on her through the night. By the time Your Majesty returns in the morning she should be alert and ready to bear the trip back to Bell Castle."

"By the time we return? You wish us to leave? Can we not take her with us?"

"She shouldn't move for a while. We would prefer that she spend the night here so that we can be on hand in case ... we don't anticipate her having a crisis but we would want to be close to care for her if she did." Alice frowned. "Your Majesty would certainly be welcome to stay here and we would be most privileged to host our king but our house is small. As you can see we have given up much of the space to the animals. Might I suggest that Your Majesty lodge at the church? My daughters can keep an eye on Meeyoo, and my husband and I will escort Your Majesty there."

With reluctance, Robin agreed.

"We'll be back tomorrow, Meeyoo," he called softly to the cat as they passed the infirmary. "We'll go back to Bell Castle and all will be as it was."

Alice, Ferree, and Robin set out on foot, his soldiers and page bringing up the rear with their horses and cart. As they walked, Alice explained that she had indeed found a stillborn kitten festering inside Meeyoo. "I removed it and cleaned her uterus, gave her potions to treat the infection. Now that her body does not have to fend off disease she will be better able to return to full strength. Care and nourishing food will help that."

"She will get nothing but that at Bell Castle where she is much loved by all."

Alice nodded. "Your Majesty understands that there is no guarantee of recovery."

Robin said, "So you stated."

"Even if she does get well—and I am optimistic that she will—she may be so injured internally that she will have no more litters. From what I observed, the coupling that impregnated her appears to have been with an extremely large tom."

That had been Sir Maxwell's assumption as well based on how large Meeyowyow promised to be.

"Then it's good that she had a least the one." Robin told Alice about the young knight who had taken one of the kittens for his own and of the name he had given it which had Alice and Ferree laughing.

The church that served all of Windham Hill proved to be not much bigger than the one at Bell Castle.

The chapel room was small and shadowed. Waning winter light shone faintly in windows that arched up to trefoils. A red runner created a path to a carved stone altar that stood in a pool of light cast by a brass lantern hanging above it. It gave the impression that something very special took place in that spot and beckoned one to approach.

Alice knelt at the altar. "Heavenly Father," she said, "thank you for giving us the skill to heal creatures when they cannot heal themselves. Even these tiny lives are precious, not just to us but in ways that we mere mortals cannot appreciate. These creatures are Your creations as much as we are. You called forth fish in the sea, birds in the air, and animals on the land. We are privileged to be their stewards. We are grateful that we can contribute in some small way to Your grand design. Be it Your will to return the cat Meeyoo to health and strength. Blessed are you, Lord God, and holy is your name for ever and ever. Amen."

"Amen," Robin found himself saying. Meeyoo was indeed precious to him but had also become important in a larger way. He had to admit that in retrospect there did seem to be quite a bit of purpose to seemingly random events, more than could be explained by mere serendipity. Had he not met Meeyoo and taken her with him on his journey, he might not have survived some of the trials and tribulations. Merely by her presence she had inspired him to carry on when he might have given up, enabling him to achieve his current lofty position.

Alice and Ferree took their leave. The church's preacher escorted Robin to a bedchamber, apologizing for its size and simplicity. Considering he had spent the previous night camping in the woods and fending off wolves, Robin found it more than sufficient. He was cozy enough under plenty of blankets in a room heated by a brazier yet he couldn't get warm. He lay awake thinking of Meeyoo. He knew that Meeyoo wasn't alone or uncomfortable—Alice promised that she would be watched and cared for. Nevertheless, he wondered if she was fearful, waking up from a soporific to find herself in pain in an unfamiliar place surrounded by strangers.

His mind drifted back to the humble residence. Ferree's words of gratitude before the meal echoed. Robin would have imagined that people like Ferree would regard their work as what they had to do to earn money to provide the necessities of life for themselves and their dependents. Anything that made that work harder was to be dreaded and avoided. That was how he had felt as a laborer. The unannounced arrival of a king with a sick cat should have presented an unwanted and fearsome challenge with dire consequences for failure. However Alice had seen only the opportunity to fix a problem and Ferree had given thanks for the chance.

Robin stared at the ceiling and wondered if indeed there was a larger significance to his own role as king. Or was "king" even the role he was meant to play? He had been other things to other people: student, teacher, laborer, soldier, entertainer, lover, husband, father, friend. What if one of those parts was the most important? Might he have a different destiny, one that was going unfulfilled in his pursuit of being king?

What about that God whom Ferree had thanked, to whom Robin had tried to pray for Meeyoo's recovery? What could He want from King Bewilliam of the Chalklands in exchange for His divine intervention on Meeyoo's behalf?

The answer came like flash of insight so startling that it made him sit upright, the breath stolen from his lungs: Conrad.

The realization was so stunning Robin felt as chilled as he had the night before when he faced down a pack of wolves.

The pieces of his life composed themselves like a completed jigsaw puzzle. It was not about Robin, it was about Conrad. Robin's destiny wasn't so much "king" as it was "father," father to Conrad. Robin's role in God's plan was to bring Conrad into the world, raise him to be the man he was today, give him the education and training that so perfectly equipped him to be a monk, even to serve in the Order of the Guardian Angels. Conrad's vocation wasn't the passing fancy of a rebellious youth; Conrad had indeed answered a genuine calling.

"We understand now," Robin said aloud. "We understand and agree to Your terms. Meeyoo's life for Conrad's service. We will no longer oppose Brother Thaddeus in the pursuit of his vocation."

Robin imagined that this was a bit like how Abraham of the Bible had felt. God had asked him for his firstborn son, Isaac, as a demonstration of faith and a test of loyalty. Perhaps this too was to take the measure of Robin's fealty.

God had demanded not Isaac's service but his life. Robin hoped that he and Conrad would be spared that ultimate sacrifice. Given the enmity and barbarity that the Guardian Angels encountered, the risk was there. Conrad had received the best military training Robin and his experts could provide. He hoped his son had heeded his lessons well.

"We will hold him back no longer but endorse his decision to join the Order of the Guardian Angels. When he has done all that You require of him, bring him back to us, please," Robin prayed. Yes, prayed that Conrad would survive his dangerous Guardian Angel mission and return to Bell Castle where Robin would give Conrad's vocation his full support.

A lifetime of questions answered, years of doubts resolved, and a decision made left Robin feeling light as if pounds had dropped from his body. He laid down, stretched out, and relaxed, confident that by morning he would return to Alice's house to find Meeyoo fully recovered. The bargain had been made.

He was therefore not surprised when he reported to Alice and Ferree's home at first light and he discovered that Meeyoo's eyes were open and bright. Her tail twitched feebly at the sight of him.

"We believe with time and care that she will regain her strength," said Alice. "We will equip Your Majesty with some preparations that we have found helpful. Powders and potions, some of which could be added to Meeyoo's food, some of which Your Majesty will have to administer by hand," Alice said. "We know forcing a cat to eat something is not the easiest thing in the world. Allow us to show Your Majesty how to go about it."

Using one of her own charges she set the cat on the trestle table facing forward. "Your Majesty should put the left hand under Meeyoo's throat and hold the medication in the right hand, like this. Scratch Meeyoo's neck and with the thumb and forefinger of the right hand, or the reverse if Your Majesty is left-handed. Tip her head back a bit so her nose is pointing to the ceiling. Apply pressure to the corners of her mouth to get her to open it. Insert the medication as far back as possible, close her mouth, and hold it closed. Rub downwards on her throat a few times to confirm that she swallows." Alice released the cat. "I've made it look easy but it does take some practice to do it without protest."

Robin envisioned a reluctant Meeyoo chomping down on his fingers and recalled the deep scratches that little Meeyowyow had left on Sir Maxwell's arm.

Alice handed him some small pots with medication mixed into pureed meat. "This will be easy for her to eat." She had also baked meat pasties for him and his men to eat on the road, a rich treat that he was certain she and her family rarely got to enjoy.

"We are in your debt," Robin said, "although we know it sounds preposterous to be so invested in an animal."

"Not at all, Sire," said Alice. "Animals extend to us unquestioned love, devotion, and unwavering loyalty. Would that we opened our hearts to our fellow man with the same lack of hesitation."

Perhaps, Robin thought, that was the role that pets played: to show people how to love and care for another being. The way of the world was indeed proving to be more intricate and complex than he had ever imagined.

"Nevertheless, we are grateful. In thanks, we have decided to name you tenants-in-chief of a property in Dulcimer, at the northern reaches of our kingdom."

A port at the mouth of the Great River, Dulcimer served as the last outpost for hunters, fisherman, and lumbermen traveling to and from the remote forests and streams beyond. It was perhaps the long chilly winter nights that kept people closeted indoors for many hours or the abundant supply of cedar that led Dulcimer to be the center of woodworking shops engaged in the crafting of musical instruments that gave the city its name.

"Dulcimer is easily reached by water or land. There is a castle there. Not the largest structure in the Chalklands we will admit, but it is sound. Quite beautiful on sunny days when the light strikes the stone. Washed with lime it gleams like marble against the green and brown of the cedars. So, White Castle it is called."

Sir Walter had once been the tenant-in-chief there. Sir Albert now had the baronage. Robin planned to name Ferree and Alice mesne lords under Sir Albert.

"You'll find plenty of room for you and your family plus generous space to dedicate to infirmaries and recovery rooms." Robin chuckled. "Dulcimer is known now for its trading posts and musical instruments but we won't be surprised when we hear that it's become a veritable sanctuary for sick and injured animals."

Alice clapped her hands together and pressed them to her mouth. When she caught her breath she cried, "Our own castle, Ferree, can you imagine? We will be like the king and queen of animal care." She beamed.

Ferree embraced his wife. "I can think of no one more deserving, dearest. Queen of my heart, there could be no finer queen of White Castle."

They helped Robin to settle Meeyoo in the cart and he and his men set out with no further delay. Robin wanted an early start to minimize the chance of having to make an overnight encampment. The return journey from Windham Hill to Bell Castle was unlikely to be any faster than the outgoing trip had been. Speed was no longer of the essence and Robin wanted to take pains that the ride be as comfortable as possible for Meeyoo.

What Robin wasn't in a hurry for was the conversation that he planned to have with Conrad. How soon would he want to leave on his mission once Robin informed him that he was free to go?

The day was cold but dry; neither snow nor rain lurked in the clear sky. Windham Hill retreated into the distance behind them. The track narrowed as the woods thickened. Every now and then Robin would spot a bird-shaped shadow cast on the track from high overhead and he wondered if it was the same bird that had trailed them on their way to Windham Hill. Would it accompany them all the way back to Bell Castle and if so, why? He made a mental note to inquire of his advisors what might cause such unusual behavior in a wild animal.

CHAPTER NINE

Robin plodded through his morning weighed down with dread. Vassals needing a decision on various trade, legal, and financial matters received only half his attention. Midmorning, he took his leave. His heart heavy, Robin climbed the stairs one reluctant step at a time and headed to the dining room in the keep. As he had requested, the shutters had already been opened and the sun flooded the space with gentle light. Bunches of fragrant herbs decorated the table and competed with fresh ale to perfume the air. Clean white linen covered the dining table laid with platters of poached fish, cold chicken, cheese, spiced apples, dried fruits, nuts and the most delicate of white breads.

Robin found Conrad in the keep's private dining room as summoned. The young man sat at the table, his hands folded. He appeared not to have touched the food.

Through the open window came the clamor of people greeting each other as they crossed the bailey, animal grunts and whines, clanging and banging from the kitchen and forge. Typical sounds of a normal Bell Castle day yet there was nothing ordinary about today.

Seemingly lost in thought, Conrad did not react when Robin first entered the room. Startled when Robin sat opposite, Conrad stood and bowed. He had traded the dark habit of his old order for a new garment: a plain robe of unbleached muslin which Robin could not imagine gave any protection from the cold. Conrad had cinched the thin covering with a belt bristling with a mace and a short, sharp rondel dagger. The strap of a baldric crossed his chest and a sword hung at his hip. The baldric was emblazoned with the insignia of Conrad's new order, the Guardian Angels: wings sprouted from the back of a T-shape with a V at its lowest point that could be a sword or a cross with a point at the bottom.

"Good morning, Sire," Conrad said.

"Brother Thaddeus, thank you for coming. We're sure you have much to do but this is a special day and we couldn't let it go by without some recognition." As well, thought Robin, it might be the last time we see you. "We didn't mean to disturb you if you were at prayer."

Conrad gave him a mild smile. "We weren't praying. We were listening to the sounds. Just another day at Bell Castle but we never really paid any attention. We realized it will be some time before we hear these sounds again."

The comment squeezed Robin's already aching heart. He forced out the words "Sit, please. Eat."

Conrad settled on a bench. "This is a veritable feast. A meal fit for a king."

And you would be king someday were you not running away from your duty, Robin was tempted to say, but he bit his tongue. In fulfillment of his vow, Robin had told Conrad he could go with the Guardian Angels if he chose. Conrad had made his choice.

Conrad closed his eyes and murmured, "Thank you, Lord, for the blessings you bestow on us."

Robin thought Conrad meant it as a grace before the meal but the young man didn't touch the food and Robin realized he was referring to his new commission. "Eat, please, Sire," Conrad said.

"You're not hungry?"

"It's rich fare," said Conrad with his usual benign smile. "We're used to simpler meals."

"We thought given the long journey on which you're embarking ...."

"Thank you. We appreciate the consideration." He helped himself to a nut. Robin wondered if Conrad anticipated eating like a squirrel as a member of the Order. "Please don't hesitate on my account." He waved his hand at the food.

Robin sighed, poured himself some ale, and cut wedges of apple and cheese.

"Good morning, Sire, Brother Thaddeus." Dale swept into the room, a diaphanous veil icing long mahogany hair like a layer of frost, a pale rose colored gown drifting from shoulders to his ankles.

"With permission, Your Majesty," she said, standing at the edge of the table.

"Please, be seated. Enjoy some dinner," Robin said.

Dale bowed, sat, and dished herself up generous servings which she ate with a decidedly unfeminine gusto. "Brother Thaddeus, are you excited about your new mission?"

Conrad gave his brother a patient smile. "Not excited, precisely. More stunned, filled with wonder. Eager to be of service. Trying not to question or worry about what we will encounter. We must trust in the Lord that what happens is our destiny."

Robin ground his teeth. In his opinion Conrad's destiny was something else entirely. He resisted dwelling on the multitude of deadly challenges that Conrad could meet as a militant monk. "May we escort you to the stables?"

"Thank you, Sire, but we have no need of a mount."

"How do you plan to get to your destination? Walk?"

"Yes, Sire, walk. Many of the pilgrims that we will protect will be on foot. We will meet our brothers at the gate."

"We will walk with you to join them, then," said Robin. "Dale?"

Dale shoved a piece of bread in her mouth and rose to follow them.

They descended the stair tower and crossed the bailey to the gate. Servants and vassals lining the path bowed as they passed.

"Bless you, Brother Thaddeus," and "Good fortune," they said. Some handed him gifts of dried flowers or pressed leaves, tokens by which he might remember Bell Castle. Others asked him for a blessing. The women's faces were drawn with the sadness and dread that Robin felt. Some of the younger boys growled, "Kill those heathens."

Conrad shook his head. "We are not an offensive, conquering force. Our mission is simply to defend those who would journey to the Holy Land to worship." He turned to Robin, "You know that, Sire, don't you?"

Robin nodded although he guessed that the distinction was lost on the natives of the land who likely saw the foreign pilgrims and their protectors as would-be conquerors and imperialists. That the conflict had been waged for so long and still endured spoke to the tenacity of the Holy Land's inhabitants in the defense of their homeland and way of life, foreign as it might seem.

Two men in Guardian Angel robes awaited Conrad at the gate. One, younger than Conrad, was but a lad who hadn't filled out his height. His robe draped from his narrow shoulders like a curtain. He had the rough look of a serf. Robin wondered if the youth hoped that service in the Guardian Angels would be his ticket to a better life.

The other was about the same age as Conrad. The right sleeve of his robe hung empty.

"Brother William, the young lad, just joined the order," Conrad said as they neared the gate. "Brother Joseph has been a Guardian Angel for several years. He has been on two campaigns. He lost his arm on the last one. He can't fight but he will be serving as our guide."

Robin gulped. All he could see was a glaring example of the harm that could befall his son. He had seen horrific wounds on the battlefield: noses smashed, entire rows of teeth shattered, eyes poked out. And worse: skulls split like gourds, limbs hacked off like joints of meat, blood gushing onto the ground like a river through a broken dam.

His barely digested dinner churned in his stomach.

The two men bowed at Robin's approach and Conrad made the introductions.

"We are most grateful to have Brother Thaddeus as a Guardian Angel," said Brother Joseph. "I can be of little service—"

"Nay, Brother Joseph. You may not be able to wield a sword but you lead us by example."

"As well, he knows the way," said Brother William. "We would be truly lost without him in more ways than one." He grinned. "But what an adventure that would be. We might discover a whole new land."

Brother Joseph's brow furrowed slightly.

"Discover it ... for God," said Brother William. "For His glory."

"Discovering new lands for God is the work of sailors and explorers," said Conrad. "We have but one mission and that is to protect those who seek to worship at the Lord's birthplace."

"Yes, of course," said Brother William but his barely bridled eagerness reminded Robin of Sir Maxwell.

"We should go," said Brother Joseph.

Now? But Robin had so much to say. He had lain awake all night rephrasing and rehearsing what he wanted to say to Conrad. Now he had only a moment to tell him to be safe, to return alive and unharmed. That he was sorry for opposing Conrad's life choice and that he appreciated every ounce of support that Conrad had shown to him. That he had forgotten every confrontational or trying moment of their life together and remembered only the joy of being Conrad's father. To tell him farewell. To tell him that he loved him.

Robin swallowed the lump in his throat. "Bless you, Brother Thaddeus."

Conrad bit his lower lip. "Thank you, Father. Your Majesty," he said and bowed. Then he and his comrades set off down the track away from Bell Castle.

Feeling small and aged, Robin turned and headed aimlessly away from the gate. If there was more that he was supposed to do today he had quite forgotten what it was. Some matter of running the kingdom but that had no importance now. In a few years Robin would be old, would take ill and die and the kingdom would crumble, if it even lasted that long. Rumors abounded that Bell Castle's king was aging and heirless and that the kingdom was an easy target. And now, with Conrad's very public departure ....

"You seem preoccupied, Sire," said Dale. "Is Your Majesty planning what to say to Lord Quentin?"

Oh, so that was what was on the agenda for today. Old business indeed. "And you know of this how?"

"We asked the steward yesterday what business would be conducted. We have made studies and given some thought to the matter, if Your Majesty would like to hear it."

Robin tried not to look as surprised as he felt.

"You have? Why?"

Now it was Dale's turn to appear surprised. "These will be our decisions to make one day. We have been following all managerial and judicial matters, noting the particulars, and evaluating the results of the decisions."

Robin had noticed that Dale now regularly attended court and appeared quite focused. He had wondered about that. It had been a struggle to get the young Prince Zachary to take, much less master, his lessons in negotiation and strategy. Now instead of pursing pastimes like trail riding or playing chess, Dale spent her time on the dry practical matters of running a kingdom.

"The ramifications are often far-ranging and long-lasting. We have learned much observing how Your Majesty rules."

"Why would you concern yourself with such things?"

"Because we intend to rule one day. We will inherit the throne now that Conrad is gone."

Absent, Robin thought. Don't say "gone" as if he has died, although that prospect was likely. Not only was Conrad's death a strong possibility, it would be some time before news that he had given his life for his mission would make its way to Bell Castle. Robin paced a few steps and turned.

"You aspire to rule the kingdom of the Chalklands?"

"Yes, Sire. It is ironic that the firstborn son has chosen to pursue the career option that normally falls to second in line, leaving us in a position to inherit. A reversal of roles, one might say."

If anyone would know about role reversal it should be Prince Zachary, now Princess Dale. "You are serious about this."

"We have the training." Dale held up her hand. "Yes, we admit, as a youngster we shirked many of our lessons. However we are applying ourselves day and night to make up for that youthful inattention. Now we see the value of that instruction."

Hadn't Conrad said something similar, that what he learned as a prince would stand him in good stead as a Guardian Angel?

King Zachary? It was not what Robin had intended. Conrad had been groomed from birth for his inevitable assumption of the crown. Robin had assumed Zachary's attraction to playacting and his immersion in different roles was the reaction of a young man whose status was that of the second son and whose future was likely going to be in service to the Church. Perhaps now his second born saw possibilities for a future that hadn't before existed.

"Of course we are delighted to hear this and you have our full support. We will give you every advantage so when the time comes for you to take the throne you will be prepared. We are looking forward to your putting Princess Dale aside and being Prince Zachary once more."

That, Robin thought, should present no problem. Surely Zachary—for Robin would no longer even try to think of him as Princess Dale—had come to his senses. Perhaps with the shock and sadness of having his brother depart for dangerous duty from which he might not return, Zachary had matured and awakened to reality. Robin felt the burden of worrying about the kingdom's future lift.

Dale frowned. "That had not been our plan."

"No? How can you intend to do otherwise? When you take the throne it will be as Zachary, King of the Chalklands. To strive for anything else would be to doom yourself to failure, would leave the kingdom vulnerable to lawlessness, anarchy, revolt, conquest. A woman cannot lead. We've discussed this."

Yes, there were exceptions to that rule, Empress Alexandra of Sea Gate, for example. That was there, not here.

"We didn't discuss it," Dale said with a pout. "Your Majesty declared it. We disagree."

No, this couldn't be happening. His firstborn son off to fight vicious and deadly battles, his second son committed to living life as a woman and aspiring to take the throne.

"Enough," Robin roared. "We have been patient. We have tried to be understanding. We gave you leave to indulge in this whimsy hoping that, like every other role you tried out as a child, you would eventually tire of this one. Well, now we are the one who is tired. This game has gone far enough."

"It's not a game," Dale protested. "This is who we are. Can't you see that?"

Robin was vaguely conscious of the attention that their raised voices drew from passers-by but there was no stopping. "No, we can't. Apparently you are of the mind to persist in this charade. You leave us no choice. We are your father. We are your king. We forbid you. We command you to cease this masquerade. Go now and change that gown for your princely garments."

Dale's jaw dropped and her face flushed. "You don't want to do this, Your Majesty."

"We do and we have. You are not to be seen outside the keep dressed in those garments. Now go."

Zachary turned and flounced toward the keep with longer more belligerent strides than Robin had seen on even the angriest of women.

In the wake of his outburst he realized that again he had lost his temper and control of the situation. Clearly it was well past the time when the king needed to take the reins firmly in hand.

CHAPTER TEN

"**Your** Majesty, what pious figure will the tournament celebrate?" Brother Leo, Conrad's replacement as Bell Castle's preacher, wore an expression on his pale unlined face that was just short of beseeching and twisted his fingers together.

Robin hadn't given that a moment's thought. He recalled the vow he had made at Windham Hill's church. Perhaps this was part of supporting Conrad's mission. Thinking quickly, he named a somewhat obscure saint, Valentine. The saint's feast day was in February which allowed for enough time to prepare for the tournament and also gave everyone something to look forward to in the middle of winter.

Each passing day brought more signs of the impending event which took on the aspects of a fair as much as it was to be a contest of athletic prowess. In front of the armory, soldiers erected targets for archery and darts. Groundskeepers cleared several square miles outside the castle walls for the tournament. Servants and carpenters constructed the stadium, setting out stakes to define the lists, the tournament battlefield. They built benches for the spectators and a stage to house plays, storytelling, and poetry readings.

The grandstand was erected a full story tall, the elevation to afford a clear view of the lists. The seamstresses, painters, and weavers collaborated on furnishing and decorating the grandstand for the comfort of the king and his honored guests.

Heralds posted the bans crying the jousting tournament and publicizing the rules. Criers in cities and towns announced the coming of the event and from there the word would spread to the villages until everyone in the kingdom knew about it.

The tournament would take place over several days, beginning with team events and the gradual elimination of competitors until the two best knights would meet in a decisive single final combat.

Knights were eager to compete. As if pride and honor weren't inducements enough, tournaments were a good source of revenue for a successful knight. The prize offered by the king to the champion knight was no small purse. Even more, the victorious knight could claim the armor and weapons of a fallen adversary during the tournament.

Knights weren't the only ones who stood to profit from the tournament. Throughout the competition, spectators would gamble on the outcome. If the contests were close, the betting could get just as fierce as the fighting. Rival nobles throughout the Chalklands issued side challenges to each other with ransoms sometimes richer than the prizes offered by the king himself.

Having invested in the competition, the nobles rallied their vassals to show their support and loyalty. Seamstresses crafted banners with the knights' colors and blazons which would be hung from the windows of the knights' lodging and those of their supporters, and created special identifying clothing for the competitors' retinue to wear in the encampment and throughout the event.

The preparations for the fair and the tournament had the desired effect. The closer the calendar moved to the opening of the fair, the fewer cases and disputes were brought to the king's court. Robin was pleased to see the Chalklands' subjects' energies productively channeled, not wasted on petty rivalries and jealousies. Nor did he receive any further urgings from his knights to act against King Ulric and he judged the matter put to rest.

Knights arrived for the competition well in advance of the opening of the tournament to set up their pavilions. Since the number of competitors with their squires and aides would far exceed the capacity of the guest rooms in the castle keep and the great hall, knights and their supporters raised tents as temporary lodgings near the lists. The knights brought draperies in their heraldic colors and other furnishings with which to decorate their pavilions, giving the tournament grounds as colorful an appearance as a fair with its canopies and stalls. Each knight tried to outdo the others in the grandeur and elegance of the temporary accommodations.

Sir Henry's was most elaborate of all, being a shed rather than a cloth tent. His servants carted in wooden panels that they quickly raised, then nailed together and roofed. They sealed up crevices with tar to keep out the winter drafts and painted the structure with Sir Henry's signature black.

Robin wondered if Sir Henry might be overcompensating for his recent humiliation. Suspected of treason, he had been stripped of his spurs, his land, and his title. Robin restored Sir Henry to knighthood when Sir Walter was declared to be the traitor and executed for his crime. Sir Henry regained his title but his campaign to repair his reputation rivaled any he had waged on the battlefield.

Contests began well before the combatants took the field in scheduled competition. The competing knights fought with fellow teammates in less formal games which gave them a chance to warm up and showcase special moves, aiming to intimidate their opponents. The evening before the opening of the tournament, vespers tourneys gave squires like Lord Quentin's young aspirant and less experienced knights a chance to try their skills. Robin strolled through the lists observing the youthful competitors, taking note of the caliber of up-and-coming knights.

At Sir Alan's pavilion Robin found Sir Maxwell readying for the vespers tourney.

"Sir Maxwell, we notice that you have redesigned your shield," Robin said. He had found it flattering that Sir Maxwell's blazon incorporated many of the same elements as his own: an orange chevron and a white bull, plus a falcon on a blue field that spoke of Sir Maxwell's loyalty. Now the emblem featured a new symbol: a gryphon, a winged magical animal with the head and talons of an eagle, the body, back legs, and tail of a lion. Combining the features of two majestic animals, the gryphon was said to be the king of all creatures, a fierce protector of treasured possessions. Those with a spiritual bent appreciated the symbolism of combining a land-based beast with one that had the freedom of a bird. In any case, the gryphon image communicated strength, courage, intelligence, and leadership, all qualities that perhaps Sir Maxwell aspired to have.

"Yes, Sire. We wanted a constant reminder of what we're fighting for and one that would inspire us to greatness." He paused. "Sire, there's something that I've been wanting to tell Your Majesty. I started to weeks ago in court if Your Majesty recalls but I was interrupted by the demands of the day. Would Your Majesty have a moment now?"

"A moment is about all we have. We would like to get around to all the knights and wish them success."

"Then I will get straight to it. I know who Meeyowyow's father is."

"Indeed, Sir Maxwell, and how do you know this?"

"Meeyowyow has distinctive features, wouldn't you agree? The sharp claws, big hindquarters. He leaps around like a rabbit."

Was he about to suggest that Meeyoo had mated with a hare? "Go on, Sir Maxwell, but be quick about it," Robin said, making for the tent's exit.

"I've seen another animal with the same features, and more. He has got to be Meeyowyow's sire." Maxwell crossed his arms over his chest and nodded with certainty. "It's a gryphon, Sire."

In an effort to stifle his laugh, Robin nearly choked on his ale. That explained the new image on Maxwell's shield. "That might actually make sense if there were such a thing."

If such a creature truly existed and if he had seen it, surely Robin would have noticed it. With a preternatural chill creeping up the back of his neck, Robin thought of the huge bird he had spotted on numerous occasions. The large bird that had trailed him to Dulcimer and back and that had followed him to the stadium yesterday and the day before. Had it the body of a lion, Robin would have been taken aback to say the least. Trying to determine what type of bird it was he had tried to make out the animal's features, but it had always been too far away to be seen clearly.

He chuckled. "And you think that this imaginary beast mated with Meeyoo."

"If any cat is worthy of such a magnificent mate it would be Meeyoo, wouldn't it, Sire? She is brave and loyal, strong and smart, according to the reports that you have given."

No argument there. She had stuck by him even in circumstances so dire even he had nearly given up hope of surviving. By cunning and sheer bravado she had saved Robin's life on more than one occasion.

"It would explain Meeyowyow's unusual features and abilities, Sire. It explains why Meeyoo took ill after having her litter."

Robin tried to stifle his mirth. Were the notion not so fanciful it would make sense. "If that's true, Sir Maxwell, and a gryphon does call Bell Castle home, we are fortunate indeed as it is a symbol of great and noble power. Should it come near, do let us know. Now, we must be off to see how the other knights fare."

The vespers tourneys seethed with the energy of participants fueled with youthful vigor and eager to prove themselves. Perhaps even fiercer competition took place the night before the opening of the tournament as each of the knights and sponsoring nobles strived to put on the largest, most boisterous, and lavish party. Robin wished that for just one night he could be a simple spectator and not King Bewilliam so he could join in the unbridled merriment without regard for maintaining royal dignity. He made his way from one tent to the next. At each stop the gaiety came to immediate halt. The partygoers bowed and hastened to be the first to provide the king with drink or refreshment.

Warmer and sturdier than that other knights' drafty tents, Sir Henry's booth was so crammed with celebrants that the host struggled to extricate himself from the crowd to greet his king.

"Your Majesty," he said with a deep bow, "welcome." He waved a hand at his pages. "Quick, food and drink for our king." One youngster brought Robin a trencher loaded with goat cheese-stuffed radishes, smoked salmon, bacon-wrapped scallops, dates, and figs. Another brought Robin a goblet which Sir Henry offered to fill with fortified wine or rum, "whichever would be your preference, Sire."

The repast was impressive and Robin was even more intrigued by the beverage selection. Both were drinks for which he had developed a taste in his travels, something that was not widely known. Not only had Sir Henry sussed out that information, he had gone to some trouble to procure the drinks. None of the rich party fare had been obtained locally and all had no doubt cost Sir Henry a pretty penny. As he sipped his rum, Robin pondered Sir Henry's extravagance. Sir Henry was current with his taxes and tributes. Robin couldn't complain that the man had spent the king's money. Perhaps some wealthy merchant was helping to host Sir Henry. Several wealthy merchants by the looks of things.

*****

Robin rose before sunup the opening day of the tournament. His page took extra pains to see that the king was outfitted in his most elegant and vivid garments, all the better to be seen by spectators at the furthest reaches of the grounds and impress subjects from near and far.

Meeyoo at his heels, Robin stepped out into the hallway and headed for the stairs. The door to Zachary's room opened and a figure emerged, a tall woman elegantly garbed in a rich gown and crown with gold and jewels. The royal crown of Zachary, Prince of the Chalklands, worn this morning by Princess Dale. "Good morning, Your Majesty. May we accompany you to the stadium?"

"No," said Robin. "Not dressed like that. "

Zachary did a little pirouette, his skirts swirling around his legs. "Do you not think our subjects will be impressed? We had this gown specially crafted by our best seamstresses to our own original design."

"You were told that in those clothes you are not to leave the keep. Either change or stay in your room. If you plan to attend the tournament and sit in the grandstand it will be as Prince Zachary, not Princess Dale."

Zachary's mouth turned down and his face turned stormy. "Your Majesty will regret this. We will rule. When that day comes we will at last be our true self. We will live the life that we were meant to live. You will be dead and you won't be able to do anything about it." He turned, stomped back into his room, and slammed the door.

Robin felt the heat of anger flood his chest and neck. Coming from anyone else that would sound like a murderous threat and be punishable by death.

He sighed deeply. Not an auspicious beginning to something to which he had looked forward for weeks. Damn Zachary. As petulant and willful as a child. Let him sit out the festival closeted in the silent and empty keep. Robin wouldn't let the festivities be spoiled.

His page and Meeyoo trotting to keep pace, Robin marched down the stairs and crossed the bailey. An odd sound from overhead caught his attention. High above, a large bird made its way across the sky, headed toward the stadium. Could it possibly be the same winged creature that had accompanied him on the journey to Windham Hill and back? Robin pulled his cloak closer around his shoulders.

Lights glowing in the woodworker's and in the weaver's hut brightened the morning-dark bailey. Smoke billowed from the forge and the cook fires of the kitchen. The chapel was practically daylight bright and a steady stream of people seeking blessings for their day's efforts filed in and out. Donkey carts snaked to and from the gatehouse and the bailey where vendors erected their stalls by lantern light. On the stage near the great hall, workers mounted backdrops and sets and made final preparations for dramatic performances.

Outside the gate, an entire new city had grown up just beyond Bell Castle's walls complete with lodgings and shops. The bright canopies of vendors' carts and knights' pavilions dotted several acres of tournament grounds turning a wintery landscape into a field of color like a meadow blooming with spring flowers. Feathery plumes of smoke wafted from small fires.

Every bench in the stadium was already filled and even more spectators sat on the ground near the lists on blankets, food baskets and beverage jugs by their side. Musicians played and jongleurs told tales to the waiting crowd.

As Robin approached the arch over the entrance to the tournament field, heralds came to attention and blew a fanfare. With bows and curtsies, late arrivals crowding the path parted to make way for the king.

Stepping rhythmically to the accompanying sounds of drums, cymbals, and bells, Robin proceeded to the grandstand. Most of the spectators were so engrossed in watching the knights warming up, the better to discern whom to back with wagers, that they hardly noticed him, nor did the contestants, occupied as they were with last minute preparations.

Robin took the wooden steps to the covered grandstand. At this elevation he had a view of the entire tournament grounds as well as shelter from sun, wind, and weather. The day was dry but the lightening sky was gray as if rain was on the way.

The grandstand was furnished with several cushioned armchairs for royalty and invited guests. Prince Zachary's was vacant. Fine, Robin thought. Let the stubborn fool sulk in his room for three days.

A sedan chair hung from the rafters by a pulley. Robin lowered it so that Meeyoo could climb in, then raised it to give her a view over the grandstand's front half wall, not that she would appreciate or even care about the spectacle. She would probably sleep most of the time. However, Robin wanted to show his appreciation for the thoughtfulness and creativity of the builder by actually using the device. He tied the rope off to a cleat using a knot he had learned during his arduous and fortunately brief stint as a deckhand.

He stepped forward and nodded to the bugler to announce that the king was about to speak. The spectators straggled to their feet. First the people directly opposite the grandstand bowed. The people behind them picked up the cue and row by row, people bowed and straightened, bowed and straightened, forming a wave of motion that ebbed away towards the back of the field.

"Welcome, subjects of the kingdom of the Chalklands and honored guests," Robin said as loudly as possible without shouting. "We are grateful for this opportunity to gather and celebrate our strength as a community."

The people nearest the grandstand stood still and honored their king by listening with rapt attention, or at least appearing to do so. Those too distant to hear milled about, anxious perhaps for the opening speeches to be done and for the games to begin.

"We are assembled here for the next three days to revel in the skill and courage of our warriors. We will compete in teams, demonstrating our ability to put striving for personal exaltation aside for the good of a shared goal. And we will have individual competitions to exhibit the results of years of training and discipline. Throughout the contests, we will have as our highest priority the spirit of fair and gentlemanly competition. We seek fame and glory, yes, as well as rich prizes."

Robin paused and knights eager to get their hands on a fat purse cheered and applauded.

"But more than that we pledge to appreciate each and every honest effort whether it results in victory or defeat. Bravery is not about being fearless; it's about being driven by something more important than fear. Let us triumph through every day in the Chalklands as we will succeed here today by helping those whom we can, and by showing our appreciation for the support that we receive."

Robin paused again for a round of applause.

"We dedicate this tournament to Saint Valentine, a courageous man who prevailed in his struggle through beatings of unimaginable cruelty and who was vanquished only when his head was taken off." That image rather robbed the saint of the spiritual significance of his sacrifice and made him sound more like an athlete of heroic proportions than a humble priest, but Robin figured that Brother Leo would redeem the saint in his speech. "With that, we give you Brother Leo, Bell Castle's newest preacher, who will deliver the invocation."

Robin directed the herald to prompt the monk. Had he been here, Brother Thaddeus probably would have thought it appropriate to sit in the grandstand with the king. Possibly Brother Leo should be so honored but the monk was in the lists circulating among the knights, aiding with last minute prayers for guidance and success.

Brother Leo hastened to stand before the grandstand. He bowed to the king. "Thank you, King Bewilliam, for the opportunity to be of service. May blessings be upon Your Majesty." The monk turned and faced the crowd and folding his hands in prayer said, "Thank you, Lord, for giving our fighting men the skill to defend Bell Castle, to keep us safe while we serve You. May their skills assist them well today and may they have Your help to use their powers to the fullest. Their performance today may result in injury. Be with them if they are wounded. Give them strength to carry on and to gain greater maturity through personal sacrifice. Free them from temptation to cheat or play foul and inspire them with the spirit of brotherhood and honor. May our efforts here today please You and bring glory to You. Amen." He turned and again bowed to the king.

The combined murmured "amens" from the crowd rumbled like distant thunder.

"Thank you, Brother Leo," Robin said when the noise subsided, "now our musicians will present an anthem, an arrangement composed especially for the Bell Castle Saint Valentine's Tournament."

The music would cue the knights to form the procession.

Young girls headed the parade carrying baskets filled with dried flower petals which they strew along the parade path.

Maidens followed, prancing and fluttering their scarves, hoping to catch the eye and possibly the heart of a knight.

Led by squires carrying standards, the knights who would fight on foot followed. One by one, each knight neared the grandstand. The herald shouted the contestant's name and the knight stopped and bowed to his king before moving on, shouting his war cry which was picked up by his supporters.

The mounted knights brought up the rear dressed in hauberks emblazed with their insignia. Manes and coats groomed to gleaming, their destriers were draped in blankets, gaiters, and blinders to match the knight's colors. The knights held their lances upright and the pennants wrapped around the end flared out in the late winter breeze.

So much color, it was like a moving rainbow. Though he had watched the tournament grow and build day by day, Robin found that even he was impressed by the spectacle. His chest swelled with pride.

The first of a steady stream of servants and merchants mounted the stairs to the grandstand to keep the king supplied with food and drink.

About to begin was the first in a series of contests, the melee a pied. The fights conducted on foot were reminiscent of the clash between vanguards of attacking and defending infantrymen. Now two teams of knights stood opposite each other in the lists and waited restively and noisily for the herald's cry to begin at which point they would rush together with a roar. Although clubs would smack and fists would fly, the object of the melee wasn't to cause great bodily harm much less deliver any mortal blows, although tales were told of a knight whose helmet was hit so hard and so badly dented that he could not remove it without a blacksmith's aid. Instead, the melee knights sought to capture as many opponents as possible. The captive would be held for ransom.

Facing off practically nose to nose against an opponent determined to wrestle one to the ground was a pale imitation of a battlefield confrontation. In war, infantrymen on the front lines knew they were about to race headlong into a battle to the death.

Nevertheless, the melee a pied called for steady nerves and mettle.

Waiting for the signal, Sirs Alan, Albert, Kenneth, and Howell stood shoulder to shoulder, huddled in menacing postures and glaring at the competing knights on the other team.

Robin heard the bugler's call but it wasn't the signal for the games to begin. Rather the tune announced the arrival of a royal personage.

CHAPTER ELEVEN

"**Prince** Zachary," the herald cried.

Robin was surprised and delighted as well as perplexed and uneasy to see Zachary make his way from the entrance to the grandstand dressed as ordered in princely black velvet trousers and gold-trimmed brocaded weskit, his long mahogany hair scraped back from his face and hanging down his back in a tight braid. The young man mounted the steps and gave a cursory bow.

"May we sit?" he asked, his voice flat.

"Yes, please," Robin replied and Zachary took a seat alongside his father and king. "We are glad to have you join us."

Robin looked askance at his son and in addition to being baffled felt a spark of pride. Zachary cut a handsome albeit slim and fair figure.

"Who's winning?" Zachary asked.

"It's hard to tell," Robin replied. The melee was a churning sea of legs and arms from which every now and then one figure would peel off with another in tow and head for the knights' pavilions. The roiling mass of color thundered with roars, grunts, groans, and epithets.

In the sea of faces watching the fracas, Robin was surprised to see Alice and Ferree, now lord and lady of White Castle, and their daughters Jewel and Joy. Robin sent his page to invite them to enjoy the games from the comfort of the king's grandstand. It was the least he could to do thank them for saving Meeyoo. Besides, Alice and Ferree's daughters were comely and charming. Either one would make a fine match for a someday king. Perhaps Zachary would take a liking to one of them.

The family entered the grandstand, Alice and Ferree leading their daughters who giggled bashfully. Robin thought Alice's costume of ice blue complemented her golden hair and fair complexion and Ferree was handsome as well in his suit and floppy hat with narrow brim and feather trim. They both looked well and Robin decided that their elevated status suited them.

Alice enthused about Meeyoo's hanging-basket seat and expressed delight at how healthy the cat had become. "She looks like she has made a complete recovery, thank God."

Or thank Alice. Yes, Robin had made a bargain with God and had honored it. Nevertheless he wasn't convinced that God had anything to do with Meeyoo's healing. On the other hand, Alice believed in God and to serve Him was motivated to help Meeyoo so maybe God had fulfilled His end of the contract through her.

"My compliments, Your Majesty," Alice said. "Apparently her recuperative care was a success."

"As you warned us it was not all that easy to administer," Robin replied with a chuckle. He introduced Zachary to the family and directed the young women to sit between him and his son.

"We thank you for restoring the king's cat to health," said Zachary without much enthusiasm.

"It was our honor," replied Ferree.

"It is we who are honored by your presence. You traveled a distance from Dulcimer to attend," said Robin.

"One of our vassals hopes someday to compete and is in the lists, assisting other knights," said Alice.

"The view from here is amazing," remarked Jewel. "I can see everything."

"Everyone from the Chalklands must be here," said Joy. "I don't believe I have ever seen so many people gathered in one place."

"So you have not been to a tournament before?" Robin asked.

"Yes, Sire, but never one of this magnitude or this well organized. The young men in Windham Hill would stage competitions sometimes but with all due respect they were more like brawls than athletic events."

Though intended to be an exercise in demonstrating one's hand-to-hand combat skills, from where Robin sat the Bell Castle melee didn't appear to be much more orderly than a public house punch-up.

Leaning far forward in her seat, Joy clenched and unclenched her hands. Robin could just barely hear her murmur "yes, yes, get him." She then sprang to her feet, threw her arms in the air, and cried, "Yes."

Everyone else in the grandstand looked at her in astonishment. She blushed and retook her seat. Robin noticed down in the huddle a knight threw a couple of punches into the air then pounded his chest while at his feet, another combatant struggled to get to his knees.

"Your knight?" Robin asked.

Alice shook her head. "That's not ours. I suspect another contestant has caught our daughter's eyes."

Robin had rather wished that Zachary might capture Joy's interest. Perhaps he should command the prince to join the contest and throw some manly punches of his own if that's what it took to earn the young woman's notice.

As the morning wore on, the ranks of combatants thinned. Sirs Howell and Kenneth had already hauled off prisoners to their respective pavilions while Sirs Alan and Albert had returned to the fray seeking to best yet more opponents. Fierce fighters likely to survive the melee and go on to fight on the morrow, Robin wanted to root for them although every man in this fight was to a greater or lesser degree one of Robin's vassals and it would be wrong to show favoritism.

He recalled his youth when as a squire and later as a knight he had been in the lists, not as an observer but as a participant. He remembered the pounding-heart thrill of challenges issued and met, of retiring at the end of the day bleeding, sore, exhausted, and exhilarated, lust for life awakened by the threat of bodily harm. How he wished he could be down there in the dirt slugging it out once again.

He chided himself at his own folly. As if he hadn't had enough mortal challenges lately. He'd gone up against dragons and sea monsters. He'd been consigned to die in a dungeon, been chased by soldiers for the bounty placed on his head. Certainly that amounted to enough adventure to last the rest of his life. Still, while the successful execution of his duties as king was rewarding, there was nothing like the thrill of having one's knee on the chest of a man he had wrestled to the ground.

The day's light waned and with it seemingly went the combatants' ardor. The last remaining pugilists brought their scuffle to a conclusion, some knights surrendering out of sheer exhaustion. Many had already withdrawn to their pavilions to nurse wounds, eat and drink to replenish their energy. It would be prudent for the winners to rest and revitalize for the second day competition but Robin knew the opposite would be the case. Parties had already started in some of the pavilions. Losers as well as winners wanted to thank their supporters and celebrate, if not a victory then at least a valiant effort, or perhaps try to drown the memory of a humiliating defeat. Many tall tales would be told of a battle lost by an unfortunate lucky move on the part of an opponent, or a contest won because of exceptional skill and fortitude.

Some might stay for the entire tournament, to learn from the performance of those who had bested them, not to mention enjoy their hospitality. Others would leave on the morrow, weighed down by the embarrassment of an early elimination.

The seneschal reported the winners of the melee a pied. Robin was secretly pleased to see that Sirs Albert, Alan, Howell, and Kenneth had all prevailed. The seneschal called out the plan and participants for the next day's contest and reiterated the rules. Robin invited the victors of the melee a pied and their sponsors to the first night celebration.

Robin prepared to leave the grandstand. "Shall we head to the great hall?" he said to Prince Zachary and the guests from White Castle. He hoped that attending the night's banquet party would advance a friendship between Zachary and either of the two young women.

Robin's page lowered Meeyoo's sedan chair.

"May I?" Alice asked and Robin granted her permission to scoop the cat into her arms. Meeyoo seemed content to be carried.

To a fanfare, the king and his party left the grandstand. Serenaded by musicians, they ambled toward the gate and bailey along a path now lit by torches. Knights, nobles, squires, and spectators rushed up to Robin, bowed, and thanked him for a glorious day of competition.

As they approached the curtain wall, Robin spied an unfamiliar gargoyle perched high atop the watchtower. No, not a gargoyle but the large bird that had winged its way overhead as he made his way to the stadium this morning.

Already aglow with candles and lanterns and warmed by braziers, the great hall thronged with early arrivals. Many of the melee's contestants had won the day and some already filled the hall, all in high spirits despite the bandages and slings they sported. The herald announced the king's entrance and the cacophony halted like a held breath. Robin acknowledged the homage and with a wave bade everyone to resume partying. Greeting guests, thanking sponsors, and congratulating the day's victors, he waded through a sea of velvet and brocade, gold braid, silk, lace, and gems and made his way to the front of the room. He invited Prince Zachary and the White Castle guests to be seated at the king's table. He pulled out the chair to his right, above the salt cellar placed in the middle of the table, and before Zachary could take the chair, Robin seated the lord with his wife beside him. To their right he sat the couple's daughters with Zachary between them. Zachary glared as if resentful about being consigned for the meal's duration with the two young women as tablemates.

Meeyoo found her seat on the dais where a platter of tidbits and a bowl of cream awaited her.

Bandaged, bruised, and bleeding, Sirs Alan, Albert, Howell, and Kenneth crowded close to an ale vat. They raised their cups and toasted each other. At Robin's approach they bowed and lifted their cups toward him.

"Did you see it, Your Majesty?" Sir Alan asked, his face flushed and eyes burning.

"It was an inspired move," said Sir Albert.

Sir Kenneth threw an arm around Sir Howell's neck and notched a knee behind the man's leg. "Sir Alan got Sir Dennis in a hold like this. Sir Dennis might be built like a brick shithouse— privy, begging your pardon, Your Majesty—but Sir Alan took him ..." Sir Kenneth tugged on Sir Howell's neck and made his knees buckle "... down."

Sir Howell coughed, wriggled from Sir Kenneth's hold, and straightened.

"I've been practicing that move for weeks but to get to use it on Sir Dennis—"

"Took him DOWN," Sir Kenneth cried.

The knights slapped each other's palms and clinked their cups.

"Well done, men." Robin chuckled and left them to resume reenacting their winning strategies, ribbing and punching each other as if they hadn't spent the day getting clobbered.

Sir Henry appeared to have no trouble keeping his cup full, so well attended was he by admirers. Robin could hardly get near him for the press of people. He bit his lower lip and felt both guilt and relief. The accusation of treason which was proven false had caused the knight much grief but the damage hadn't been irreparable. Sir Henry had apparently made a successful comeback.

Robin recalled the execution of Sir Walter, the true traitor. The fatal blow Sir Henry delivered may not have been so much of a coup de grace after all but rather struck in vengeful anger over the needless humiliation that Sir Henry suffered.

Robin shook the grisly image from his mind. Tonight was no night for such gruesome remembrances. He bade the herald to trumpet a short fanfare.

Standing at the edge of the dais, Robin said, "We will ask you to pause in your celebration for just a moment while Brother Leo gives the invocation, after which we will formally congratulate the day's victors. Please, hold your acclamation until all the knights have been named."

Brother Leo's invocation was thankfully brief.

"Ladies and gentlemen, honored guests, and most excellent knights," Robin cried, "it is our great pleasure to formally acknowledge today's winners." The hubbub stilled and Robin hastened to reel off the names of the knights who had prevailed in the melee and who would compete again on the morrow. "Valiant knights, collect your trophies and prize money from the officers at arms before your return to your pavilions. Which we would suggest that you do at some point tonight and get some rest because the next event will sorely test you."

Robin's audience laughed but not a single knight took the advice. Robin chuckled. Some would no doubt wish that they had. Tomorrow's melee a cheval would be no simple trail ride.

When the cheers and applause subsided, he said, "We have one more announcement and then we bid you to resume your merrymaking." With that he introduced the kingdom's newest lord and lady and their daughters. "They have our thanks not just for the service that they provided to us personally but also for the knowledge and skill they contribute to the kingdom. We are proud to have among us such talented and caring stewards of our animal charges."

The applause was polite if not unanimously enthusiastic. Quite a few of his subjects had pets such as prized trained hawks, fighting cocks, and hunting dogs who were so valued that they were coddled and treated as well or better than some serfs. However, for the most part animals were regarded as lesser beings or in some cases menaces and threats. That anyone would be devoted to their welfare was considered odd, as Robin's doctor had noted.

Before returning to the king's table, Robin drew Brother Leo aside. "Any word about Conrad—Brother Thaddeus?"

Brother Leo pressed his lips together. "News from that distant and embattled region is slow to reach us. I would imagine that when they are available, the abbot gets detailed reports on how things fare in the Holy Land, but the monks are not privy to them. I'm afraid that I would hear about Brother Thaddeus only if something exceptional had transpired."

"In other words, no news is good news?"

"I'm sorry, Your Majesty. I will try to find out something."

Robin thanked him and moved to take his seat.

"A moment first, Sire, if you would," said Zachary. "Your Majesty, have we given offense?" he said. "We did as you required." He swept his hand along his jacket and trousers.

"Indeed and your garb is most pleasing, as is your spirit of cooperation."

"Yet Your Majesty denies us our place of honor at your side."

"We mean no insult. It was simply our intent to be gracious hosts to our guests."

Zachary frowned. "What will others in attendance think? They may attribute meaning to Your Majesty's placing Lord Ferree in the prince's chair."

"Should anyone have a question about who is the prince of Bell Castle or who is next in line to rule the Chalklands?"

Robin could see the muscles in Zachary's jaw clench. "No, Sire," he said with a snort.

"Surely you don't find it objectionable to have a charming and beautiful woman at each elbow."

"No, Sire."

"Excellent. Then may we return to our place and enjoy the evening?" Or at least as much enjoyment as Robin could muster. Good news about Conrad would have done much to lighten his mood. His first-born son should be here, not wandering around some forsaken desert in a monk's robe.

Between courses of food, entertainers played music, sang, told stories, and performed juggling acts. As part of their retinue, Alice and Ferree had brought a young musician. "If it would please Your Majesty, he would like to perform for the king and his guests."

The musician did prove to be an accomplished player of the dulcimer, the stringed instrument whose manufacture had given the city a reputation which looked to be matched or even overshadowed by White Castle's growing fame as an animal sanctuary.

The couple's daughters expressed an interest in their host, asking Robin questions about the Chalklands and courtly life. In the spirit of competition, Jewel and Joy contested for the privilege of being Robin's dance partner.

Joy won, which Robin didn't mind. She was a nimble and graceful dancer and a delightful companion. Throughout the evening Joy fended off her sister's attempts to enjoy Robin's company. Between songs and courses, Joy kept him entertained with stories about some of the more curious animals that had been brought to Dulcimer to be healed, the odd and challenging illnesses and injuries that her parents had tackled, and the near-miraculous rescues.

"So, is the Queen of Bell Castle not able to attend tonight's festivities?" she asked.

"There is no Queen," said Robin.

"Oh, my apologies, and my sympathies. I certainly did not mean, that is, I—"

"No apology necessary," said Robin. He didn't explain that his queen wasn't dead, just no longer his wife.

Had he been worried as host that Joy's sister Jewel was neglected, a few glances at the table eased his concerns. Prince Zachary and Jewel's heads were bent in conversation. Robin smiled. Prince Zachary could do worse than to consort with a lord's daughter. Lord Ferree and Lady Alice had proved to be intelligent, resourceful, and kind people; their daughters came from good stock. Jewel would make a fine princess and one day, a fine queen.

Perhaps at last Robin could put aside worries about his kingdom's future. The first day of the Saint Valentine's Tournament had truly ended on a high note with Robin winning the greatest prize of all. As drunk with delight as if with wine, he returned his attention to dancing with Joy.

CHAPTER TWELVE

As he had the day before, Robin headed for the stadium without Zachary. Maybe he would find the young prince already in the grandstand because he wasn't in his room nor anywhere else in the keep. Perhaps he had spent the night with Joy or Jewel.

Cold weather had crept in overnight and showed no signs of departing. Even the evergreens looked pallid in the gray light. The air was icy. Rain, sleet, perhaps even snow were possible, making for an especially challenging tournament that would be uncomfortable for the contestants and even more so for the spectators.

Robin passed a display of the helms belonging to the knights who had fought the day before. Ladies crowding around it inspected the helms and remarked which knights had fought fairly and which not so fairly.

Zachary was not in the grandstand but the lord and lady of White Castle were already in attendance as was their daughter, Joy. At Robin's entrance they stood and bowed.

"Where is Jewel?" Robin asked. "Is she unwell?"

"Not at all, Sire, and thank you for asking. May we say that was a most marvelous feast last night and we greatly enjoyed ourselves."

"As did I," said Joy, and Robin thought there was a special twinkle in her eye. "Prince Zachary has also been a most gracious host and has made Jewel feel quite welcome. I believe this morning they are perusing the vendors' offerings and taking in the entertainment at the stage."

Well, well, well, maybe there was hope for Zachary after all.

The herald called the combatants to order and Brother Leo blessed the day's efforts.

Robin addressed the combatants. "Gentlemen, congratulations are in order. Yesterday's winners have been rewarded handsomely but the losers are to be commended as well for while you took no prizes, you won nevertheless. You could have stayed home but you aimed higher. You challenged yourself to do more. You conquered your fears. You gave your best effort. Next time, you will have the benefit of experience.

"We commend you all for upholding the principles of gentlemanly competition. Those principles should be foremost on your mind today. Remember, we are not at war. You are to respect not only your fellow competitors but the residents of the lands through which you will pass. Do not damage any property, royal or privately owned, nor seize any possessions. Do not frighten or disturb noncombatants, in particular the women."

Mounted knights would be demonstrating their skills in riding, racing, and tracking by chasing and fleeing from each other for miles through the countryside. Past melees a cheval had become notorious for the hordes of young men who would charge into a settlement, hot-blooded from the previous day's contest. Caught up in the frenzy, they would smash wares in shops, set fires to hovels and fields, and carry off young women. At first flattered by the attention, the maidens would later resent having been taken like war trophies, used and then discarded like playthings. The subjects' complaints had nearly removed the melee a cheval from the program of competition until Robin had drawn up the rules which he strictly enforced. Knights found violating the injunctions were banned from further competition, fined, and forced to compensate the injured parties.

"Nor is this a battle to the death. You are reminded that the objective is to capture your target, not kill him." Some years ago a melee a cheval had indeed gotten out of hand and resulted in the pointless death of a valuable knight.

Robin gave the signal to begin and mounted knights stampeded from the tournament grounds. Throughout the day, winners would return with their captives. Sir Kenneth was one of the first to arrive with his hostage: Sir Howell. Believing the two knights to be on companionable terms if not actually friends, Robin left the grandstand for the lists to see if a sudden enmity had sprung up between the two men.

"I sought to spare Sir Howell the ignominy of being captured by someone else, especially someone who would insist on a punishing ransom and on taking his armor," said Sir Kenneth. "My terms are more forgiving." He turned to his captive. "You pay for all the ale today."

Sir Howell glared. "You got lucky, that's all."

"Howell," Sir Kenneth said, "you are no good on a horse. You would have had a better chance of getting away from me had you fled on foot."

"I'm not that bad."

"Yes you are."

Amiably jostling and elbowing each other and trading insults, they headed for Sir Kenneth's pavilion.

While the arrival of each triumphant knight with his captive caused a stir in the victor's camp, for the spectators in the stadium there wasn't much to see and the tournament became more of a fair. Outside the barracks, soldiers and youths competed at archery and darts. Vendors sold food, drinks, and souvenirs. Toy horses and weapons were especially popular with young boys who staged their own jousts and melees. So as not to show favoritism, Robin stopped at every booth. Each merchant pressed a sample on the king which he in turn gave to the lord and lady or handed to delighted passers-by.

The children enjoyed puppet shows and magic acts while their parents delighted in performances by musicians and storytellers who circulated throughout the grounds. Having considered himself something of a jongleur in the day, Robin himself took in a few of the performances.

Nearly continuous entertainment was offered on the stage in the form of plays, comedies, and dramas. During the tournament preparations, Prince Zachary showed an avid interest in and devoted a considerable amount of attention to the readying of the stage and the theatrical events. Fearful of what he might discover, Robin was reluctant to go near it. The last time he had stopped to watch a play at a fair he was confronted by the sight of Zachary dressed as a woman and portraying a seductress altogether too convincingly for Robin's comfort. However, the guests from White Castle were eager to take in dramatic delights of a caliber unlikely to be found in Dulcimer.

As he feared, Robin found his son at the stage. Robin breathed a sigh of relief to see Zachary properly attired as Prince of the Chalklands. With Jewel by his side, he appeared to be giving directions for the next performance.

Jewel hastened from the stage to join her parents and sister. She bowed to the king and said, "It's so exciting, Your Majesty. Mother, Father, there will be comedies, dramas. Recitals of epic poems. Prince Zachary is an accomplished dramatist. The stage, the playbill, the costumes are all his doing." She clasped her hand. "Did you know that the prince has a talent for acting?"

Indeed. Robin began to wonder if by behaving as a charming prince, Zachary was simply playing another role. Which was genuine and which was an act, Prince Zachary or Princess Dale? And were there other identities yet to emerge? It made Robin's head ache.

He looked toward the stage but Zachary was now nowhere in sight. The master of ceremonies spotted Robin and announced that the king himself was in the audience, which brought the spectators to their feet to acknowledge their ruler. With a wave, Robin bid them retake their seats.

The Master of Ceremonies announced the next performance, *In My Dreams*, an original play written by Prince Zachary specifically for the Saint Valentine's Tournament.

The drama told the story of a sad princess condemned by her evil father to spend her life cloistered in the castle keep for the crime of having been born female when the king had wished for a son. At last the princess was rescued by a dashing prince who killed the king and freed the princess. She became queen and ruled in her father's stead.

Zachary played both princess and prince, cleverly switching roles even within the same scene by swapping a veiled hennin for a crown and reversing a neck-to-ankles cloak to hide or reveal a man's costume.

Jewel clapped her hands in delight. "Isn't Prince Zachary just brilliant?" she exclaimed. "His Highness gave me a preview of the performance last night. I suppose he spent a lot of time rehearsing the role of princess and working out just the right costume because he has many gowns. He modeled a couple for me." Jewel giggled. "His Highness is as beautiful in a gown as he is handsome in breeches."

Robin felt sick. Here he had imagined that Zachary and Jewel had left the feast in the great hall and repaired to the keep for a romantic assignation. Robin dreamed of a wedding, of grandchildren, but instead of making love, Zachary and Jewel had been playing dress-up like a couple of children.

Worse was the play Robin had just witnessed. The play's message was clear. Robin found especially disturbing the death of the evil king. It had its dramatic impact, drawing gasps from a stunned and titillated crowd. Zachary's threat from yesterday morning resounded. "We will rule and when that day comes we will do as we please. You will be dead and you won't be able to do anything about it."

Zachary couldn't really have murder on his mind. Could he?

CHAPTER THIRTEEN

Robin would have thought to find the great hall to be nearly deserted. Knights, supporters, and guests had partied the night before the opening of the tournament and all throughout last night, not to mention the fact that the knights and their squires had put in two grueling days competing in the melees.

Robin snickered at himself. It hadn't been that long ago that as a prince and even a young king he had fought all day, partied all night, and gone back for more the next day on little sleep and less food. How easy it was to forget the indefatigable spirit of youth. Perhaps more than wrinkles and gray hair, the diminishing of one's energies was an unmistakable sign of growing old.

A little weary, he primed himself to put on the display of vigor that his subjects needed to see.

The herald moved to announce the king's arrival and Robin bade him wait a moment. A carole was in progress and Robin saw no need to make his guests stop dancing in the middle of a song.

He spied Sirs Howell and Kenneth dancing with their wives and Sirs Albert and Alan with young female admirers. Sir Maxwell's knighthood curriculum included dance and the young man was gamely trying out newly acquired moves and coordination with a young woman. The lord and lady of White Castle were also on the floor.

Prince Zachary and Jewel sat at the king's table deep in conversation. Robin hoped that they were planning an assignation and not exchanging fashion advice. A seat away, Joy sat alone toying with her food, a slightly sullen expression on her face.

The music ended and the herald announced the king. Robin addressed the crowd and as he had the night before, requested that Brother Leo deliver the invocation, after which Robin named the day's winners and awarded prizes. No prize for Sir Howell who had been "captured" by Sir Kenneth.

"I thought it best to bring him to the feast lest he try to escape," Sir Kenneth said and laughed.

"I shall appeal to my king about the cruel and unusual punishment I am receiving at the hands of my captor," said Sir Howell.

"Cruel and unusual?" Sir Howell retorted.

Sir Howell hoisted his tankard. "My cup has gone dry. Perhaps you intend for me to die of thirst."

Sir Kenneth laughed harder, linked arms with his "prisoner" and led him away to the ale vat to refill his cup.

Joy appeared at Robin's side and with a curtsy said, "Your Majesty, may I again thank you for a most splendid time? This tournament has been the event of my lifetime."

"We're pleased that you are enjoying it," Robin replied, his attention half on Zachary.

The musicians resumed playing. Joy fidgeted and caught Robin's eye. By her hopeful expression it was clear that she wanted to be asked to dance and Robin complied.

As they traversed the floor in the round, Robin could see Zachary and Jewel were still together. *What could they be discussing at such length?* Robin longed to return to the table and perhaps get some notion of what had the two so thoroughly engaged, but Joy wanted another dance and then another ale. She fetched a drink for herself and for Robin. She then took a turn on the dance floor with her father, leaving Robin to partner with Lady Alice.

More ale and then it was Joy's turn again. When he next looked at the king's table it was empty. Zachary and Jewel had left the table and were headed for the door.

Still stewing about the play, Robin found himself imagining the unimaginable. First, that Zachary was complaining to Jewel about his treatment at the hands of his father. Robin wished he could be present to defend himself and provide Jewel with his side of the story. Then, that Zachary had gone beyond merely complaining to plot against Robin, find a way to remove him from the throne. A young and impressionable woman like Jewel could easily be swayed by Zachary's cunning speech and promises of rich rewards for her cooperation. Worse, were they plotting some ultimate solution to Zachary's discontent?

"Sire?"

Robin looked at Joy and realized that he had come to a complete stop in the middle of the dance floor. "Our apologies," he said and resumed, but with little enthusiasm.

"Oh, not at all. I was just concerned that Your Majesty had become unwell."

"No, just preoccupied." He should go, intercept Zachary and Jewel, try to get an inkling of what had them so completely engrossed. "I wonder where Prince Zachary has gone."

"Oh, no doubt His Highness is with one of the other guests. Your Majesty needn't worry." She looked up at him, her blue eyes sparkling, her face flushed from dancing. "I'm sure Your Majesty always has some concern of the kingdom on his mind." She brushed a stray tendril from her forehead and her lips parted in a smile. "I wish that I could give Your Majesty at least a moment of happiness. Would it please Your Majesty to leave the hall, perhaps get away for a moment from all these people who seem but to remind Your Majesty of obligations?"

It might indeed be a good idea to leave the hall. Maybe Robin could see where Zachary and Jewel had gone. Nodding to and greeting his guests who bowed as Robin and Joy made their way arm in arm across the room, Robin noted their curious glances and smiling faces.

Outside, a cold wind slapped Robin's cheek. Frost crunched underfoot. Star- and moonlight glinted off the surfaces of puddles that had iced over. "It seems that Winter is not at all ready to give way to Spring," he said. "We thought this morning that cold weather was on its way. We should go back inside. We would not want you to get sick." He could ask the officer at arms where Zachary had gone.

Though she wrapped her arms around herself against the cold, Joy pouted prettily. "Oh, but I don't want to go back to the feast so soon. Perhaps we could tour the gallery. I've heard that Bell Castle is privileged to have in its collection some fine works of art. And Your Majesty can observe the hall from the promenade," Joy said, which was true enough.

They mounted the stairs to the hall's second level which housed the gallery, chambers for guests, and quarters for the castellan and the captain. Along the walls, console tables displayed bowls, trays, and pitchers of precious metals and outstanding craftsmanship. The walls themselves were hung with paintings and tapestries as well as a number of swords, maces, and hatchets. Some were more decorative than functional. Highly ornamented ones had been gifts from the realm's lords, and still others had been working weapons retired from service and given a place of honor to commemorate an important battle.

"This one," Robin said, "won the battle of Otter Crossing."

Joy smiled. "I'm sure it was only as effective as the man who wielded it."

A flush of pride warmed bones chilled by the winter night and a soul hardened by his burgeoning anxieties. "With this one," he said, "we took off the head of a dragon."

"I heard that Your Majesty fought dragons but I never imagined it was true,." Joy said in open-mouthed astonishment. She stifled her gasp with her hands and her eyes went wide. "How fortunate are the Chalklands to have a king who is not only handsome and kind but fearless too."

Robin endeavored to be nonchalant but it was hard. He was proud of his dragon-slaying skills. He was such a formidable dragon slayer, he had traded his services to many a distant realm to rid them of the beasts. The generous purses had handsomely enriched Bell Castle's treasury.

The kill memorialized by the displayed sword hadn't been the most fearsome dragon Robin had ever fought. That had been a three-headed monster and while Robin had prevailed, he had come away from that expedition minus his sword. He lost far more than his weapon as a result of that campaign, a memory he did not care to revisit. *Best not to mention that one.*

At least it hadn't been his last. That had been the beast he fought near Rocky Port. "A place very far from here."

"Indeed, I have never heard of it," Joy said. "So you go to strange lands to battle even stranger beasts."

Robin thought to elaborate but that was not an episode he wished to dwell on, either. Not all of his experiences in Rocky Port had been pleasant. He had hit his lowest point there at a desperate time in his life when he couldn't imagine that there were deeper depths. A sage old man had told him that from such a point in life, one's future could only improve and fortunately that had proven to be true.

Still, the sight of the sword made him smile. "We made that sword," he said.

"Made it? Is that not the job of blacksmiths?"

"It is but we made that one with our own two hands." Robin held up his and noticed how soft and smooth they had become, no longer cracked and blistered the way they had been when he labored in a forge and made the sword that now hung on the walls, replaced by a newer better model crafted by Gregory, Bell Castle's smith.

"A dragon slayer and a craftsman?" said Joy. "I am astounded."

Robin felt proud, justifiably, he thought. Not only could he wield a sword with fatal proficiency, he could make one, give it edges and a point that would cut and pierce flesh and metal. With Robin's handcrafted sword, he had killed yet another dragon in a land even farther away than Rocky Port and had saved a fair lady. Robin grinned at that recollection. He and the rescued woman had shared an intimate night. She invited him to her bed not because she was grateful for the rescue but rather because she liked him, despite the fact that at the time he wasn't King Bewilliam. He was simply Robin, a penniless vagabond for all she knew. Yet she had treated him with respect and affection. The memory was bittersweet. The Empress Alexandra was an exceptional woman and Robin's life would have taken a different direction had he stayed at Sea Gate Fortress.

That was in his past and had no place in his present or future. When he found thoughts about it intruding as they sometimes did on dark and lonely nights or the rare quiet afternoon, he pushed them aside.

"Sire?"

Robin realized that he had again drifted off and he returned his attention to Joy.

"Here I had intended to give Your Majesty a pleasant diversion but it appears that I am failing. Your Majesty's thoughts are elsewhere. Is there anything that I can do to take Your Majesty's mind off weighty matters for even just a little while?"

The invitation was clear and one that Robin was not going to decline. Thinking about Alexandra had roused a longing for tenderness and passion, to be appreciated simply for being himself. "There is." He took Joy's hand and led her into one of the guest chambers.

*****

They returned to the great hall to find that Lady Alice and Lord Ferree were ready to depart for their lodgings.

"I can see by your flushed cheeks that it must be very cold outside," said Lady Alice, pulling her cloak about her shoulders.

"Yes, that wind can rub you raw if you stay out in it overly long," stammered Joy, cheeks reddened not so much by a brisk wind as by Robin's stubble.

Robin looked about the hall. Though some guests had left, the room was still crowded. He strained to spot Jewel or Zachary and saw neither. "Your daughter, Jewel?" he asked.

"Departed with Prince Zachary, about the same time Your Majesty and Joy went to get some air. We thought they meant to catch up with you," Lord Ferree replied. "Did you not encounter them?"

"No," said Robin. They hadn't come up to the gallery and it was indeed far too cold to be out walking around the bailey. "But they could easily still be here," he said, hoping that they had gone to Zachary's chamber in the keep. "Who could find them in this crowd?" With a sweep of his arm he embraced the mass of partygoers. "We will search them out and tell Jewel that you have left."

Lady Alice and Lord Ferree bowed. "Thank you. We are most grateful. We are so looking forward to tomorrow."

Joy curtsied deeply. "Thank you again, Your Majesty. It has been a most memorable day, and evening. I hope I was pleasurable company."

"Most enjoyable," Robin said, half his attention still seeking out Zachary or Jewel. The other half wondered; had it been his irresistible charm that had inspired Joy to distract him away from the hall or was there some other reason? Had she an ulterior motive for discouraging him from finding Zachary?

He regarded Joy with suspicion. Had it all been a ruse to engage the king while the prince and his henchwoman planned regicide?

It wasn't easy to kill a king, as well guarded as he was. He was rarely alone, not even at night. A page was always right outside the bedchamber door in case his king needed something in the middle of the night and at least one guard always stood watch. Because of such security measures it took more than one man to kill a king. With whom might Zachary conspire? Who would aid him?

It would have to be someone who had access to the king, who could get close. Someone whose loyalty could be bought.

Robin thought about his page. A young man who aspired to a life better than the one he seemed destined to lead as a chandler's son, he had left his home and faced fourteen years of training before he could even be considered for knighthood. Might it seem more expedient to accept a bribe and enable an assassin?

Just to be on the safe side, Robin would dismiss him. The same for his house carls. Robin had no complaints about their performance and they would wonder why they had suddenly been discharged, but he was the king and he owed no explanation. Instead there was the now urgent matter of new personal attendants and guards to be vetted and trained. The training wouldn't be a problem; in fact he welcomed the opportunity to work with fresh recruits. The vetting was another matter and one that called for someone possessing discretion, diplomacy, objectivity, and irreproachable integrity. He knew of one such person, an advocate upon whom he relied to investigate Queen Daya's betrayal. He could send for Terrowin to be brought with all possible speed knowing from experience that "now" had much less immediacy for an advocate than it did for a king. Perhaps Robin would be lucky enough to learn that Terrowin was in attendance at the tournament. Robin dispatched several servants to search amongst the partygoers and those encamped around Bell Castle with orders that the minute Terrowin was found, he was to be brought for an audience with the king, day or night. Meanwhile, before he retired, Robin would outline his concerns in a sealed letter to be sent on the morrow if Terrowin were not at Bell Castle.

Until now, Robin hadn't felt vulnerable enough to require a food taster, but beginning with his first meal tomorrow he would. The most effective candidates for this essential but hazardous duty would be found among the kitchen servants. Knowing that he would have to partake of anything offered to the king, the food taster would take considerable pains to make certain that anything coming out of the kitchen was safe. Robin would decree that the duty would be rotated and on any given day, anyone could be pressed into service at the king's discretion. That reduced complacency and the likelihood that any particular servant would be set up to take the fall in an attempted poisoning. In addition, all foodstuffs provided for the king's consumption would first be tested by the person who delivered it, and so would Meeyoo's food.

Robin glanced around the hall. Near one of the ale vats, Sirs Howell and Kenneth shoved each other and laughed. Were they simply joshing about the melee or were they chortling about the better life that they would lead serving the man who ousted King Bewilliam? Among his most trusted knights, they had served by his side on a perilous campaign to the Palisades to seek justice from King Ulric. Robin had gotten a legal judgment; Ulric had been penalized. Yet Robin's knights urged him to take further action. Was it a ruse to expose him to deadly danger?

Sirs Albert and Alan danced with their ladies. They had been part of that campaign too and also pressed Robin to wage war against King Ulric. *Could the four be part of a complex plan to lure Robin away from the relative safety of the castle and deliver him to a murderous enemy?*

Who was the instigator? Did King Ulric mean to avenge himself for the penalty that Robin caused to be imposed? Had King Ulric always had designs on the kingdom of the Chalklands, covetousness that had been thwarted and festered unsatisfied? Did King Ulric conspire with Zachary or did Zachary conspire with King Ulric? Who had eyes on the throne?

Robin's heart sank at the thought that no one could be trusted, not his guests, his knights, or his son. He couldn't afford to waste time on sentimentality. He needed to be unemotional and prudent.

He scanned the room for allies but all he saw were people who could use their position or advantage against him. Expressions that he had taken to be smiles of delight and merriment now appeared to be the smirks of conspirators who already saw him as vanquished. The lords, ladies, and knights were gone, replaced by devils, gargoyles, and leering jesters.

Robin shuddered. This was what it meant to be king: to be ever a target, always on guard, trusting no one. More than the fact of his royal birth, more than his accomplishments, more than his crown and embroidered cape, it was this isolation and vulnerability that made him king. Until tonight, he had reveled in the feeling of satisfaction for the fine edifices he had erected, the people he had served, the legacy that he built and would leave behind. This was the price that he had to pay for that: the feeling of never being safe, of always being on alert, alone because there was no one to whom he could get close.

He thrust back his shoulders and puffed out his chest. Anyone who thought that King Bewilliam was an easy target was so very wrong, and that included Prince Zachary.

CHAPTER FOURTEEN

Robin rose with his rondel at hand. He had dozed only lightly throughout the night and roused many times, alert for any sounds outside the door that might be signs of an imminent attack. On several occasions he was tempted to visit Prince Zachary's room to see if the young man was even abed and if so, was he alone or with Jewel.

The third day of the tournament dawned even colder than the last two; late winter weather held the Chalklands in an icy grip. Even Meeyoo was reluctant to leave the cozy warmth of the bed and Robin saw no need to disturb her. Despite her fluffy fur, she felt the cold as much as he did. A heated bedchamber in the keep might be a better place for her to spend the day than a drafty grandstand.

Robin selected layers of insulating clothing and dressed himself, having excused his page on the pretext of giving him the day off to enjoy the tournament. It wasn't a prohibitively taxing chore but Robin did miss the convenience of having assistance. While he would be occupied all day today with the final events, the first order of business clearly would be vetting new pages and guards.

The advocate, Terrowin, had been located and presented with the king's summons. Robin met him in the keep's private dining hall for a brief conference before the day's tourneys commenced.

Terrowin bowed. "We apologize for our attire, Your Majesty. We did not anticipate that we would be called on business."

When Robin had last seen him, the young man had been formally outfitted in a suit and a cloak bearing his coat of arms, a silver shield with three black martins. Today he wore rougher, bulkier clothes fit for a day in the stadium.

"No apologies necessary. We did not know we would be in need of your professional service but such is the case. We consider ourselves fortunate that you are in attendance as there is urgency to the matter." Robin outlined the task at hand. "We regret that this will keep you from viewing the jousting."

"That is regrettable, Sire, but my wagers likely will be won or lost regardless of whether I'm there to cheer on my knight."

Robin suspected that whatever Terrowin lost on the joust would be more than compensated for by his fee for services, but it would be money well spent for peace of mind. As Robin strode to the stadium, he studied each face that greeted him. Did this person intend the king harm? It would be a welcome relief to get Terrowin's reports.

Robin made his way to the grandstand with little interference, the business of readying for the final events keeping competitors and aides occupied.

The knights who would compete barked orders to stable boys readying their steeds, to the smiths putting the finishing touches on their weapons, to their squires who would help with their armor and stand by with replacement weapons, and to their kippers—lads who aspired to be squires and knights one day— who would scramble after a scuffle and collect the weapons and armor of a fallen adversary.

Fatalities were rare and injuries infrequent; nevertheless, each knight's pavilion housed a surgeon to stop bleeding or splint broken bones. The physicians got their ewers of water, towels, and bandages at the ready and stocked plenty of strong drink to help lessen pain.

Knights who wanted to compete in the jousting hung their shield on a tree. The seneschal made note of the candidates and prepared a list of pairs of knights who would ride in the joust. In match after match, the contestants would be eliminated and an overall winner would be determined.

Robin was surprised to see Sir Kenneth attended not by a squire but by Sir Howell. Robin wondered if Sir Howell was still paying off his "ransom" for being captured in the melee a cheval or if the two were forming a treacherous alliance.

Having lost in the melee a cheval, Sir Howell was disqualified from the joust which was probably for the best. The man was a better tactician than a horseman. Had he been able to compete he likely would have lost, Robin thought with a snort, and this tournament would prove costly for him.

Could and would Sir Howell's agile mind be employed to plot against the king? Robin sighed. He didn't like thinking of the knight as capable of treachery. Let him not be a traitor, Robin found himself imploring. The man's perceptiveness and knowledge made him a unique and valuable asset.

Robin found Prince Zachary in the grandstand alone nursing an ale. None of the guests from White Castle were present. Robin didn't know what to make of their absence until he recalled them saying that they had a vassal in the lists who might be interested in competing. Naturally, the lord and lady and their daughters would want to be on hand in the knight's pavilion to lend their support.

Vendors hastened to supply the king and his son with food and drink, all of which the food taster discreetly sampled first. Fortunately the steaming pies and mulled wine produced no ill effects. The warm spiced wine provided welcome relief against the icy air.

As he had for the melees, Robin welcomed the crowd and reviewed the rules of engagement. "Each knight will run the lists three times with his opponent. Only standard tournament lances can be used and the tips must be blunted. When in the lists, knights may be assisted by one squire and one squire only. Knights, school your kippers. They may take weapons over which a fallen knight has lost control but only after he has been completely unhorsed. There will be no striking a fallen knight in order to strip him of more of his armor or clubbing of another kipper in order to gain an advantage."

In their zeal to serve their knight by seizing as much armor as possible from an unhorsed knight, kippers had been known to brawl with a ferocity that rivaled the melee a pied.

"May we remind you that the objective is not to run your opponent through. Instead the man who breaks the most lances in each bout wins unless one of the competitors is unhorsed. Unseating an opponent automatically wins the bout unless you are also unseated in that pass, in which case you both count as one lance break. If it is a draw after three passes, it goes into sudden death, which is not to be taken literally."

The spectators closest to Robin guffawed.

"Instead it means that the first person to get ahead wins." Robin continued, "We want to emphasize the importance of sportsmanship. Do not seek an unfair advantage. Indeed, the competitor who merits the greatest honor is the one who overcomes the most obstacles, who comes from behind to score a victory."

Brother Leo's invocation stressed the virtue of honest competition.

The third day of the competition was to open with the naming of the umpire who would rule contested decisions. Robin had planned to name Gregory, the senior blacksmith.

"But Sir Maxwell has hung his shield on the tree; he intends to compete," said Zachary. "Gregory cannot be the chevalier d'honneur. He will be accused of having bias."

"We're sure he can do it," Robin protested, ready to summon the man to the grandstand. "He can be fair."

"We can't take the risk. People have been fighting on and off the field for three days. Reputations and a lot of prize money are at stake. Who knows what riots would ensue if we hand down an unpopular decision." Zachary folded his arms across his chest. "We volunteer to be the judge."

"You?" Robin said.

"Why not? When we were young we were trained in the martial arts and sciences."

Robin grimaced. "Resisted being trained" was a more accurate description of Zachary's early education but it didn't appear that Robin had any other options. "So be it, then." Robin directed the herald to call for attention and declared, "We name Prince Zachary as chevalier d'honneur."

The first pair of knights lined up for the charge. At the blast from the herald's bugle, the men would ride at each other and meet with levelled lances. If they remained on horseback they would turn quickly for another pass, the action which gave rise to the name "tournament."

The opportunity for jousting at this point was customarily first offered to the new, young knights like Sir Maxwell. Robin fully expected the youth to compete, yet he did not respond when the seneschal called his name nor did Robin see him about. Perhaps Sir Maxwell had stayed too late at one of last night's parties and was still sleeping off too much ale. Had the young man taken ill or worse, was he off somewhere conspiring with Robin's enemies? Sickened to even think of Sir Maxwell's perfidy, Robin sent a page to find the young man's father, Gregory, and inquire about the lad's whereabouts.

Robin watched with morose interest as the youngest knights jousted. Should he have to dismiss any of his veterans he would have to rely on these less experienced fighters. He made note not only of which lad seemed to be the most accomplished fighter but also which performed in closest accordance with the guidelines for proper conduct and demonstrated the strongest moral fiber.

Zachary watched in silence and as the morning wore on, Robin found himself missing the more companionable presence of the lord and lady of White Castle and their daughters. He imagined Joy leaping up to cheer the competitors and Jewel enthusing about the spectacle. Perhaps he should go seek them out. They'd be better company than his petulant son and it might behoove him to become acquainted with their ambitious vassal.

Robin rose to excuse himself and take his leave when he spied a figure approaching.

Sir Henry strode to the grandstand and stood with his feet spread wide. Not a tall man, he was broad and solidly built. "Hear ye," he cried. "This competition has been thrilling and suspenseful with impressive performances by the realm's most estimable knights. But I mean to raise it to a level worthy of the kingdom of the Chalklands." Standing firm as a tree trunk he planted his standard into the ground. "I, Sir Henry, issue a greater challenge. I will take on any opponents until there are none left and I will win."

A stunned hush answered the announcement and even Robin was at a loss for words. Like Sir Henry's opulent pavilion and lavish parties, was this bold dare part of his campaign to restore, even elevate his standing? Should Sir Henry be able to deliver on his boast, it would certainly demonstrate great prowess to his king and fellow knights. His brazen posture threatened to change the tenor of the tournament from friendly competition and tests of skill played by certain polite rules to something more barbaric.

"In honor of our king, to show the world the caliber of our fighting men, so that any who have designs on us dare not challenge us," Sir Henry continued.

Robin felt chilled. So someone did covet the kingdom of the Chalklands and had an eye on the throne. Were rumors of such already in circulation? Had it been that and not boredom that made his subjects restive? It would explain his knights' interest in heightening defenses and making preemptive strikes.

Who would be casting an acquisitive eye on his kingdom? Despite his humiliating defeat, did King Ulric still want Bell Castle? Did one of King Bewillam's vassals mean to move against him? Robin resolved that after the tournament was over he would investigate the possible threat.

However, the here and now of Sir Henry's boast probably had nothing to do with the kingdom's reputation or appearance of vulnerability. A more likely explanation was that the fever of competition had overheated Sir Henry's blood.

Robin tried to read the expressions on the faces of the other knights. It was hard to tell what they thought of Sir Henry's dare as their heads were bowed together in conference. When they straightened and squared their shoulders, Robin could see that the tournament had left them hot blooded as well. They nodded and punched the air with their fists, eager to accept Sir Henry's dare.

Maybe the greater stakes would be a good thing. That would ignite the pride of his subjects and reinforce their fealty.

"For the ultimate prize that we have already put up?"

Sir Henry nodded. "That and one other favor."

Robin wasn't so carried away as to agree without having heard what Sir Henry desired. "And that would be?"

Sir Henry turned slightly to face Prince Zachary. "A token of appreciation from Princess Dale."

Something about Sir Henry's avid expression struck dread into Robin's heart. His face burning with embarrassment, he gasped in gratitude that only Zachary and he occupied the grandstand, sparing him from having to make an explanation to the guests from White Castle.

Before Robin could object, Zachary stood, clasped his hands, and cried, "Oh, Sir Henry, how flattering. You do us a great honor. We accept and will reward you most handsomely."

Robin hoped that Sir Henry's scandalous request and Zachary's even more shocking reply had been drowned out in the clamor of spectators eager for an all-out contest with heightened stakes. As Robin framed a reply, the crowd roared louder. Punching the air with their fists, spectators and combatants alike cried, "Yes. Yes. Yes." Zachary's glare defied Robin to refuse.

So be it. By the end of the day Sir Henry's arrogance would either be quashed by one of the knights or he would prove himself to be more of a man than any of them knew. Robin sighed, stood, and said, "Your challenge has been accepted, Sir Henry."

The knights hastened to the shield tree and struck Sir Henry's heater to enter the fray. Robin had misgivings but there was no stopping this now. "Who will first meet Sir Henry?"

CHAPTER FIFTEEN

A voice piped up from the lists. "I will." Sir Maxwell stepped forward.

Robin sighed with despair. *Now? This was the dare that Sir Maxwell chose to take?* The impetuousness of which the young man's trainers had spoken would indeed be his undoing. He had nowhere near the necessary training and experience to go up against a veteran combatant like Sir Henry. Robin moved to object. "We're sorry, Sir Maxwell, but you can't—"

Sir Maxwell folded his arms across his chest. "Sir Henry said 'all comers,' Sire."

Indeed he had and the older man grinned the way Meeyoo did when she had cornered a mouse. Sir Maxwell was certain to lose but Robin decided that might not be a bad thing. The chastisement might encourage Sir Maxwell to apply himself to his training instead of trying to rush through it. "Proceed, then."

Having been so recently knighted and still undergoing training himself, Sir Maxwell did not have a squire to stand by him. Robin was touched to see Sir Albert adjust Sir Maxwell's armor and help him onto his horse. Sir Albert took up spare lances and stood nearby, the better to supply Sir Maxwell with a replacement weapon if need be.

Sir Maxwell acquitted himself well but his rashness and inexperience proved to be his undoing. He charged quickly, perhaps meaning to take Sir Henry by surprise, but failed to heed the signals his own horse gave him. At the confrontation, the mount turned aside, leaving Sir Maxwell vulnerable. He was easily unhorsed. Head bowed, he trudged to Sir Albert's pavilion. There he was greeted with handshakes and back slaps from Sirs Alan, Albert, Kenneth, and Howell. Straightening, Sir Maxwell accepted an ale and stood with Sir Howell to watch the next contest while Sirs Kenneth, Albert, and Alan made ready to compete. Robin didn't take Sir Howell's eschewal of the joust as a sign of cowardice but a triumph of honest self-appraisal over bravado. Jousting was very much an equestrian event, not Howell's strong point. Undoubtedly he would have lost and likely would have been injured.

When the knight failed to vanquish Sir Henry, Sir Kenneth took up the challenge. It required several passes for him to lose, but lose he did as did Sir Albert who followed him. They joined Sir Maxwell and Sir Alan at Sir Howell's pavilion. Already suited up, Sir Alan made as if to enter the joust but Sir Howell held him back. The knights put their heads together in what seemed to Robin to be a heated debate. No doubt the three knights who had already gone up against Henry had advice to share. In Robin's opinion, the most effective tactic would be simply to wait. Surely as the day wore on Sir Henry's energy and focus would flag.

With each skirmish, what had begun as a dignified and organized display of athletic prowess and skill degenerated into a barely organized brawl no more sophisticated or polite than a set-to between two drunks, each confrontation becoming more brutal. Bent over the necks of their mounts with intensity, Sir Henry's challengers rushed to charge seemingly with little regard for strategy or skill. Like tree limbs breaking in a windstorm, lances shattered with a resounding crack and flew into the air to land yards away. Shields cracked and splintered and scraps of their leather coverings littered the ground.

Kippers raced to collect broken lances with which they would build a bonfire at the conclusion of the tournament. As a child, Robin had snuck away from the royal pavilion to participate in the scavenging, much to the dismay of his parents. A young prince training in the martial arts, he had conspired with knights, squires, and kippers to build a record-breaking pile and create a truly spectacular fire. Now king with resource management ever on his mind, he saw the bonfire as a waste of good kindling but there was no stopping tradition.

As each knight fell, the kippers became more aggressive and vicious. They rushed in to capture his weapon before he could even rise, clubbing each other and even the fallen knight. Out of loyalty to their knight, some strove to salvage anything of value so that their knight, albeit cheated of victory, would not go home empty-handed. Others switched loyalties, ran to join the camp of the apparent winner, and tried gain notice for themselves by beating out the other kippers.

At first the spectators were behind Sir Henry, cheering him on as he racked up win after win. Side bets were made and side fights broke out. Then the tide turned. People grumbled about unfair maneuvers. They grew to wanting to see a seemingly invincible fighter knocked from his pedestal and started cheering for the underdog—whichever the underdog happened to be.

The challengers were also angrier. Visors slammed down over murderous expressions as they readied for combat.

Throughout the tournament, Prince Zachary maintained his silence. Yet with each tilt, he scooted closer to the edge of his seat and leaned farther forward.

At last Sir Alan strode from the pavilion with his squire and horse. The two knights faced off and it seemed to Robin that Sir Henry showed no signs of fatigue. He sat just as tall in his saddle as he had hours earlier. The squires handed the knights their weapons. The two opponents spurred their horses to a gallop with lances held high, lowering them as the distance between them shrank. On the third pass, it appeared to Robin that Sir Henry had carried his lance too low and deliberately smacked Sir Alan's thigh. Armor afforded some protection but a blow from a heavy lance delivered at that speed would cause agony and no trifling injury. Hunched over in pain, Sir Alan nevertheless turned his horse and seemed prepared to make another run.

"Not fair," Robin cried, prepared to disqualify Sir Henry and declare Sir Alan the winner but Zachary said, "We're sorry, Your Majesty, but we are the decision maker here. It is our view that Sir Henry carried his lance level. To our eye it was just a last misstep by his horse that resulted in the injury to Sir Alan. We declare it a righteous victory."

From atop his horse, Sir Henry bowed.

"As there are no more challengers, we declare these games to be concluded," Robin said. Reluctant as he was to name Sir Henry the ultimate victor, he was weary and cold and longed for the comfort of the great hall. He beckoned to the herald, ready to direct him to close the tournament.

"Begging your pardon, Sire," came a voice from the lists, high pitched but steady and strident. A figure stepped out of the crowd of knights and squires and came to stand before the royal grandstand. "The games are not quite concluded. Not all combatants have had their turn. I struck the shield when Sir Henry issued the dare. I have not yet had my chance to ride against him." With finality the slim young man planted his standard. The breeze fanned out the pennant. Against a field of blue was emblazoned the orange chevron of ambition upon which stood a white castle with crenellated towers, suggesting safety. Albeit masked by a helmet, the young contender was still no one that Robin recognized. Although the cry had gone out to knights of the Chalklands, it was not inconceivable that a competitor had come from a distant realm to compete.

The figure hidden by armor and helm was that of a personage probably younger and of even smaller build than Maxwell had been when he served Robin as a squire. Not a knight perhaps, but some knight's squire. Too young and too small to have a chance against Sir Henry who bested every challenger including Sirs Kenneth, Albert, and Alan, although Robin was still of a mind that not all the contests were won fairly. Fair or not, this green stick of a squire didn't have a chance and Robin was loathe to see him injured, maybe crippled while still little more than a boy.

"The time for squires to battle was days ago, at the vespers tourney. We have declared these contests to be concluded," Robin said.

The young warrior stamped his standard with the same assertiveness that Sir Henry demonstrated when he issued the dare. "But I am no squire."

"Let the boy have his chance, Sire," cried Sir Henry. "I promise not to hurt him—too badly."

"Your Majesty." Zachary's voice was tinged with warning.

The young challenger stood his ground.

"Fine," said Robin. "Proceed." He prayed that the match would end quickly and without too much harm done to the boy.

With a bow, the young contestant headed toward the pavilions. As he passed Sir Howell's, Sir Kenneth rushed out. The result of their brief conversation seemed to be that Sir Kenneth would serve as squire.

Sir Henry mounted his horse and the two opponents took their starting positions. They charged at each other. As they came abreast, the lad's lance struck Sir Henry's shield, snapped, and slammed Sir Henry's forearm.

Clutching his injured arm Sir Henry slipped from his mount and cried, "Foul!"

"Yes, Your Majesty, that was foul, an affront to the rules and unfair," said Prince Zachary.

Robin gave him a stern look. "No more wrong than the move that Sir Henry made which injured Sir Alan, an error that you attributed to the mount, not the man, and declared to be fair."

Scowling, Zachary said, "Fine." To the combatants he said, "Decision to the young challenger."

"Another pass, then," Robin declared. Being right-handed, any injury Sir Henry would have sustained would be distracting but not disabling. "Agreed?"

The two opponents bowed. "As Your Majesty wishes."

"Continue."

Sir Kenneth rushed to the young fighter's side and provided a fresh lance.

The second pass went to Sir Henry who broke his lance against the other knight's shield. Though the impact left the young man visibly reeling in his saddle, he kept his seat.

Prince Zachary sprang to his feet. "Sir Henry wins," he cried.

"Not so fast," said Robin. "Best of three matches."

Zachary scowled and slumped into his seat.

Robin heard a clatter at his side and turned to see Sir Maxwell rushing up the stairs into the grandstand. He skidded to a stop, dropped to a bow, and popped up all in one move.

"Sire," he said, so breathless the word came out as a gasp.

"Not now, Sir Maxwell," The third and final pass was about to begin, the last challenge of the tourney. If Sir Henry triumphed he would be announced the winner of the entire tournament, the best knight in the land. For some reason that rankled and Robin found himself hoping that the brazen knight with the white castle blazon would be victorious.

"Apologies, Sire, but Your Majesty will want to hear this. Please." Maxwell looked askance at Prince Zachary. "Privately," he whispered to Robin.

"What, then, Maxwell, and make it fast," said Robin. He did not want to miss a minute of this last fateful pass. He rose from his seat and followed Maxwell to the rear of the grandstand while trying to keep his eyes on the lists.

"Sire, Sir Henry has been cheating." Maxwell's voice was a low hiss.

Robin whipped his head around to face Maxwell so quickly that he pulled a muscle in his neck. "Sir Maxwell, that is a serious allegation. To bring a charge of cheating, you must be very certain. Do you wish to make an official protest? You had best have evidence."

"I do, Sire." Maxwell fumbled at his purse. "He's been using strengthened lances. See?" Sir Maxwell held out a fist full of wood shavings and scraps. "I picked these up near his pavilion where his men have been making and readying Sir Henry's weapons. Look, his lances are maple, not ash." Maxwell pointed to a wood scrap. "Your Majesty can tell from the grain. Denser, you see? Look, here's a piece of ash to compare it with."

The difference was subtle but undeniable, the maple smoother and more tightly knit.

"It makes for a stronger lance. Less likely to break."

Robin smirked. "Now why would Sir Henry want a stronger lance when he would gain points for breaking his?"

"He's been using his lance defensively, holding it out almost as one would in stick fighting. When other knights' lances strike his, they're deflected before they can come anywhere near hitting Sir Henry. As well, he's been able to unhorse his opponents more easily so no one has a chance to accrue any points against him."

Robin frowned. "In all fairness, this doesn't necessarily constitute cheating, Sir Maxwell. Perhaps Sir Henry has simply hit upon a valuable improvement in the manufacture and use of lances. We have to wonder if maple is superior why we all don't use it."

"It's heavier, Sire," said Sir Maxwell. "For prolonged battles it would exact the price of fatiguing the man who carries it. As well, maple takes a long time to dry and is hard to work with. While a maple lance might give Sir Henry an advantage, isn't that contrary to the spirit of the contest? I thought the bravest knight was the one who won despite being the underdog."

"True, but that isn't the same thing as cheating."

Maxwell pouted. "But it is. Your Majesty specifically instructed 'standard tournament lances only.'"

"Right you are, Sir Maxwell." Robin felt his pulse race and his breath came shorter as though readying for a fight.

"And there's more."

"Quick with it, Sir Maxwell." Sir Henry and his opponent had lined up for the final charge.

"He's been sabotaging the shields."

"What? How?"

Maxwell pressed his lips together. "While the knights' shields hung on the Tree of Shields. He's loosened the glue holding the leather coverings so they will separate when struck. And has taken a knife to some and carved a flaw into the wood, then reglued the leather so it would not be detected. Sometimes the glue hasn't even dried when the time comes for the knight to take his turn."

Now that Maxwell mentioned it, Robin realized that there had seemed to be an inordinate number of shields failing, the leather flying off or the shield splintering on impact.

"He's also loosened the rivets on the straps," Maxwell said.

"These are serious charges, Sir Maxwell. You have seen Sir Henry do these things?"

Sir Maxwell regarded his feet for a moment then looked up. "Not Sir Henry himself, Sire. His kippers and pages. After I ... lost, I had time to tour the other pavilions, review my performance with the other knights, hoping to better my skills for the next time. That's when I saw the activity at the Tree of Shields."

"Perhaps Sir Henry doesn't know," Robin said, more to himself than to Maxwell. He didn't want to believe that one of his knights was capable of such perfidy. Perhaps it was the misguided efforts of overzealous vassals.

Sir Maxwell sneered. "Really, Sire? Your Majesty thinks he isn't aware? And anyway, even if he's not, he should be held accountable for his men's actions, should he not? At the very least, he shouldn't get to claim the ultimate prize since he's had an unfair advantage all along."

Robin had to admit that Sir Maxwell raised some valid points. His anger mounting, he hastened to the front of the grandstand, intending to pause the contest until Maxwell's accusations could be investigated. Before he could speak, the bugler launched the third pass.

Hunched over in a posture of near homicidal menace, Sir Henry charged at his opponent, then straightened and steadied his lance as they closed in. The coronal spiked his opponent's shield squarely in the center and even the allegedly-strengthened lance shattered from the force. As if hammered by a battering ram, the young man flew off his horse and crashed to the earth with a thud.

"Yes," cried Prince Zachary. "Well done, Sir Henry. Sir Henry rules. Forgive us our poor choice of words, Your Majesty," he said with a dissembling smile. "Sir Henry wins."

The challenger lay motionless in the dust and for a long moment Robin feared he had been killed. The participants and spectators stood in stunned silence. Sir Kenneth and his squires rushed toward the fallen contestant but before they reached him he rolled over and struggled to his knees. He lifted his arm and raised a gloved hand.

"He admits defeat," said Zachary.

"Perhaps not. He may just want to show he is all right and doesn't need assistance."

"In any case, he has lost and Henry has won. He is the ultimate victor."

"Not so fast," said Robin. "There is one more challenger."

CHAPTER SIXTEEN

"**There** is? But no shields remain on the tree," Zachary said.

Even as he said it, Robin knew it could be a mistake. He called to the seneschal, "We accept the challenge."

The seneschal gaped, eyebrows raised. "But Your Majesty …."

It wasn't unheard of for a king to participate in a tournament but it was unwise, even risky. He could be injured or killed, but the potential danger was burned to a cinder by Robin's red-hot rage. "Announce it."

The seneschal bowed and passed the word to the herald who declared that there would be yet another contestant, King Bewilliam himself.

Behind him, Sir Maxwell said, "Begging your pardon, Your Majesty, but is that wise?"

Zachary cried, "Sire, you can't, you shouldn't," but the protests were a meaningless murmur lost in the roaring in Robin's ears and the stomp of his boots as he descended the grandstand's steps.

Maxwell trotted up behind him.

"Sir Maxwell, get our armor." Safely stored in the armory there was little likelihood that anyone had interfered with it.

"Let's see what Sir Henry can do against a fighter who hasn't been sabotaged by faulty equipment. Get our horse."

"Hope, Sire? But Hope is no destrier,"

"No, but he's a good sturdy courser. He's fast and strong and agile and we have become a good team. He will respond to our instructions and we do know what instructions to give. And we want those spurs that we designed." The king's spurs were not simply a pick affixed to a heel band but a more versatile rowel, a star-shaped wheel with sharpened points that rotated on a shaft. "And get us an ale."

Robin's nerves twanged, his blood sang, and his muscles twitched in anticipation. He felt light on his feet like the youth he had been the last time he jousted. That may have been some years ago but he hadn't forgotten the moves nor lost his edge.

Sir Henry signaled for the seneschal and their heads leaned together. The seneschal nodded, approached Robin, and bowed.

"Sire, Sir Henry is honored to have such an esteemed opponent. He wishes you to know that he promises to grant no favors nor hobble himself due to his opponent's status."

Robin didn't miss the insinuation. He knew that Sir Henry's statement wasn't a promise. *Was it a question: did Robin expect special treatment? Or was it a dare?* "Indeed, we would expect no less than Sir Henry's best effort," Robin replied, trying not to sound sarcastic. "We would be offended by anything less. We intend to fight fairly according to the rules."

While they waited for Sir Maxwell to return with Robin's armor, Sir Henry paced.

Let him carve a path in front of his pavilion and burn off what is left of his drive. Robin thought Sir Henry would be wiser to rest but he was pleased at Henry's agitation, a sign perhaps of apprehension.

Pacing wasn't a bad idea though. Walking would help Robin to warm and stretch muscles stiffened by a day of sitting. As well, Sir Henry might think that his adversary was nervous. It might give Sir Henry false confidence.

You are mine. Robin breathed deeply and set his jaw. He realized with a start that he no longer thought of Sir Henry as his own vassal whose loyalty was an important element of the

Chalklands' security. Instead, the man was a foe to be vanquished.

He reminded himself of Sir Henry's question about granting favors and holding back. Clearly Sir Henry had no qualms about doing battle with his sovereign.

Maxwell arrived, breathless with the effort of having made all speed weighed down by fifty pounds of armor. "Why did you not have Hope carry it?" Robin asked.

"Your Majesty, the stable master thought it advisable to give Hope a little exercise. He will be along shortly."

Sirs Alan, Albert, Howell, and Kenneth and a small horde of pages crowded around with offers to help affix each individual plate. Robin had no reason not to trust them but he had every reason to minimize the risk of any one man impairing his protection. However, Sir Henry's impatient scowl and Robin's eagerness prevailed over his prudence. He watched closely as the men quickly but carefully fitted him with his armor, starting at his feet, applying riveted plates to cover his ankles, calves, shins, knee caps, and thighs while Sir Maxwell strapped the uniquely-designed spurs to Robin's heels.

Robin's armor was suited for a commander on the battlefield. It afforded protection not so much in hand-to-hand combat as from missiles and long-range weapons such as swords and spears. As such, it offered none of the specialized advantages of which Gregory had spoken. On the other hand, it was of the finest materials and no expense had been spared in crafting it.

The stable master arrived with Robin's horse, Hope. "I made haste, Sire," he said, "but I hope Your Majesty will agree that the mount will respond better if his muscles are warm and flexible."

Draped in a caparison bearing Robin's heraldic signs, the horse held himself tall, dipped his head, and pranced almost as if he knew of the exciting event to come. The iron chamfron that covered his face, the back of his neck, and chest to protect him from lance strikes was embellished with filigrees and the iron spike between his eyes gave him the appearance of a fearsome unicorn. Hope had been fitted with a high backed saddle that would give Robin more leverage during the charge and better support if he were hit.

Robin scrutinized his outfit and his horse's barding and found no fault with any of the preparations. Buoyed with excitement, he planted himself firmly in the saddle, the heavy armor helping to root him in place. He sat Hope perhaps a bit more solidly than he had when he was slimmer, and while his bigger bulk might present a larger target, it would also be harder to budge. He thrust his feet fully in the stirrups. He thought he could feel Hope's energy vibrate between his knees even through the armored caps.

Maxwell had also brought him his buckler. Robin hefted the shield. Smaller and therefore lighter than that of infantrymen who needed neck-to-knee protection, it was a swordsman's shield, rounder and more convex than a heater. Robin had noticed that properly employed, the curved shield could do more than simply prevent a piercing weapon from impaling its target; it could deflect the weapon, turning a head-on strike into a glancing blow. The polished steel surface showed no signs of tampering.

Maxwell handed him his lance, the first of three.

Spectators crowded as close as they could to the lists but Robin had eyes only for Sir Henry. Robin narrowed his focus on his target. The knights' vivid pavilions, the throngs of brightly dressed spectators, musicians, and jugglers became a featureless wash of color in his peripheral vision; the chatter of the crowd a mere hum. What would be Sir Henry's first move? Hidden by his helm, his face was unreadable. Robin tried to gain intelligence from the man's posture and the position of his mount. Covered in armor, his face obscured by his helm, what stood opposite Robin was no longer Sir Henry, a man, but the target. Robin focused on the shield centered on the figure's torso. A heater shield, its sides were tapered down to a point and an upper corner was notched to allow the lance to pass. The shield's black ground could have been meant to speak of constancy but more likely grief, the grief that the bearer would cause his foes. An arrow signified readiness for battle and an axe stood for the execution of military duty. The mythical antelope that Robin had once taken for a symbol of harmony and peace could also connote political cunning. The raguly line across the top spoke of difficulties that had been encountered, a recent addition to the original design. The canton in the right corner reminded Robin of a reward he had once given Sir Henry for exemplary service. That would not advantage him now.

Of course, one's insignia was intended to communicate a message about the bearer, and for fighting men, to intimidate the viewer. The symbols on Sir Henry's shield might strike a fearsome first impression but Robin would not let his emotions overtake his reasoning.

More daunting was Sir Henry's performance. Robin tried to recall every move he had seen the man make and wondered how many of his successes owed to skill and how many to the trickery of which Sir Maxwell had accused him. It would be smart to give Sir Henry's abilities the benefit of the doubt.

Robin sought to discern whatever he could of the man's strategy from his posture. The man would have to know that Robin's shield was intact, calling for a different tactic. Henry's eyes were unreadable black coals behind his helm's slits but Robin thought he could feel the menace.

Henry had fought throughout the tournament, could well be bruised, in pain, and wearied but his muscles and joints would be warm and loose. Having been but a spectator Robin was fresh but stiff. He was also aware that he hadn't jousted since he was a prince.

Readying for the charge, Robin clenched and released his muscles.

As if stirred by the noise and color of the surroundings, Hope, too, seemed eager to move. Robin could feel the animal quiver and prance. A sturdy horse more suited for work and endurance, Hope lacked the speed and agility of jousting destriers. Robin hoped that the horse's strength and fortitude would compensate.

A blare from the herald's bugle signaled the start and propelled Robin from planning to action. He spurred Hope forward.

Holding the lance upright and keeping the tilt barrier to his left, Robin leaned slightly forward and urged Hope straight ahead, hard and fast. Jousting knights could collide at speeds up to sixty miles an hour and Robin aimed to achieve that speed. Henry could have gotten a fresh mount and maybe should have. He seemed to Robin just a beat late to the charge. Robin had already lowered his lance and pointed it forward across the barrier, aiming straight for Henry's midsection.

Though Hope raced down the track at top speed, each moment seemed to last a lifetime and Robin tried to glean as much information as possible from every second. Sir Henry couldn't know that Robin was privy to the enhanced strength of the maple lance and it appeared that he aimed to hit Robin dead center. Robin responded by twisting his torso to present less of a target. He aimed for his rival with an eye to snagging his shield.

From the way Sir Henry's body angled, it seemed to Robin that the man sought to deflect Robin's lance with his own. At the last possible moment, Robin lifted his elbows and keeping the lance level raised it slightly. Spurring Hope on, he clamped the horse between his legs, pressed his hips against the back of the saddle, and thrust the lance with all his might. It skimmed over the top of Sir Henry's weapon and the prongs lodged solidly in his shield. It took every ounce of strength Robin had to keep hold of the lance as Hope's momentum carried him forward. The lance yielded with a loud snap, the stub still planted in Sir Henry's shield.

Point, His Majesty. Robin heard the cries of dismay, cheers, and applause only as a distant drone. He gave Hope the signal to slow, reined him in, and turned him back toward to the start. Sir Maxwell rushed to his side to see if he required anything. "Just a fresh lance, Sir Maxwell," Robin said, and reached for it with an arm that still shuddered from the impact.

Sir Henry's horse turned with alacrity and the man snatched a fresh lance from his squire who stood at the ready.

Before Robin had a chance to review the first pass and revise his strategy the second pass began. The signal blared and Hope took off with a palpable eagerness as if to say "I get what we're doing. Leave this to me."

This time Robin planned to aim for Henry's head, giving him two points. It would be virtually impossible for Henry to beat that score.

It was a good plan and clearly Sir Henry thought of it too. Just as Robin lifted his lance to strike Sir Henry, Sir Henry moved to thwack Robin's head. Too late did Robin edge Hope to the side to evade Sir Henry's lance. Already committed to his course of action, Robin could do no more than duck. The lance still struck home, rang Robin's helm like a bell, and cracked. Dazed, Robin felt himself slip from the saddle. Hope stopped and rose up on his back legs, sliding Robin towards the saddle's high back. Then the horse sidestepped to the barrier, wedging Robin in place. His lower back ached where it had slammed against the saddle and his neck screamed with whiplash. Just barely managing to keep his seat, Robin clung to Hope, every bone throbbing, his brain rattled. Even the horse seemed shaken.

Two points for Sir Henry, but at least Robin had managed to stay mounted. Had he been unseated it would be game over.

They lined up again for a last and final pass. The initial exhilaration that had fueled Robin's performance had evaporated and he felt pounded from the high speed sprints. His head throbbed from the hit he had taken and he could barely focus. He needed to end this.

He aimed to hit Sir Henry squarely in the chest and unhorse him, but just as he was about to land his blow, Sir Henry's horse stepped off at an angle. Robin's lance made contact with Sir Henry's shield and snapped but the man managed to keep his seat.

They were tied.

CHAPTER SEVENTEEN

The herald announced that there would be another pass: sudden death. Whichever contestant scored would be the winner.

This could not go on all day, Robin decided. How was Henry doing this seemingly with no ill effects? Something that Alice of White Castle said to him echoed. For the operation she had given Meeyoo something to dull the pain. Had Sir Henry also taken a preparation that would make him oblivious to injury or worse, availed himself of some magic?

Robin had done neither. He couldn't take another hit. There was nothing for it but that Robin would have to unseat his opponent. It was the only way to end the contest with the next pass.

Sirs Albert, Alan, Howell, and Kenneth crowded against the barrier and hollered suggestions. According to the rules, only Sir Maxwell could attend the combatant. Robin wished he could hear what his men had to say, especially Sir Howell. An innovative strategy would be welcome.

Robin took several deep breaths to energize and clear his head and vision. He squirmed deep into the saddle and positioned his feet in the stirrups, got a firm grip on his lance. He had an idea. It was a risky maneuver, but if luck was with him it would pay off.

As he had in previous runs, he spurred Hope forward at high speed and aimed not for Sir Henry's head which would be the daring move. Instead he chose the larger target, the man's chest, with the sole aim of unhorsing him. As they closed ranks he felt Henry's lance make contact but instead of stiffening and resisting, Robin rolled with the blow, letting the lance slice across his shield. The glancing blow would earn Henry no points but determined to have a decision Robin struck out with his own lance. Robin aimed for Sir Henry's neck. The knight's helm provided adequate protection but at the sight of the lance coming for his neck and face, Sir Henry instinctively leaned away. Robin lowered his lance and drove it home with such force that Henry teetered. Robin turned Hope in time to see Henry struggle to center himself then lose his seat altogether and slip from the saddle.

Decision, King Bewilliam.

The whole of the tournament inundated Robin's awareness. The smell of sweat, blood, horse manure, ale, cook fires, and dust. The herald's blaring trumpet. The spectators hollering and jumping up and down, some delighted that their king had won, others dismayed at having lost a bet. The throng writhing as toasts were made, money changed hands, and small fights broke out. Robin saw several figures race towards him: Sir Maxwell, followed by Sirs Albert, Alan, Howell, and Kenneth. Sir Henry's squire and kippers sprinted to his side. Prince Zachary dashed down the grandstand steps and rushed to the lists but then seemed torn as to whom to greet, his champion or his father, the king.

Sir Maxwell helped Robin from his saddle. Stretched to the limit, every muscle throbbed, every nerve shrieked, but drunk with his accomplishment, Robin felt elation more strongly than pain. Exultation buoyed him on weak knees. In the morning he would receive the bill for his bravado to be paid in full; he would be too sore to rise from his bed. That would be tomorrow. For now he was eager to shed his heavy armor and wrap himself in something warm and soft.

Sir Henry's squire and vassals helped him to his feet and removed his helm. With a murderous expression on his face, he turned on his heel and limped towards his pavilion where his crowd of followers had thinned.

Zachary gazed wistfully after him. "Someone should run after Sir Henry and tell him that he is the true victor."

No one made a move to do so.

"He fought all day, only to lose it all at the end for one error?"

"Sir Henry proposed the challenge," Robin replied. "He lost according to the terms that he set and you know it. Why are you defending him?"

"Because he has supported me," said Zachary, his pale face dark with anger. "Is it fair that after three days of competition Your Majesty takes the prize?"

"We don't intend to." He summoned the seneschal. "There will be prizes and awards for every knight who jousted," he said. That might stifle protests about the outcome of the challenge especially should Sir Maxwell's charge of cheating be proven. "Make sure they know and that they know they are invited to the closing banquet where we will make the announcements." Sometime between now and then Robin would have to dream up appropriate honors so that all the competitors would be rewarded for their effort. *Most Innovative Strategy, Fastest Takedown, Most Honorable Comportment. Most Colorful Pavilion, Best Maintained Equipment ….* "Maxwell, find that young man, the one who fought Sir Henry just before us. Have him meet us at the grandstand."

Robin followed Sir Albert to his pavilion where knights, squires, and kippers vied to help remove the king's armor. *Most Efficient Squire,* Robin thought, *Most Respectful Kipper, Best Trained Horse ….* The winter air stung his cooling flesh and he hurried to get into warm clothes. Comfortable at least for the moment in his cloak, coif, and crown, he strode to the grandstand where Zachary sat brooding.

"You would name this unknown knight, this straggler, victor?" Zachary said.

Robin would name them all victors. The latecomer knight came to stand before the grandstand. He too had shed his armor. A rough woolen cape covered him from shoulders to knees and a cap instead of helm covered his head. With a grand sweep he removed his cap and bowed. A long braid like a coiled rope unwound from around his head. When he straightened, Robin could see that the knight wasn't a knight at all, or even a squire, or even a boy, but a young woman. The spectators nearest the grandstand gasped.

"Victor, approach," Robin said with somewhat less conviction than he had intended.

"Victor?" cried Zachary. "He—she was not," said Zachary. "None of them were, save you."

"It may be proved otherwise." Robin would have the charge of cheating investigated. That would take time. Were it proved to be true, the results of each tilt would have to be reevaluated.

"It's a woman. She never should have been permitted to enter the tournament much less be declared its winner," said Zachary.

Robin glared. "Of all people, you are the last one I would expect to raise that objection. If a woman can't compete in a joust, certainly she can't rule a kingdom," he said. True, the idea of a woman competing in a joust was shocking, was controversial, and to his knowledge had never been done before, but was it wrong? Sir Henry had challenged "all comers."

Robin found himself thinking of the woman he had met when he was a vagabond, a lost king. Empress Alexandra was a dragon slayer in her own right. He didn't doubt that she would argue that under the circumstances, skill, not gender, should be the deciding qualifications.

He thought of other women he had met, intelligent, fearless, and committed to their goal. Certainly no one begrudged them fighting to defend their children. Would it completely disrupt the world order if they were allowed to fight for their king, their glory, or whatever else they valued?

Too thorny a question to be answered here and now. Robin had never given the matter much thought and if pressed couldn't present a well-reasoned defense of either position, but Zachary certainly should have. Robin hadn't planned to set a precedent today but his son's obstinacy needled him and he couldn't help needling back.

The young woman glared at Zachary and he glared back. *A prince who wanted to be a princess, and a maiden who wanted to be a fighter, what was the world coming to?* Robin sighed. He was getting too old for this.

"Alright, then, putting the matter of her gender aside for the moment, this so-called victor isn't a knight," said Zachary. "She isn't even a squire. She never should have been permitted to enter the tournament much less be declared its winner."

The contestant stood tall. "May I present myself? I am Deidre, Your Majesty, of the baronage of White Castle."

Lady Alice had said that they had a knight in the tournament. Had she meant Deidre?

"I am the niece of Sir Walter. It was not my intent to rob any of your most worthy knights of the tournament's purse. Only to avenge my uncle's betrayal by Sir Henry and restore honor to our family name."

"His betrayal?" As if he had encountered a ghost, the pronouncement filled Robin with dread. He shivered with a chill unrelated to the winter day's temperature. He forced his speech to be even and firm. "Your uncle was tried fairly and found guilty and punished as befitted his crime."

"A crime that he did not commit. During his imprisonment, his sister—my mother—and I visited him in Your Majesty's dungeon to bring him whatever comfort we could while he awaited his execution. He swore to us on all he held dear and holy that he was innocent of what he had been accused of doing."

Robin willed his knees not to buckle and his legs not to quiver. "Your uncle was given the opportunity to speak in his own defense and never did," Robin said, trying not to sound as defensive as he felt. The death sentence pronounced on one of his most trusted knights had been painful to declare and even more agonizing to carry out. It had left him and his knights wounded, a scar that to this day had not healed.

"Because to declare his innocence would have required that he accuse another, besmirch the name of a comrade, and violate his knightly vows. My uncle would not do that. He prayed that the culpable party would embrace his guilt, admit his wrongdoing, and accept the punishment that he deserved for betraying his king and fellow knights, any of whom would have given their life for his. As my uncle ultimately did. My uncle paid the highest price to honor his vows, vows that the true culprit betrayed. Sir Henry has gone on to enjoy a happy and prosperous life blessed with the respect of others while my family suffers." Deidre turned, extended her arm, and pointed in the direction in which Sir Henry had fled. "It was Sir Henry who collaborated in the disaster at Grimstaff Castle, not Sir Walter."

Zachary gasped. "These are serious charges."

"I don't make them lightly, Your Highness," Deidre said.

"This is not a conversation for a tournament stadium." Robin wondered who else might have overheard. "We would hear your charges in a proper setting, in court."

Deidre squared her shoulders and tipped up her chin. "We have tried to bring the matter to the king's court," she said. "Nothing came of it."

Robin frowned.

"We talked to the usher, asked that our petition be heard. Many times. We waited in court but were never called to speak."

Something about consulting with the usher about the court calendar made Robin look at Zachary. His son's face was flushed and he seemed discomfited. Robin had an uneasy feeling about why Deidre's petition was never brought to the fore. "We hear your accusation and we will reopen the investigation. If your uncle is proved to have been unfairly judged, we will make redress. Your uncle's death and dishonor will be avenged."

Deidre bowed. "It was justice that I sought. Being thwarted, I sought vengeance instead. That was the prize that I fought for in this tournament." With that, she curtsied as best she could in leggings and a cloak and withdrew.

Robin summoned the seneschal. "Instruct the gatekeeper. Ensure Deidre does not leave Bell Castle." he said. Robin hoped that she would attend the final banquet to be acclaimed and awarded the purse, but her declarations about justice and revenge being the prize led Robin to suspect that she meant to depart. As well, he wanted to know what she had learned from her uncle, Sir Walter. "Detain Sir Henry as well." From the way the knight stomped off, Robin did not expect that he would appear at the final ritual. Before the combatants left the stadium, they all were to meet in the center of the lists and embrace each other in the true companionship of gallant competition. Robin doubted that he'd see Sir Henry there much less at the banquet.

He turned to ask Zachary what if anything he knew of Sir Henry's guilt or innocence, but the prince was no longer in the grandstand. "Prince Zachary?" Robin asked the guards.

"His Highness stated that he would go to the Great Hall to see that all was in readiness for tonight's festivities," said one of the men.

That was possible, but what was more likely was that since Prince Zachary's "champion" had not only lost but had been declared a traitor, he had gone off to sulk.

Yards away from the pavilions, lodgings, and stadium benches, kippers put the finishing touches on the stack of shattered lances in preparation for the bonfire. Instead of simply heaping one pole atop the other, the knights directed their kippers and squires to stand the staffs upright and lean them together to create a cone-shaped pile. Thus constructed, the structure grew to an unprecedented height of almost twenty feet.

Parties were already underway at the lodgings of various knights. Those who were disqualified early were now well and loudly into their cups. In the spirit of good sportsmanship, even the losers would attend the banquet in the great hall to celebrate the winner, leaving their kippers, vassals, and supporters to party on. It was anyone's guess which would burn out first, the bonfire or the revelers.

The herald announced the closing of the tournament to anyone who was still listening and summoned all contestants to come forward to congratulate each other. Brother Leo blessed the knights and gave a benediction, expressing hope that they would strive to give their best effort in all that they did and uphold the values of honesty and fair play. From the grandstand, Robin thanked everyone who had made the tournament a success. "The kingdom of the Chalklands' most valuable resource is its subjects," he said, "not just those who provided the entertainment and reassured us that we are defended by the bravest and most capable warriors, but also those who made it possible for them to put on this most impressive display of fighting skill."

As he headed for the hall, his euphoria seeped away like air from a leaking bladder. It had been a successful tournament and had achieved the goals he set for it, but now it was over. Tomorrow it would be back to business as usual. And business not so usual. He would be sorely tasked without trustworthy pages and house carls. The charge that Deidre had levied against Sir Henry would have to be investigated and Prince Zachary's ambitions channeled.

People lined the path to deliver thanks and congratulations, slowing Robin's pace which was slowing anyway, his muscles seizing. He was handed cup after cup of ale or wine which he accepted but did not drink. Instead, he surreptitiously spilled the contents. As desperately as he wanted strong drink, concerns about his personal safety proved sobering in more ways than one.

A breathless Sir Maxwell pulled up beside him. "Your Majesty, your armor has been stowed away. It took a beating. I will personally see to its maintenance."

"Delegate and supervise, Sir Maxwell. Repairing and polishing is not a job for a knight for but squires, a good way for them to familiarize themselves with the equipment too. Besides, you have earned a place at the banquet tonight and you should enjoy it."

Sir Maxwell inclined his head in acknowledgement. "Supervise, Sire, that I will do. And Hope has been returned to the stable, none the worse for wear I am pleased to report.

"I see that Your Majesty's cup is empty. Has Your Majesty had his fill or can I get something else?"

Robin could barely speak with his tongue stuck to the roof of his dry mouth, and his aches and bruises cried out for relief. "There is a jug of wine in our bedchamber. We have been saving it for a special occasion. This is it." The "special occasion" was a fabrication; the wine had been given as a gift some time ago and put aside. Stoppered with a cork and sealed with wax there were no worries about tampering. "Fetch it, please. We would be most grateful."

"Special occasion, I should say. The entire tournament was outstanding, but the final contest with our king as the conquering hero was something I'm not likely to forget. The Chalklands will be talking about that for years to come. I will make all speed and bring that wine to Your Majesty in the hall." With a bow Sir Maxwell raced off to the keep.

Robin resumed trudging toward the hall wondering how he was going to make it through what promised to be a long night when all he wanted to do was crawl into bed and curl up with Meeyoo.

As he neared the hall, the officers at arms came to attention and the herald announced his entrance. Partygoers rushed to the door to usher in their king, victor of the dramatic winner-take-all challenge, crowding as close to him as protocol permitted. Again, food and drink was pressed upon him. Food he didn't need but he was elated to see Sir Maxwell arrive with the jug of wine. Robin examined the wax seal. The light coating of dust reassured him. He broke the seal and took a long swig.

Impeded by well-wishers, Robin made slow progress to the throne dais to deliver one last speech. It took two fanfares to quiet the jubilant crowd enough for Robin to speak and once he announced that every combatant would be recognized and rewarded in some way, the acclamation could not be silenced. The only ones who could benefit from Brother Leo's invocation were the few who were standing close enough to him to hear it.

His body stiffening and his head a little light from strong drink on an empty stomach, Robin grabbed a handful of nuts still safe in their shells and took a grateful seat at the king's table. In what possibly was a preemptory move, Prince Zachary had already established himself at the king's right. He stood, bowed, and retook his position. "Your Majesty, congratulations on a stunning performance," he said with a smile that was frostier than the night air.

"We assume you compliment us on our jousting skills," Robin replied. "To be honest we surprised ourselves. We have not had an opportunity to comment on your theatrical presentation." Interrogate would be more like it and he would. He had to know the validity of the sedition implied by Zachary's play. "Your Highness received accolades from our White Castle guests, especially Jewel. Where is Jewel by the way?"

CHAPTER EIGHTEEN

"**With** her parents, celebrating with their retinue."

"Of course." Robin longed to know as well what his son and the lord's daughter had discussed when they left the hall last night, but he would have to wait for those disclosures. Interruptions from servants bringing courses of food and guests appearing at the table to pay their respects prevented further conversation.

Robin smelled the smoke and dismissed it. Although house fires were all too frequent catastrophes, he knew this particular blaze was under control. The ceremonial burning of the broken lances was an orderly fire that had been carried out without mishap for many years at tournaments throughout the land. It was only when he noticed smoke threading through the chinks in the great hall's shutters that he suspected much more was burning than a simple celebratory bonfire. No sooner had it occurred to him than an officer at arms hastened to his side. He bowed quickly and in a hushed voice said, "Sire, I don't wish to alarm Your Majesty or the guests but there is a great fire. The bonfire is out of control and threatens to spread to the stadium."

Robin stifled a dismayed reply but couldn't keep his eyebrows from rising. Just as quietly he said to the officer, "Go, calmly but quickly. Get soldiers and rally a fire brigade."

"Some are already on their way."

"Go. We will join you speedily."

With another economical bow, the officer made for the door with long but measured strides.

Robin turned to Zachary. "There is a fire at the stadium grounds. We are going to attend to it."

Zachary pushed back his chair. "We will come too."

"No, stay here. Entertain our guests as if nothing is amiss. Keep them here in the hall. We don't want a panic to ensue." Robin could picture a hall full of people hastening to the stadium to see the blaze and being trampled by people rushing to flee it or extinguish it.

Robin no sooner stepped outside the hall than he was overwhelmed with the smell and sight of a smoke-filled courtyard. The wind carried the smoke across the curtain wall where it dropped to pool at the base of the wall and fill up the bailey. Beyond the wall, an orange glow bled into the black night sky like an eerie sunset.

Robin thought to run to the stables and grab a mount then decided he could get to the stadium just as fast or faster on foot.

He emerged from the gatehouse and saw the commotion in the distance. Frightened people fleeing the area on foot were knocked aside by those on donkeys and horses. Squires chased after people who had appropriated the knights' steeds to make their escape.

In stark contrast, a neat line snaked from the burning woodpile to the moat, and knights, squires, soldiers, and spectators rhythmically passed filled and empty water buckets up and back. Others scurried like ants to the stadium and tossed water on wood where wind-blown sparks landed and touched off fires. Standing roughly at the line's midpoint, Sir Howell had taken command, outstretched arms pointing this way and that. Robin raced to his side.

"You, there," Sir Howell shouted to a dairy maid, "we need more buckets." At Robin's approach he made a quick bow." "Sire, it's not safe here. Your Majesty should put more distance—"

"We're fine, Sir Howell. Quickly, tell us the status."

"We're trying to extinguish the flames as well as remove anything flammable from the fire's path to control its spread."

The area immediately surrounding the fire was little more than open fields. Beyond that lay forest land and the rickety hovels of a few squatters. Robin didn't wish to see either consumed by flame. Far worse would be if the wooden stadium seats caught fire or if sparks traveled over Bell Castle's curtain walls. Once aflame, the wooden structures on the castle grounds would feed a fire that would rage for days. Robin cast his gaze upwards. The winter weather that had loomed all day had arrived, bringing with it light snow that did little to douse the flames and a brisk wind that fanned the fire and carried sparks towards the castle.

"And we're drawing water from the moat," Sir Howell continued in a rush, "but the distance makes it a slow bucket-by-bucket process. I'm having vats of water brought closer to the fire by wagon."

"Sand, too," said Robin. "You can smother it with sand." He spied Sir Kenneth escorting a young man to a pavilion where, Robin discovered, the tent and several of the knights' doctors had been pressed into service to treat injuries. The wounded took comfort in their king's assurances.

"Is Brother Leo here?"

Sir Kenneth shook his head. "He might be on the fire line."

"Send a page to find him and make sure that he reports here as well to give hope to those who are despairing."

Robin returned to the brigade encouraging the bucket handlers as he made his way along. He found Sir Albert at the end near the moat barking orders at youngsters to fill the vats that had been brought up in a wagon. He acknowledged Robin with a bow then returned to the line, pulling out those who had tired and recruiting fresh replacements.

Sir Alan had taken position at the head of the line nearest the fire. The tinder shifted with a crack and flame spurted out like a dragon's tongue. Falling snow set off bursts of steam.

Sir Alan spotted Robin, bowed, and stayed bent over, coughing mightily.

"We think you have stood at this position too long," Robin said. "You should be relieved to go clear your lungs."

"I'm fine, Your Majesty."

"You're not. You are ordered to get respite, there." Robin pointed to the pavilion where Sir Kenneth was leading a maid clutching her injured arm. "Sir Henry can take your position."

"If you can find him, Sire," Sir Alan said, limping away.

Robin located Sir Maxwell midway down the line and directed him to take Sir Alan's place. Robin searched the crowd for Sir Henry, but as Sir Alan had submitted he was nowhere in sight.

As Robin surveyed the scene, something about the smoke disturbed him: an odor of something more than burning wood and foliage, something slightly sweet like perfume.

The brigade worked through the night to control the conflagration. Sir Howell sent a small army of children a safe distance from the bonfire to clear fallen timber and dried foliage down to the bare earth, creating a fire break that left a ragged scar but successfully kept the flames from spreading to the forest. He charged others with bringing back sacks of sand to pour on and smother the flames. Sir Albert dispatched pages to find a pump and draw greater volumes of water from the moat to fill vats.

The day dawned gray and it wasn't just smoke that darkened the sky. The murky clouds overhead promised more snow. Not good news for homeward-bound knights and spectators, but at least the cold wet blanket would aid in cooling and smothering what was left of the fire. The brigade braved the choking smoke and steam to stir the ashes ensuring that there were no live embers that could reignite. Exhausted from the effort but relieved that the fire had not spread, knights, squires, and pages trooped to their pavilions. Robin directed the kitchen staff to supply bedraggled spectators with food and drink for their journey home. Huddled against the cold, they staggered down the path away from Bell Castle.

Robin toured the scorched and ashy pile that remained. Sirs Maxwell, Kenneth, Alan, Albert, and Howell drew up alongside him.

"Gentlemen, you fought for days and then fought all night. Please, retire to your lodgings and get some well-deserved rest," Robin said.

"This was tragic," said Sir Kenneth.

"That anyone should die as a result of this," said Sir Albert. "This was supposed to be a celebration."

One poor man had indeed succumbed. Whether to the smoke or the stress was yet to be determined. In either case, Robin intended to knight him posthumously and award a stipend. The remunerations wouldn't lessen his survivors' grief, but it would reduce the impact of losing the family's breadwinner.

"We can be grateful that there was but one death and no loss of property."

"Indeed," said Sir Kenneth. "The death is tragic but at least all the other injuries were minor. Scrapes and bruises, some burns, a twisted arm, and a crumpled foot. For the most part people were stricken by panic and fear or overcome by smoke. The physicians are optimistic that the injuries will heal."

Sir Howell's expression was so thoughtful, Robin was moved to ask what was on his mind.

"I find it curious that the fire burned so hot," he said.

"Surely that can be attributed to the different way in which the pile was constructed, vertical instead of horizontal," said Sir Albert. "Wouldn't that feed more air into the fire, direct the flames more efficiently?"

Sir Howell shook his head. "Not really. Just because the pile was tall shouldn't have made it burn hotter than usual. It was more or less the same amount and type of material as always."

"I'm not so sure about that," said Sir Alan. He kicked at a piece of charred wood. "This is no broken lance."

Robin stooped to pick up the cinder. Indeed, instead of being a pole it was the remains of a plank of wood.

"Perhaps someone added some trash to the pile," said Sir Maxwell.

Sir Alan peered over his shoulder. "It appears to have paint on it. Black."

"And tar," Robin murmured. The odor he had smelled; it had been burning tar. He looked up to see all four knights frowning.

"I think I can see a bit of an emblem here. An antelope? Does this look like an antelope to you?" said Sir Albert. "It looks like a piece of lumber from Sir Henry's pavilion."

"Sir Henry used tar," Sir Maxwell said.

"Tar would make a fire burn hotter," said Sir Howell.

For a moment Robin stopped breathing. When he could speak he said, "You don't suppose that Sir Henry contributed this to the fire?"

"Deliberately to make it burn so hot as to rage out of control?" Sir Howell nodded.

Robin shook his head. "We didn't say that. Perhaps a member of his retinue was simply trying to dispose of some debris."

"Sire," said Sir Albert. "It's kind of Your Majesty to give Sir Henry the benefit of the doubt, but he was angry, very angry at having lost the tournament."

Robin wondered if Sir Maxwell had shared with them his concerns about Sir Henry's cheating. "Angry with us? Angry enough to cause a conflagration at Bell Castle and risk so many lives?"

The knights nodded.

"You know, he has never completely regained our trust," said Sir Albert.

Sir Alan glowered as only Sir Alan could. "Sire, I never did care for the story he told me when I found him hiding like a coward at his own manor, or his explanation for why he ignored Your Majesty's summons. The actions of a guilty man, in my opinion."

Robin held his breath and his tongue. Had any of knights been close enough to the grandstand to hear Deidre's accusations?

Sir Alan prodded the heap with his sword and turned over more of the blackened debris, revealing other rectangular pieces where there should have been only poles and finally a small badly-scorched and cracked stone pot of the type used in the application of tar. He looked up at Robin. "I, for one, would like to ask Sir Henry about this fire." He spit out the word "ask" in a way that indicated he really meant to say "beat the man senseless."

"As would I," said Sir Kenneth and the other knights agreed. With more energy than they rightly should have had after the night's ordeal, they set off in the direction of Sir Henry's pavilion. Robin followed reluctantly, sick with dread.

They neared the cluster of pavilions and stopped. Most of the competing knights had already disassembled their pavilions or were in the process of doing so. One of the missing pavilions was Sir Henry's. Robin and the knights drew close to where the shed had stood. Nothing of it remained except an area of trampled ground. Sir Henry's elaborate booth had been completely dismantled and carried away along with all its furnishings. It would have taken hours to disassemble the pavilion and pack up. Rather than lend a hand with fighting the fire, Sir Henry and his vassals must have been taking apart his encampment.

Even if the man was angry after having competed gamely for three days and leaving empty-handed, what knight abandons a raging bonfire at his king's castle?

"Gone," said Sir Kenneth. "Every stick, every scrap."

"Completely," said Sir Howell.

Glowering, Sir Alan said, "We need to find him. He needs to answer some questions."

"He needs to answer more than just questions," said Sir Albert. "If he intensified that blaze, he needs to answer for the death it caused." He looked to Robin. "Sire?"

The blaze wasn't the only thing that had intensified. Three days of tournament challenges and a full night fighting a fire hadn't dampened their savagery. It seemed to have exacerbated it. Either that or their simmering resentment of Sir Henry had come to a boil.

"Should we need to take action, you need to be ready. Get something to eat and drink, get some rest. We will investigate Sir Henry's whereabouts and send for you as needed."

"Until further notice, we will not leave Bell Castle," said Sir Albert, and the other knights nodded. "We will be in our pavilions awaiting our lord's command."

Robin returned to the great hall to find that, in spite of its distance from the flames, smoke hung in the air. The stench also clung to his cloak and he wished that he had shed it before rushing to the fire. It was doubtful that he would be able to get the smell of smoke out of it and it would forever remind him of the tragedy.

Most of the guests had departed. Those who remained sat huddled together clutching tankards of ale. The leavings of last night's feast lay scattered across the tables, ignored by diners too anxious to eat and neglected by servants too busy attending the fire to carry away. The officer reported that some guests had retired to the rooms on the floors above in the hall. Others, he regretted to say, had left to ogle the conflagration and had yet to return. "I hope that they lent a hand in controlling it, Sire," he said.

"We suspect that they did. There were a great many people there. As many arrived to help as left in fear. It was exhausting work and they are resting in the knights' pavilions. We are happy to report that the fire has been contained and has been extinguished. It will smolder for some time and will have to be monitored for fear it may reignite. For now, however, we are confident that it will not spread and take any more land or buildings. There have been injuries and one life was lost. We will compensate those who suffered." Robin scanned the room but didn't see Sir Henry or for that matter Prince Zachary and asked the officer of their whereabouts. "Prince Zachary was instructed to stay here, out of danger and in charge of the welfare and safety of our guests," Robin said.

The officer at arms frowned. "Sir Henry arrived with different instructions. He reported that Your Majesty had said that the prince was needed at the fire and he had been sent to fetch His Highness."

A sense of dread crawled up Robin's spine and spread across his shoulders. Not only had he given no such command to Sir Henry, he hadn't even seen Sir Henry at the fire the entire night. It was possible that in the confusion and commotion he missed the man but that seemed unlikely.

Why would Sir Henry lie about Zachary being needed at the fire?

Robin recalled the man's bluster in upping the tournament from a sportsmanlike melee to something more personal and barbaric. The prize? Nothing grandiose like more money or the expansion of his holdings. Just a token from "Princess Dale."

By means fair and possibly foul Sir Henry had bested every knight, including Robin's top fighters. As for the means foul, there were Sir Maxwell's allegations of cheating. Compounding that, Zachary had appeared to be complicit in swaying decisions in Sir Henry's favor, but how could that be? Zachary didn't know until the last minute that he would be named chevalier d'honneur. Or did he? Had he known that Maxwell would enter the contest and disqualify his father as arbiter? Had Zachary and Sir Henry conspired to achieve his victorious outcome and if so, why? Zachary had called him his champion.

Questions swirled around Robin's brain like the smoke that eddied about the great hall's ceiling. "And they left together?" he asked the officer.

"I'm sorry, Sire. I didn't see them leave."

Not certain what he hoped to find, Robin left the great hall and made his way to the keep wishing he had not left his cloak behind, smoky as it was. He hurried up the stairs to get out of the cold.

Empty of people, all of whom were either in the great hall or at the scene of the fire, the keep echoed. Robin climbed the stairs to the floor that housed the royal bedchambers. He stood before the door leading to Zachary's room. For a moment he remained still, head bowed, his thoughts and emotions tumbling over themselves like leaves in a gust of wind. He knocked on the door. In the silence of the vacated keep, his knock echoed. "Zachary," he called but got no answer. He sighed and called, "Dale?" but there was no reply.

Taking a deep breath, he pushed open the door.

The room was deserted. The clothes chest was gone. Cupboard doors standing ajar showed the shelves to be clear of jewelry, goblets, hairbrushes. The bed was made and did not appear to have been slept in. Some paintings still hung on the wall, but others, like one of a knight battling a monster on behalf of an imperiled maiden whose cloak was painted with costly ultramarine, had been removed.

Robin's son was gone.

CHAPTER NINETEEN

Stunned, Robin stood in the hallway. Sir Henry appeared to have fled and Zachary as well. Had they absconded together and to what purpose?

Now Robin's need to find and interrogate Sir Henry was dire. Grabbing a warm cloak, Robin hastened down the stairs, headed for the garrison. He scanned the sky to determine what challenge the weather would present and noted how thin were the ranks of soldiers on the wall walks. Though it was midmorning, the barracks were unusually quiet, filled with worn-out soldiers resting after their exertions fighting the fire. Robin ordered that every soldier man his post.

"We are not heedless of the men's exertions in the brigade," Robin told the captain.

"No, Sire, of course not. None worked harder than our king."

"Nevertheless, a new dilemma threatens Bell Castle. Our defense is to be at full strength. In addition, we need men for a search party."

"We'll need to recruit manpower from your lieges," the captain said, "many of whom are en route to their homes after the tournament."

"Then intercept them," Robin said. "Have the men for the search party report to us in the hall and tell the knights still on the grounds to find us there as well."

Robin trudged through mounting snow. Foul weather would impede the progress of tournament knights returning to their manors and it would also delay efforts to apprehend Sir Henry.

Sirs Albert, Alan, Howell, Maxwell, and Kenneth arrived, their faces drawn and expressions grave. From the gaiety and giddiness of a tournament and the focused intensity of fighting a raging fire, they had plummeted to worried and wary.

Robin bade them take seats. Servants bustled around them setting out bowls of mulled wine. Soldiers reporting for duty stood at attention.

"Curse this snow," Robin said, warming his hands around his bowl. While not typical, a snowfall this late in the season was not unheard of, but the timing couldn't be worse.

"A damned unfortunate inconvenience. It will make following Sir Henry difficult, especially since we don't know where he's headed," said Sir Kenneth.

"It will slow him down too," said Sir Howell.

"Don't you think he will make for his castle?" asked Sir Albert.

Sir Alan shrugged. "He might indeed try to seek refuge at Windbrook. He's familiar with the resources there and the fortifications."

"We will issue a summons and command him to return to Bell Castle," said Robin.

Sir Kenneth smirked. "Sir Henry has demonstrated utter disregard for the gravity of the king's summons in the past. I wouldn't be surprised if, as before, he will need to be arrested."

Sir Kenneth had a point. "At least he won't be holing up at Cedar Creek now that you are its tenant-in-chief," Robin said.

"Windbrook isn't Cedar Creek, it's true, but it's still a formidable stronghold. He's put some work into it. I assayed it some time ago. Just to see how he fared." Sir Alan's smile was full of menace.

"We should try to apprehend him en route before he has a chance to dig in," said Sir Kenneth.

"Indeed, we need to move now," said Robin. He had to know about Zachary's fate. Was he a victim of Sir Henry's machinations or was he a conspirator? If he was with Henry against his will, could he be rescued? If Zachary was with him willingly did he deserve to meet the fate that they intended for Henry? Could he be extracted and punished less severely? "There's something else you should know before planning any offensive."

Questioning faces turned toward him.

"Prince Zachary is also missing."

The curious expressions turned to frowns.

"Missing?" said Sir Maxwell.

Robin described the prince's vacated bedchamber.

"It's a strange coincidence," Sir Alan muttered.

Sir Kenneth asked, "Did he leave of his own accord? Does Your Majesty believe the prince to be with Sir Henry?"

"His Highness was taken?" asked Sir Albert. "A hostage?"

"If we could have a look at the bedchamber, we might be able to ascertain ...."

Robin nodded.

"We should launch a reconnaissance," said Sir Kenneth. "A small lean squad that can travel swiftly despite the weather, bring back information."

Robin nodded. "At the very least." As exhausted as he was, he knew that he would get no rest until he knew more about Zachary's circumstances.

"If we're going to send spies, we may as well send assassins and be done with it." Sir Albert slammed his tankard onto the table. "Be done with him."

"Assassins? Execute him without a trial? What do you think we are, pagans?" said Sir Howell.

Sir Albert sprung from his seat, planted his hands on the table, and leaned forward. "Who are you calling a pagan, you bastard cur?"

Sir Howell vaulted out of his chair to face him. "You're the one who wants to forgo a trial, you stinking son of a sea cook."

"Now wait a minute," said Robin.

Sir Alan leaned across the table and stuck his face in Sir Albert's. "Lousy bag of fleas, do you mean to set civilization back a thousand years?"

"As if it's civilized to mount a siege and sacrifice tens of thousands of lives simply to punish one man, you biscuit eater." Sir Kenneth, got to his feet.

"Lily-livered coward," Sir Albert replied.

"Men," Robin shouted over the storm of insults. Too much ale, too much wine, too little food, and too little sleep had unraveled nerves already frayed by the tournament's shocking outcome, the raging bonfire, and Sir Henry's mysterious disappearance. "Enough. This isn't getting us closer to action. Less arguing, more thinking and planning."

The men eased back into their seats.

Robin wanted to rub his temples and settled for clenching his mug instead. "We will begin today. We have put out a call for soldiers but yes, we also need intelligence."

Looking down, Sir Kenneth drew a small circle on the table with a gloved forefinger. "What if—?"

"What if what?" asked Robin.

Sir Kenneth raised his head. "What if Sir Henry did take Prince Zachary prisoner? What if we demand Henry's surrender and the price of the prince's ransom is Henry's freedom?"

What if, indeed? Could Robin strike a bargain with a criminal? Could he sacrifice his offspring in the name of justice? If he met Henry's terms, the fathers and mothers of the Chalklands would understand but would they think it right? Would that not tell everyone that the king could be bought?

The officer at arms announced another caller, Deidre, the late Sir Walter's niece.

She strode across the great hall floor. She was no longer trying to pass for a knight or even for a male; her cloak parted to reveal more appropriate wool dress. Sir Maxwell's gaze narrowed in bafflement and ended in wide eyes as he realized Deidre was the latecomer knight from the joust.

She curtsied and stood. "I, Deidre, have heard the call for soldiers to join the campaign against Henry and I come to offer Your Majesty my sword arm," she said.

Robin heard chuckling and snickering from the knights and soldiers. One man doubled over and stifled outright laughter with a gloved hand.

"Gentlemen, you have not been properly introduced. Deidre is Sir Walter's niece and was the last to joust with Sir Henry before we took the dare."

The disclosure was greeted with murmuring and muttering and not a few surprised gasps. Sir Maxwell was agape.

Robin hardly knew what to say to Deidre's offer. He understood her desire for vengeance but there was no way she could possibly join the ranks as a fighter.

"You hesitate, Sire, no doubt thinking that a woman cannot serve in combat. May I remind you of my performance in the lists?"

"How could we forget?" Robin replied, more out of politeness than serious consideration. Like the other spectators, he had been impressed with her jousting skills, but an organized meeting of athletes was one thing. The battlefield was quite another. The troops needed to have complete confidence in each other. How would the men feel fighting alongside a female?

"Yet Your Majesty is not convinced that I am up to the task. Shall I remind Your Majesty of other warrior women of renown? The Amazons; Artemis, the daughter of Zeus; Atalanta; Athena."

"Those were fictional characters, the stuff of legend," said Sir Howell, but his tone was matter-of-fact, testing without being confrontational as though he thought Deidre's candidacy worthy of deliberation.

Deidre nodded. "True. Think then of Deborah, Jael, and Judith in the Bible. Surely you believe that they and their victories were real. You do believe the Word of the Bible, don't you?" She turned to Robin. "Your Majesty?"

Sir Kenneth chuckled. "Howell, you don't truly think ...?"

"Should we find ourselves under attack, it's every man for himself. We couldn't be expected to come to your defense," said Sir Albert.

"I can hold my own. I would not expect any more assistance than you would extend to any other comrade at arms who was in trouble."

Sir Alan shook his head. "Bivouac conditions are primitive and harsh."

"I'm a country girl. No stranger to camping. I can fish, hunt—"

"You'd have no privacy," said Sir Albert.

"That needn't be a concern. I can make my own privacy."

Sir Alan said, "The presence of a female would be distracting, even disruptive. You may envisage yourself as a warrior but there's no escaping the fact that you're a woman. The men—"

"Would not be mindful of their chivalric vows?" Deidre asked.

None of the men present rushed to admit that he would not be able to control his baser instincts. Still, Deidre's rejoinders weren't anything Robin wished to debate now. What brooked no argument was her fervor. Perhaps he would see his way clear to put that zeal to good practical use in a way that wouldn't endanger her or the fighting fraternity.

Robin was reluctant to go on the offensive until he knew more about Zachary.

"We have decided," he said. "We will recon first. We want to know where Sir Henry is and who is with him."

"As in how many troops? Take measure of the strength of forces?" Sir Kenneth asked.

"As in 'is Prince Zachary with him?'" Sir Howell said softly.

Robin affirmed Sir Howell's conclusion with a nod. "Dispatch a small troop. If Sir Henry is found on the road and can be arrested without hostilities, bring him here. If he has already taken refuge at Windbrook, observe, do not engage, and return to report. Speed is of the essence."

CHAPTER TWENTY

Robin wished that the tournament was yet to come rather than in the past. Then he would have something to look forward to while he bided his time, eager for the report on Sir Henry's and, he hoped, Prince Zachary's whereabouts.

Robin's suspicions that Sir Henry had availed himself of some potion, magical or otherwise, Sir Maxwell's allegations of cheating, and Deidre's charge of treason all had to be addressed, matters that would have to be brought to trial. Sir Henry's accusers would need to present evidence of his wrongdoings: a sample of the potion, a representative of the maple lances, a damaged shield.

What sort of tonic could Sir Henry have used? Who at Bell Castle knew of such things? If it was a magic charm, no one in Robin's court could be of help. Robin disliked magic so there were no wizards among his counselors.

As for those maple lances, had they all gone up in smoke? Had the knights already repaired damaged shields? Sir Maxwell might know.

The snow in the bailey had been stamped flat by many feet, but the cold did not do any favors for Robin's joints. Feeling older than his years, he plodded rather than strode to the smithy.

The floor of the smithy was crammed with buckets of scrap metal and wood scavenged from the tournament. The metal would be melted down and crafted into something else. Even wood fragments and sawdust were collected to feed the fire for the forge. The smiths themselves were busy and barely acknowledged the king's entrance before returning to their tasks.

Gregory left his workbench and bowed to Robin.

"You're on both feet today, I see."

Gregory smiled. "I have good days and bad, Your Majesty. Today is a good day. Well, every one of my days is good but my foot doesn't always agree.

"May I compliment Your Majesty on a fine tournament? That it ended so tragically is a shame because it was the most splendid three days I have ever spent. That's the part that I want to remember."

"Thank you. It's the tournament and that bonfire that we would like to speak with you about. We are looking into how that fire could have gotten so out of control so we never have a repeat of that calamity. We wanted to ask Sir Maxwell a question or two about it."

Gregory's brow furrowed with concern. "Your Majesty doesn't think that my son was responsible in any way. I can assure you—"

"Not at all. He just may be privy to some relevant information. Is he about?"

"He is not." Robin thought that Gregory seemed slightly put out. "Can I be of help in any way?"

Robin said, "He had mentioned something to us about maple wood lances. We were going to ask him if he had happened to retain a sample."

"As a matter of fact he did bring some pieces to show me. He wondered if maple were to be used instead of ash would we need to alter the design of the coronals or make some other change in the fabrication to adjust for the sturdier wood. We may still have them." He looked about the smithy. "I wouldn't have discarded them."

"Would they have ended up in the scrap wood bin?" Robin said.

"If they haven't already been used for fuel. I should go check without further delay." He reached for a bucket but Robin stopped him.

"Don't interrupt your work. Sir Maxwell can search. Where is he?"

"He said that he wanted to work on his tracking skills so he went off to the woods." Again, Gregory seemed somewhat irked. "I will send one of the men to go after him."

"Don't take anyone away from his work. We will find Sir Maxwell. And when we find him, we will tell him to return to the forge." That he would not neglect his duties in the smithy was a condition of his knighthood.

At the gatehouse Robin asked the gatekeeper if he had seen Sir Maxwell depart.

"Yes, Sire, not that long ago, and on foot, so I don't imagine that he's gone far. Shall I send a guard?"

Robin waved away the suggestion. "We'll find him ourselves. Have a stable lad bring our horse around." A little jaunt in the woods suddenly had appeal. It would be revitalizing to get away from the castle for an hour or so. A gentle ride would stretch and loosen his muscles. In a different setting he might get some fresh ideas about solutions to his dilemmas or perhaps not think about them at all for an hour or two.

Foot traffic and oxcarts had cleared the path but once Robin's horse stepped off, it was in snow up to its fetlocks, even deeper in places where the wind had piled up drifts. Robin found it easy enough to spot the tracks of many different animals and yes, one human. Robin set off across the snow-covered field toward the woods.

If Sir Maxwell was practicing tracking, Robin couldn't discern what the young man was following as the animal prints were random and unremarkable. He spotted Sir Maxwell's cloaked figure pressed against a pine tree up ahead. So as not to startle him, Robin dismounted and waited until he was closer before calling to him.

Sir Maxwell turned and bowed, then pressed a finger to his lips. Leaving the horse where it stood, Robin picked his steps carefully to avoid crushing a twig under the snow and making a noise that could startle Sir Maxwell's prey, whatever it was.

"What are you doing here, Your Majesty?" Sir Maxwell whispered.

"We came to find you. We have some questions." He told Sir Maxwell of his need for samples of the maple lances.

Sir Maxwell said, "I did bring my father some pieces of broken lances."

Robin nodded. "I talked to him. He's looking to see if any remain in the scrap bucket. We also need to know about those damaged shields. Do you know if there are any yet to be repaired?"

"Possibly. The carpenters ... they may also have some stubs of those maple lances. I know I talked about it with Arnold, Claude's son. He was the one who pointed out the difference in grain between the maple and the ash and told me about the different properties." He hung his head. "I should have given him credit for that insight."

"That's of no importance now. We will inquire of the carpenters. Meanwhile, your father said you were polishing your tracking skills. May we ask what your quarry is?"

Sir Maxwell beamed. "Some time ago I said that there was something that I wanted to show to Your Majesty. If fortune smiles on us, I will be able to show that to you now. I'm trying to spot him. Do you see him, Sire?"

"See who?" Robin squinted, trying to bring the details of the glade up ahead into focus. Light filtered down through the lacy canopy of bare trees and shadows dappled the ground below. The shapes of dark and light shifted as the wind moved the tree limbs.

"Not 'who,' Sire, 'what'." Maxwell craned his neck forward and then looked up. "The gryphon. Can you spot him? He can hide, I'll give him that."

Gryphon? Robin recalled their conversation the night of the vespers tourney when Sir Maxwell had explained the changes he made to his blazon. Apparently Maxwell was not only convinced a gryphon existed, but that one inhabited Bell Castle's grounds, had mated with Meeyoo, and sired her kitten, Meeyowyow.

Surely there would be no mistaking a gryphon if one prowled the woods ahead. Something with the body of a lion? They didn't have lions in the Chalklands, but Robin had certainly seen enough representations of them to imagine what one should look like.

And with the head of an eagle, and wings? They would have to be enormous wings to lift such a big animal.

"He should be somewhere around here, Sire," Maxwell said. "He wouldn't stray far from this spot where he can keep Bell Castle in sight. It's because of Meeyoo. Gryphons mate for life you know. He wants to be close to Meeyoo. When she was ill and it looked like she would die, he acted as if he was in mourning. He didn't hunt, he didn't eat. He slept a lot and when he was awake, he just lay here, gazing at the castle, sighing."

Maxwell had truly seen the beast and on more than one occasion? Had gotten close enough to a gryphon to hear it sigh? What would the sigh of a gryphon sound like? It would be loud, Robin imagined. Doleful.

"When Your Majesty took her to the healer in Dulcimer, it was as if he knew she was no longer at Bell Castle. He left his post here in the glade. I did not see him again until after Your Majesty returned."

Because the gryphon trailed us to Dulcimer and back?

There was no question that a large airborne creature kept them ever in sight. Had it been the gryphon? Robin recalled their overnight encampment and the unearthly roar that had not only startled him and his soldiers, but had also scared off a pack of hungry wolves. Had that been the gryphon, protecting Meeyoo?

And then, Robin thought, the gryphon shadowed Meeyoo to the stadium and back during the tournament.

"Had she not survived he would have lived out the rest of his life alone, never taking another mate, gryphons are that faithful," Sir Maxwell said.

Mate for life. Robin found himself thinking about that. Had he himself mated for life? With his marriage over, would he spend the rest of his years alone? The church was of divided opinions about remarriage in the aftermath of an annulment.

"That's why I thought to capture him and bring him to Bell Castle, so that he could be closer to Meeyoo. And to Meeyowyow, his son."

"Surely if he wanted to be close to Meeyoo, he could find his way inside the walls. Apparently he has at least once or there would be no son," Robin said, more musing aloud than participating in a serious conversation about an imaginary beast he couldn't see. "He can fly after all, can't he?"

Find his way inside the walls. Robin found himself thinking about walls that he had put to his back when he left a sojourn where perhaps he should have stayed. He shook his head. No, it wouldn't have worked.

"I realized that finally," said Maxwell. "Maybe when the weather warms up Meeyoo will come out to see him. Maybe they will have another litter."

"It's possible that Meeyoo can't have any more children."

"Kittens, you mean, Sire?"

"Yes, kittens." *That was what they were talking about, right?* Robin wondered if Meeyoo questioned where her kittens had gone. Did she miss them?

Maxwell frowned. "That would be sad. At least there's Meeyowyow to carry on the family line."

"Indeed," Robin said, his thoughts turning to Conrad and Zachary. Conrad, now Brother Thaddeus, had taken a vow of chastity and worse, volunteered for the front lines of a deadly conflict with no end in sight, but Zachary had taken no such vows. Could, would Zachary father a child? The idea of "Princess Dale" having a son seemed as fantastic as the notion of a gryphon.

Robin could have more children. He was still vigorous. He might not live much past their majority but that didn't matter.

There would be no end of candidates willing and even eager to provide the king with an heir, but the woman he found himself thinking about was not eligible.

"Sire?" Maxwell said.

"Yes?" Robin replied, pulling himself back to the present.

"You see him now, don't you?"

Was there a creature there in the high branches or just a trick of the light? Maybe one needed to believe gryphons were real in order to see them. By the same token, did one need to see them in order to believe in them? No one had ever seen God, yet everyone believed He existed.

Questions for another day. More urgent matters demanded attention. "Shall we return to the castle?" he asked. "Walk or ride?"

"Walk is fine with me, Your Majesty. but please go ahead and ride if you prefer. I can keep up."

"We can ride double, Sir Maxwell."

They left the covering of the trees and set out across the snowy field, Sir Maxwell reeling off the names of knights whose shields might still show signs of damage.

Robin heard the whizz of the arrow but not soon enough to avoid it. It pierced his robe and sleeve and bit into his arm like a viper.

"Oh my God, Sire," Sir Maxwell cried. "Get down."

Robin didn't need to be told twice. He pressed himself against Hope's neck and felt Sir Maxwell flatten himself against his back, an arm wrapped around his chest. Sir Maxwell tugged on the arrow's shaft. "No, Maxwell, leave that in place, otherwise there will be much more blood." Robin spurred Hope across the field to Bell Castle's gates. He dared not raise his head to try to identify the source of the attack against which he was defenseless. He had his dagger and sword but they were useless against a bowman.

He heard Sir Maxwell cry and felt him shudder. "Another arrow, Sire. I'm hit but I'm—"

He felt the young man's weight slump against his back. Robin didn't hear the flight of the third arrow but he did hear it plop into the snow behind them. "Faster, Hope," he urged the horse. Would that he had the spurs he wore in the joust. Robin raised his eyes as they neared the gate. The guards straightened and then sprang into action, raising the alarm and racing towards the approaching riders.

Robin didn't slow Hope until they were through the gate into the bailey and he heard the portcullis clang closed. He reined in the horse and tried to straighten but the young knight still lay on top of him. "Sir Maxwell, we are safe."

"Ah, yes, Sire." Sir Maxwell slipped from the horse as soldiers and servants crowded around. Robin heard "Get the doctor," "Get more men on the gate," and "Get more soldiers on the wall walks," all of which were excellent ideas and commands that he was about to issue. He was most grateful to hear someone cry "someone bring His Majesty some ale."

Sir Maxwell moaned. Robin wondered had it all just been an elaborate ruse to get the king away from the castle, out in the open and vulnerable? No, he decided. Gregory could not have known that he would call at the forge, that he would ask for Sir Maxwell, or even that he would go searching for him. Had the young knight been some kind of bait he had certainly redeemed himself by shielding his king and getting shot himself.

So who was the bowman? Did Sir Henry lurk in the woods or was it a confederate of Prince Zachary's?

Servants carried Robin and Sir Maxwell into the great hall. Some hastened to bring braziers to warm the room while others cut clothes away from the wounds.

The doctor and his assistants examined the injuries. "Thank God you did not try to remove the arrow," the doctor said. "The shaft might have separated from the point making it harder for us to find it." He ordered servants to bring strong drink for the two patients.

There was rum in Robin's private stock and he told the servants where to find it.

"We have to remove the arrowheads," the doctor said. "We cannot leave them in place. The wounds will never heal, they will just fester around the points. I will have to enlarge the wounds. I must probe to see if the arrowheads have lodged in bone and let us pray that they haven't. May we find that they are not barbed." He bowed to Robin. "My apologies, Sire, but my examination and treatment are going to be more painful than being shot was in the first place."

"Do what you must," said Robin, swallowing his first mouthful of rum. Would that he had the soporific that Lady Alice used in Meeyoo's operation or whatever preparation Sir Henry might have fortified himself with during the joust, magic or not.

"Scream if you are pained and you will be," said the doctor, "there is no shame." Robin knew well the heart-rending sound of agonized cries on the battlefield. He could not let his subjects think their king weak. Even as he felt the doctor's knife pierce, he held his silence though he thought he might grind his teeth down to the gums, he clenched his jaws that tightly. Sir Maxwell didn't cry out but his moans were pitiful. Servants poured out more rum for him and helped him to drink it from his prone position stretched across a long table.

As they worked, the doctor and his assistants pronounced that the arrows had penetrated skin and muscle only, not bone; that the points had gone in straight and appeared to have clean smooth edges for which he was grateful. "Had they been barbed or had they twisted upon entry they would be embedded more deeply in the tissue, making them harder to remove. Nevertheless, these are serious injuries. For Sir Maxwell's wound which is severe I have an instrument," he said. "I will be sliding it into the incision that I have created. It will enclose the arrowhead so that I may remove it without causing further damage," which sounded to Robin like the doctor proposed to dig the point out with a spoon.

"The arrow," Robin murmured, rum already slurring his speech. "Put it aside for safekeeping."

The doctor gave him a quizzical look, no doubt wondering if the king meant to keep it as some battle souvenir, but he did as commanded.

Later, Robin thought, when he had his wits about him, he would study the fletching. If it didn't come from Bell Castle's armory it might hold a clue to the identity of the bowman.

The doctor gestured to his assistant who brought him a saw. "For Your Majesty's injury I'm afraid I must try a different operation."

Robin felt himself go suddenly hollow. "You must amputate?" he said, trying to keep his voice steady. "Perhaps you could just remove the shaft and leave the point in place. Isn't there a slight chance that it would heal?"

"Oh, Sire. I apologize if I alarmed Your Majesty. I don't need to remove the arm, just the fletching. For this injury I'm afraid the best treatment will be to push the arrowhead the rest of the way through and out."

This didn't sound any more pleasant than having the point dug out of the wound. Robin thought to drink to oblivion but even with his already muddled mind he wondered about the wisdom of being that vulnerable. If he kept his wits about him, could he bear the pain? He steeled himself for the torture to come.

*****

Robin opened his eyes and then just as quickly closed them against the harsh light. His mouth felt dry. His left arm throbbed as if to a drumbeat. He lifted his right arm and shielding his eyes with his hand, cracked open the lids. Adjusting to the light, he lowered his hand and gazed at the ceiling. It appeared that he was in his own bedchamber. He made to lift his head which proved to be as heavy as a rock. He turned his face to one side just enough to confirm that he lay in his own bed. The quality of the light said it was the middle of the day, but what day he could not be sure. The last thing he remembered was being in the great hall at the mercy of a doctor driving an arrow through his arm. Despite Robin's resolve to remain conscious, he must have passed out.

He turned his head to the other side and was greeted by a pair of sympathetic eyes. Stretched out on a pillow beside him, Meeyoo blinked and made a little mewling sound. She crawled closer to him, patted his shoulder with a paw, and nudged his cheek. He reached across and scratched her head, smiling despite his pain.

He rolled on to his good side and tried to raise himself.

"Your Majesty, you are awake," he heard.

A youngster appeared at the side of the bed. About eleven years old, with olive skin, dark hair and eyes, he was no one that Robin recognized. "Who are you?" Robin croaked.

"Your Majesty's nurse," said the boy, helping Robin to sit upright. "Nurse, page, whatever Your Majesty needs. My name is Jacky. The advocate, Terrowin, assigned me this duty."

Robin nodded. "Need drink," he said.

Jacky filled a mug from a pitcher. "Well-watered wine with some herbs to aid your healing." He held up a finger and sipped from the mug. "So you may be assured it is safe to drink," he said and then passed it to Robin. "If there's something else that you'd rather have I will get it for you."

Robin whet his mouth and throat and then was able to say, "You said Terrowin?"

"Yes, Sire. He says to tell you that he continues to work on the task you gave him. Meanwhile, in light of your concerns about your security he said that I should attend you. Of course, that's only temporary until my lord approves. We would have consulted Your Majesty but—"

"We had passed out," Robin guessed. "How long?"

"Just since yesterday, Your Majesty. Any man would have, Sire. It's just as well. It allowed the doctor to proceed with his operation. Which I am pleased to report was a success. The arrow has been completely removed, Your Majesty's wound cleaned and dressed. I am told that with care Your Majesty will mend nicely."

"And Sir Maxwell?"

"His operation too went well. It's a more serious wound; he will need much time to rest and heal. You, Sire, are advised to rest for at least a week. The doctor says the best therapy is simply to do very little."

"Easy for the doctor to say. He doesn't have a kingdom to run." Robin made as if to get up from the bed.

"Sire, please, if there's something that you need, allow me to fetch it for you," said Jacky.

"Something to eat. Let Sir Maxwell know we are concerned for his health and recovery. See if there's anything that he needs."

The boy bowed and left to do Robin's bidding. Robin slumped against the pillows and cast his mind back to the attack in the woods. When the first arrow struck, he wondered if it was a hunting mishap. The second arrow and then the third made it clear it was no accident but a deliberate attack. Who could have been behind that? Who even knew that Robin would be at that spot when Robin himself didn't know until he arrived there? Had an enemy been lying in wait just on the off chance the king would happen by undefended? It seemed too unlikely a coincidence.

Might there be more assailants staged at various locations outside the castle walls and if so, who would mount an offensive like that? Sir Henry? The thought was chilling. Robin yearned to talk it over with his knights but could any of them be trusted? What if one of them was behind it? What if they were all in together? Could Sir Maxwell be part of the conspiracy? Was his injury just part of a ruse to divert Robin's suspicion?

Questions buzzed like swarming bees. His head throbbed worse than his arm. Robin closed his eyes.

When he next opened them, he saw a platter of food by his bed. A discreet slice had been taken from each item by the taster. A few other bites were missing, but from the ragged looks of them, Meeyoo had done the nibbling. The sauces had congealed, the bread looked dry, and the edges of some of the dishes were slightly brown, so the platter had sat a while.

Jacky appeared at his side. "I brought some food as requested but you had fallen asleep, Sire. I thought it best just to let Your Majesty rest."

"Thank you, Jacky." Robin struggled to a sitting position and helped himself to an apple. His arm ached and felt as if it was twice its normal size but his head was clearer.

"I report that Sir Maxwell is being cared for in one of the great hall's bedchambers," Jacky said. "He is resting but does have moments of wakefulness. He asked about Your Majesty's condition. And the captain of the guard also wishes to meet with you, Sire, when Your Majesty has healed. Terrowin is also ready to report on his progress at Your Majesty's convenience."

Robin threw back the covers and swung his legs to the side of the bed. "Have word sent to the captain that we will meet with him in the great hall. Have food brought there for us. Help us to dress."

Jacky bowed and did as Robin commanded.

*****

Robin dropped onto his throne, exhausted by the effort of dressing and walking to the great hall. Several guards insisted on escorting the king. They offered to carry him but he refused out of concern for the message that would send to his subjects. As Robin lumbered to the great hall, he noticed with approval the increased number of guards on the wall walk.

The captain fairly trotted towards the throne, bowed, and with no further delay said, "Your Majesty, we are grateful for your speedy recovery."

Robin was by no means recovered but that was beside the point. "You have something to report."

"Indeed. Our scouts have returned from their mission. Sir Henry has returned to Windbrook. He does not set foot outside the castle walls which are well-guarded."

"Castle, you say?" Windbrook was no castle.

"Yes, Sire. A keep with curtain walls and a fortified city."

This was news. Robin frowned. It bore out what Sir Alan had said about Sir Henry putting work into Windbrook.

"I hope that the additional information I bring is useful though I confess that I found it confusing," the captain continued. "To inquire of Prince Zachary without arousing suspicion, we approached servants of Sir Henry's household on their travels to and from the castle. No one mentioned seeing the prince however there is a princess, Princess Dale, whom the lady's maids found ... strange. One servant said that Princess Dale is really a man masquerading as a woman. Could that not be the prince in disguise? If it is Prince Zachary, I would have to assume the point of the disguise is to remain undetected at

Windbrook Castle. In any case, it didn't sound like this Princess Dale was being held against her will." The captain held out his hands. "I apologize, Sire, and wish that I had something more definitive to report."

"Thank you. Be at the ready for further commands but for now that is all," Robin replied. That Zachary may have gone willingly with Sir Henry complicated the matter and now Robin had to take seriously the possibility that Zachary was part of Sir Henry's treachery or had even engineered it.

So Sir Henry had holed up behind castle walls? Sir Kenneth would be proven right. It would take more than a summons to pry Sir Henry loose.

CHAPTER TWENTY-ONE

In a chamber on the upper floor of the great hall, shields, swords, and maces hung on the wall along with tapestries depicting classic battles. The belligerence of the décor was deliberate; implements and images of armored men bristling with weapons were meant to stir the blood of the war room's occupants.

One by one, the knights and Deidre arrived in answer to Robin's call. The fighters bowed and stood behind the seats surrounding the sturdy wooden trestle table at the room's center.

Standing at the table's head, Robin was about to address them when one more person entered the room. Looking as if he had aged many years, Sir Maxwell made slow progress across the floor to the table.

"Sir Maxwell, you are far from recovered from your injury. You are supposed to rest."

"My body may still be healing but my brain is fully functioning, Sire. I hoped to be of some service."

"Be seated then." Robin detailed the captain's report and his suspicions. "Not only do we suspect that Sir Henry was complicit in the arson, but he has also been accused of cheating at the joust."

Deidre caught his eye and Robin knew that she wanted him to add the betrayal of Sir Walter to the list of charges. He gave her a stern look and she bit her lip.

"We are investigating all these accusations, but we want Sir Henry here to provide answers."

"Lies. They would be lies, not answers," said Sir Alan.

"Nevertheless, in the interest of justice we want to hear him tell them so that we may disprove them if in fact they are untruths." The judgment passed on Sir Walter still haunted him; Robin wouldn't be so quick to pass sentence again.

"Once again, he has ignored the king's summons. It sounds like he has burrowed in at Windbrook," said Sir Kenneth.

"He might find it hard to refuse his king's command with His Majesty standing outside Windbrook's very gates." Sir Howell sounded almost glad to have an excuse to act.

True enough, but now Robin wondered if the proposed strategy was intended to draw him away from the protection of Bell Castle and leave him exposed. He hated not being able to trust his men, to have to think and double-think every word, every action.

His mind raced ahead, projecting the outcome of such a plan. If it failed, if it were in fact a ruse to kill the king and leave Bell Castle vulnerable for takeover, what were the chances that the knights would survive the battle? If this was part of a cleverly disguised conspiracy, did it include a plan of escape? Had any one or all of these men offered their cooperation in exchange for protection or a ransom to be paid to their families? Did these men have so little invested in their own king that they were prepared to sacrifice themselves, their comrades, and all of Bell Castle so that their heirs might prosper?

Robin's thoughts chased each other like Meeyoo chasing a mouse. It was impossible. He could not rule a kingdom if he had to second-guess the motives and moves of his vassals. He slammed his tankard on the table and leaned forward.

"Sir Howell, tell us now. Are you conspiring for the undoing of Bell Castle? If you confess, we will show you mercy. If you deny it and your betrayal is proved, not only will you suffer, but so will your family."

Mouth agape, his eyebrows raised, Howell looked more stunned than guilty, although Robin was not about to determine a man's innocence based on what could be a carefully rehearsed expression.

Howell looked a question at the other men at the table, who shrugged. He frowned, pressed his lips together, and eased to his feet. "Excuse me, Sire?"

"We asked if you conspire against your king. Tell us now and we will go easy on you."

"Conspire? I would be insulted if that wasn't such a preposterous notion, begging Your Majesty's pardon. What have I done that would lead Your Majesty to doubt my loyalty?" His tone was even but he clenched and released his fists and his face was tight with fury. "If I had such traitorous intentions there would be no need to expose myself and my fellow knights, whom I have sworn to protect, to danger. I could simply kill your Majesty right here, right now." No sooner had his words left his mouth than he flew to Robin's side, got his left arm around Robin's chest, and with his right hand held his dagger to Robin's throat.

The other knights gasped. Chairs shoved roughly aside crashed to the floor as the other men sprang to their feet, knives at the ready.

They all intended his death, Robin realized. It was going to be a massacre. He would die many times over, his life streaming from a dozen wounds like water from a sieve.

He might as well die. All his fears had been justified. His closest and most trusted men plotted against him and wanted him dead so badly that they were prepared to murder him in cold blood. He deserved such a humiliating fate for having so innocently placed his trust. Of course, any of these men could have killed him at any time; he had given them plenty of opportunities. Now he would pay for his ingenuousness and stupidity. Everything that he had wished and fought for had come to this ignoble end. He would die at the hands of traitorous knights.

"I could kill you now and who would stop me?" Sir Howell's voice was steely.

"I would!" Brandishing his dagger, Sir Maxwell leaped onto the table, wincing with the effort.

"I would," roared Sir Kenneth, drawing his weapon.

"Unhand our king, you dog," said Sir Alan.

"Harm His Highness and there won't be enough of you left to bury," said Sir Albert.

Agog, Deidre unsheathed her dagger.

"No need, gentlemen. Relax." Sir Howell's voice was firm and calm. He released Robin and held his hands away from his body. "It seemed that a demonstration of my loyalty, our loyalty was called for." He turned to Robin, held out his dagger for Robin to take, and dropped to one knee. "Sire, my abject apologies for my assault on Your Majesty's royal personage. I hope I have shown that had I any such evil intentions, I could have acted on them long before now, as could have any of us. If you still don't trust me, Your Majesty may as well behead me right here where I kneel. My life has been about service to my king, the kingdom, and my fellow knights. If I can't perform my sworn duty then I am as good as dead." He bowed his head.

Robin felt his lungs fill with air. The blood returned to his head, dispelling his icy fear, and also warmed his face with embarrassment. "Rise, Sir Howell," he said and gave the man his weapon. "Sir Maxwell, get down from the table before you reopen your wound. You may all sit."

Rigid with tension and with puzzled and wary expressions, the men righted their chairs and took their seats but remained perched at the edge in positions of readiness. Bewildered, Deidre looked about.

"May I know, Sire, what gave rise to your doubts?" asked Sir Howell.

Robin sighed and took his own seat. He was the king and owed no one an explanation or an apology, yet he felt Sir Howell deserved an answer. "It all began during the Saint Valentine's tournament. You were all at the melee a cheval. Well, you weren't, Sir Howell, having been captured, nor you, Sir Kenneth, being otherwise engaged keeping your 'prisoner' under control."

Sir Howell coughed and the other men chuckled nervously, but Robin's attempt at humor seemed to break the tension.

"While we awaited the victors' return, we took in a theatrical performance at the stage that was written and performed by our own Prince Zachary." Robin described the play and its unsettling implications, how the seed of worry had been planted and grew over the days and weeks until he became lost in a forest of unease and suspicion.

"I missed the play," said Sir Howell. "I was suffering at the hands of my captor."

"Suffering?" Sir Kenneth retorted. "The only thing that suffered was my ale vat which you sought to empty singlehandedly."

"I was drowning my humiliation."

More chuckles followed and Robin appreciated Sir Howell's and Sir Kenneth's efforts to lighten the mood.

"I saw that play," said Sir Maxwell. He frowned. "I never thought ...." He shook his head. "Had Prince Zachary plans to murder the king, would it have been prudent to make his intentions known that way, thereby putting the king on notice?"

Well, no, Robin had to admit. That would be foolish and whatever else he was, Prince Zachary was no fool.

"How could such unfounded suspicions about us have ever taken root?" Sir Albert asked, a hint of peevishness in his voice.

"A king must always be on guard," said Sir Howell. "He needs to see every angle, be prepared for every contingency, imagine every possible outcome."

"These are stressful, uncertain times," said Sir Kenneth.

Sir Alan slammed the table with his fist. "Then let's restore our king's confidence. Let's take back the upper hand. Let's prove Sir Henry's guilt and then let's punish him."

"Hear, hear," replied the other knights.

Robin felt himself carried aloft by their zeal like a ship wafted to shore by a stiff breeze. When the clamor died down he said, "We presume you have a strategy in mind for that, Sir Alan."

The men turned their attention to the knight. "Yes, Sir Alan, how do we apprehend Sir Henry from outside his fortress?" asked Sir Albert. "What are the chances that he will surrender as easily as he did the last time?"

"Who said that was easy?" Sir Alan demanded.

"We have commanded his presence. We hoped for the best but we must prepare for the worst. We will proceed at once with a show of force to Windbrook." Robin stood and slapped his palms on the table. Pain shot up his injured arm. "In light of the recent attack, however, we must take special measures to safeguard Bell Castle in our absence. One of you must stay and see that peak defenses are maintained."

He was greeted with a moment of silence as none of the knights was eager to sacrifice his place in any offensive against Sir Henry.

Sir Albert stood and bowed. "I will, Sire."

"Excellent. Sir Maxwell, you will also remain and aid Sir Albert."

Sir Maxwell pursed his lips as if about to protest.

"Yes, we heard your assertion that you are fit for duty in mind if not in body. In that case, we will all be best served by your remaining at Bell Castle. You can continue your recovery and be of assistance to Sir Albert."

Sir Maxwell took a deep breath and bowed. "I will, Your Majesty.

"Men, make ready to go on the offensive."

"And I, Sire?" Deidre's expectant expression was mirrored in the faces of the men around her.

CHAPTER TWENTY-TWO

Servants, pages, and squires gathered food, fuel, and supplies for the journey and an encampment at Windbrook. Soldiers loaded barrels of arrowheads and quarrels for longbows and crossbows, sheaves of arrow shafts, and stacks of spears onto donkey carts along with bows and bowstrings, maces, axes, and clubs. Retrieved from storage and fitted onto sturdy wheeled platforms, the heavy machinery of warfare would lag behind, drawn by slower oxen.

The caravan included a canopied cart that was outfitted with cushions and blankets for the comfort of a king still recovering from a severe injury.

Though Robin wished to show no weakness, the knights urged him to take advantage and get some restorative rest. His arm did ache and his energy flagged and the closer they drew to Sir Henry's Windbrook castle the more he would need his wits about him. Yet even as he stretched out in the cart and closed his eyes, his mind would not rest. They were headed for Sir Henry's castle. *Had Henry heard any of the charges leveled against him by Deidre? Had he indeed created the bonfire inferno and if so, out of spite over losing or out of a greater enmity?*

Unable to sleep, Robin rejoined the traveling party, riding alongside Sir Howell. Howell was in many cases a man of thought before action.

"What are the chances we'll find him still at Windbrook?" Robin asked. "He knows that there is a warrant out for his arrest and detention. We would imagine he'd find somewhere else to hide."

"I believe we will find him there, Sire. He could seek refuge elsewhere in the kingdom but he would be aware that he would be found sooner or later. He's been on the run before and knows how difficult it is to remain hidden. Even if he has some ally who will give him sanctuary, we will be able to suss out his whereabouts. On the other hand, at his castle he has the full advantage of its defensive structures, all his armaments and men."

His armaments and men, Robin thought. *Those men are my men, too, my subjects.* It felt strange enough to be making war on his own knight much less his own people.

"What are you thinking, Sir Howell?" Robin asked. "Blockade first, then siege?"

Howell never sought guess what strategy the king might prefer so as to deliver the most politic reply. "Your Majesty, I would suspect that Henry has already begun to strip the countryside with intent to stockpile food and materials while at the same time depriving us of a local supply source. Assuming he has called up his vassals, he will have their service for forty days. He will be in a good position to hold out that long behind his fortification."

"I say we move immediately on the city," said Sir Kenneth. "Before Henry has a chance to build his defenses to full strength. Once we have control of the city we can call for his surrender. If he won't concede, we can continue to blockade him until we break his will."

"I'd rather break his walls," said Sir Alan. "Mount an immediate siege. Smash our way in, drag him out. Spare the city and his subjects. It's Henry who should be punished."

Sir Alan's suggestion appealed to Robin who sickened at the thought of attacking innocent citizens. Although they owed service to Sir Henry, ultimately they were subjects of the kingdom of the Chalklands.

"By the time we get there he will have had more than enough time to make complete preparations for any attack," Robin grumbled. The snow had stopped falling and had melted where struck by the sun but drifts lingered in shaded and sheltered areas, the accumulation sometimes slowing their progress. "He will have stockpiled food and supplies, called up his army, had his smiths working day and night making arrowheads …."

"I suggest that we take the ancient roads," Sir Howell said. "I've been making something of a study of them. They were built true then, better in some ways than we build them today. The transportation systems were laid out for speedy and efficient travel; our vehicles will move more easily on them. I know the routes may be unfamiliar to many of the men but I say we will make good time."

Howell was unlikely to gamble the success of the campaign to prove a personal point. "Set the route then," Robin said.

With each plodding step toward Windbrook Castle, Robin's heart grew heavier. He felt none of the fire that had heated his blood on previous campaigns. This was simply a sad mission.

What of Zachary? What would Robin find when they took the castle, that Zachary was once again Princess Dale? Would Dale side with Henry? Would she put aside her gowns, don armor, and fight alongside the duplicitous knight? If Robin met her on the field of battle, would he be able to strike her?

As for women on the field of battle, he had misgivings about including Deidre in the army. At best, the other soldiers kept a polite distance. Every now and then Robin would catch a glimpse of her and be reminded of Sir Walter whose execution weighed heavily.

Robin had Sir Alan brought closer to the front.

"Sire, you seem preoccupied," said Sir Alan. "I suspect that Your Majesty is concerned about every aspect of the campaign, but I have ridden throughout our army. I can assure you that we are ready and able."

"We have no doubt," said Robin. "We have full confidence in the ability of our men. Nevertheless we find ourselves troubled. We have need of your special skills," Robin said. "Play us something especially rousing."

A fearless and competent fighter, Sir Alan had another talent that proved useful especially during long campaigns and fierce combats. His expert drumming enlivened soldiers' spirits on marches and fired their passion on the battlefield. Robin needed both.

Sir Alan smiled. "I have the very thing in mind. An opus that I have composed especially for this campaign to capture the essence of our mission. I am calling it *The King's Redress*."

Sir Alan proceeded to play a composition full of clattering strokes that captured the clash of weapons, and beats that called to mind the pounding of thousands of feet on march and the heart's throbbing pulse in the heat of battle. Sir Alan's drumming mounted in speed and fury, foretelling of the fierce combat to come. A sudden pause like a held breath spoke of the eerie stillness following the battle's conclusion as the combatants took stock and numbered their gains and losses. He broke the silence with light frisky rapping that hinted at the shouting and jubilation of the victor. The piece ended with steady strokes to the rhythm of an overheated heart slowing to rest.

They drew close to Windbrook and Robin could see the top of a keep on the horizon.

He commanded the army to stay well back and establish a temporary base out of sight of Windbrook's guards. Servants swept away snow and erected tents in the wood at the edge of a clearing. Unlike the colorful pavilions of the tournament knights, the dun-colored shelters blended with the surroundings.

Robin and Sir Howell climbed to the crest of a rise. The captain had not exaggerated in his report. Sir Henry had indeed made improvements. Where once had been a manor house and a stockade village, a walled and gated city lay at the base of a motte-and-bailey castle surrounded by a moat. The walls surrounding the city were of stone except for the section of stockade abutting the moat. Robin could just about make out black pennants and the figures of soldiers manning the wall walks.

Where had Sir Henry found the money, the men, and materials for the expansion?

Cleared of snow, tracks led to a drawbridge over a dry ditch protecting the city's main gate, to the postern gate in the stockade, and to the drawbridge over the moat defending the castle gate. Ox and donkey carts carried raw materials and finished goods to and from the city and the castle. The density of the traffic suggested that Sir Henry anticipated a blockade and was stockpiling supplies.

The winding brook from which the castle took its name snaked across the landscape. The stone bridge fording it was certain to be strongly defended, could in fact be a deadly snare if Sir Henry knew adversaries were on the way. Were he Henry, Robin would emplace soldiers behind the approach to the bridge to ambush the enemy's army from the rear as they crossed.

"We should send scouts to reconnoiter that area," said Sir Howell. "Look for Henry's soldiers who might be protecting the access to the bridge or planning to attack our rear flank."

Robin almost chuckled. "Just what I had been thinking."

"What about that mill bridge?"

"Timber. Too easy for Sir Henry's men to knock it or burn it out from under us. We should plan to make our own crossing. The brook may be shallow enough to build a temporary log bridge or we could construct barges and ferry our men across. We should recon the city too. We should take it first." The people, food, and materials would be useful to Robin's army. Otherwise his men would have to travel far from the field of battle to secure supplies.

He spotted puffs of smoke rising above the city walls. From where he and Sir Howell stood, it appeared to be the exhaust of ordinary domestic fires but that could change. Either out of loyalty to or under threat from Sir Henry, the inhabitants could torch their own buildings to deny Robin's army the use of them, thereby sabotaging a siege.

"Sir Alan was right. Henry hasn't made it easy. We could send flaming arrows into the city, set the buildings on fire. The villeins would have to open the gates to flee. That would give us access to the city, its remaining supplies, its forge, and give us a staging area close to the castle."

"That's one strategy," Robin said, but half his attention was focused on the castle. *Was Zachary behind its walls?* He needed to know and a risky plan to find out took shape.

CHAPTER TWENTY-THREE

Robin and Sir Howell turned and descended the rise. "We'll keep the troops off that mount for now."

"If we can see Henry's soldiers from there, they can see us."

"Exactly. For now, we don't believe they are aware of our presence although we don't doubt that they soon will be. We will give Sir Henry one chance to surrender. Meanwhile, intercept traffic bound for the castle, commandeer the supplies for ourselves. We need iron, hides, charcoal. Tools and weapons. Food. Send soldiers into the countryside. Enlist fighters from those who owe us service. We also need carpenters, masons, and blacksmiths, archers and miners. Sir Howell, convey the order to the other knights and the commander."

Robin waited until Sir Howell had departed then sought out Deidre.

Dressed for battle, her armor fit better than the mismatched assortment she had worn to the joust. A light coating of road dust dulled its gleam but otherwise the armor appeared sound. Robin thought that she might have used some of her tournament winnings to have armor tailored to her form. Armor was costly and Robin could think of a great many other things that a young woman might want to buy than a chainmail hauberk and metal plates that covered her from toe to head.

The young woman bowed. "Your Majesty, how may I be of service?"

"You spoke of Judith."

Her eager expression turned thoughtful.

"Judith, in the Bible. One of your heroines. As we recall the tale, she insinuates herself into the enemy's camp."

Deidre's face brightened. "Holofernes, yes, the general of the Assyrians. Judith beheads him. Without their leader, his troops disperse and the Israelites are saved. Your Majesty wishes me to sneak into the castle and behead Sir Henry?"

"No. Not at all." Such savagery in such a young woman, Robin thought. It was baffling. If Deidre didn't work so hard at looking fierce she would be an attractive woman who could anticipate a bright future as wife of a worthy husband. "We wish for you to take a page from Judith's book but you needn't go quite as far as she did. Dress yourself in a woman's attire and smuggle yourself into Windbrook Castle."

Deidre frowned. "You Majesty means I am to seduce Sir Henry? Sire, I am a warrior not a—"

Robin cut her off with a glare. "The heroines you admire did not hesitate to use any and all of their assets in service of the mission, be it their fighting skills or their feminine wiles."

Deidre pressed her lips together and nodded. "Your Majesty, whatever my lord requires, if it is within my power I will do it."

"We want you to find Prince Zachary. You remember the prince from the day of the joust?"

"Yes, Sire, His Highness was with Your Majesty in the grandstand."

"Do you think you will know His Highness even disguised as Princess Dale?"

"I do, Sire. The prince's features are distinctive. Fair complexion, dark red hair like chestnut."

"Sir Henry won't recognize you, however, having seen you only covered in armor. That will enable you to get close to Prince Zachary. Do not let him out of your sight. Stay at His Highness's side, protect him throughout the battle. There will be loss of life but Prince Zachary is to survive. Do you think you can do this?"

"I will, Your Majesty, or die trying."

Robin sighed. Sir Maxwell had once made a similar vow. *What was it about these young people that they were so eager to give up a life that they had yet to live?*

Hostilities seemed inevitable. Henry was not about to surrender. The Bell Castle knights thirsted for vengeance. With every throb of his wounded arm, Robin did too but he feared for Zachary who was likely to be the victim of the assault, killed as collateral damage or by Sir Henry in retribution.

"Follow us." He led Deidre to the top of the rise where he and Sir Howell had made their survey. "Did you bring other garments?"

"I do have a chemise and a cloak."

"That will do for these purposes. Change into those clothes. You will leave your horse behind. And your sword."

"My sword, Sire?" Deidre frowned.

"You must to all appearances be a simple solitary woman who would pose no threat to anyone."

"Judith at least had a knife."

"You're certain that it was her knife and not just a weapon of opportunity?"

"Well, Sire, I—"

Robin sighed. "A knife then, but nothing that a maiden wouldn't carry under normal circumstances. Go on foot through the wood. Come out there, where the track meets the mill bridge." Robin pointed to the right. "Hide and wait until a wagon or cart comes along that's headed for the castle. A laden one, obviously, as you will conceal yourself in the cargo. Once inside, infiltrate Sir Henry's court as a servant. Seek the greatest access without calling attention to yourself. Find Prince Zachary. Stay by His Highness's side. Protect him." Robin studied Deidre face for any signs of fear. "You can do this?"

She pressed her lips together but then took a deep breath. In a steady voice she said, "Of course. If this is what Your Majesty requires it shall be done. I will leave my mount with the cavalry master, change, and be on my way." She bowed and strode back to the encampment.

With misgivings, Robin watched her go, then went to join the knights and make ready for a battle he hoped he would not have to wage.

Robin dispatched a single rider to deliver one more subpoena demanding that Sir Henry answer the charges against him. Henry had already ignored one summons and Robin did not expect a conciliatory response. He wasn't surprised when the emissary returned and reported that he was greeted with a burst of arrows from the gatehouse. "I was not able to deliver this, Your Majesty," the emissary said and handed back the summons, "but I believe Sir Henry got the message."

Robin needed no clearer declaration of war. He commanded his knights to fan out immediately throughout the kingdom to conscript fighters, laborers, and materials. Robin was reminded of the melee a cheval that Bell Castle has just hosted, but this was no game. The mission was grave. The outcome of Robin's offensive depended on its success.

"Spread word of Sir Henry's contempt for his king," Robin ordered, so that the locals' allegiance would be swayed from their lord in favor of the king. To the remaining troops he gave orders to start felling trees. "Strip the branches. We'll use the debris to fill the dry ditch and the castle moat. Fill the spaces in with rocks, earth, whatever you can find. The bed that you build must be stable. It must support animals, carts, men, and heavy wheeled machines.

"Cut and split logs to lay across that bed and make a roadway for the cat." The fancifully-named wheeled shelter would carry soldiers to the base of the castle wall and afford them some protection at that position.

He ordered servants to gather boulders and cut stones with which to load the war machines. Catapulted by a mangonel or a trebuchet against the castle walls, the projectiles could smash battlements. Such apparatus would come into play only weeks and months from now when the hostilities reached a certain intensity. Anything could happen between now and then—a truce or even surrender—but it would take almost that long for the parts that had been retrieved from storage at Bell Castle and loaded onto oxcarts to travel the rough winter roads and reach the encampment whereupon they would have to be assembled.

"Build ladders." Scaling the castle walls would be their first strike. Under the protective cover of archers from the ground, soldiers would scramble up, leap onto the battlements, and attack Windbrook's defenders. Conducted quickly and from several different points, the escalade could insert soldiers into the castle where they could overtake Henry's men and even capture Henry. The same archers could shoot flaming arrows which would ignite wooden rooftops, sending the castles' occupants scurrying to extinguish the flames or flee. Robin smirked; there would be a certain satisfaction in using a conflagration to beat Henry.

Night fell hard, dark and cold. In the encampment men hammered, sawed, and nailed by firelight. The smoke trapped under the canopy of trees rendered the copse as suffocating as a forge.

Under the concealment of night, Robin scaled the rise and studied the castle. Where might Zachary be? In the dungeon? In the hall dining with Sir Henry? Robin shook his head. He had entrusted his son's welfare, his very life, to Deidre, a mere slip of a girl.

He looked up at the featureless sky and prayed that Zachary would be safe. Pray. Was there a God up there, high above in Heaven, eyeing the proceedings? Maybe this was indeed another bargaining moment. *What would God want in exchange for Zachary's life?* Robin couldn't think what else he had to give. He had already surrendered Conrad into the Lord's service. Did He want Zachary too? Could Robin make that decision for his son? The Bible was filled with tales of parents who had done exactly that: Hannah prayed to bear a son and pledged to give him back to God. That turned out well for Hannah and her son, Samuel, who became a judge and anointed kings. Not so well for Jephthah who had to sacrifice a daughter in fulfillment of a rash vow.

No, Robin decided, this was between King Bewilliam and Henry, not King Bewilliam and God.

Throughout the night, the ranks of Robin's army grew as vassals reported to the encampment along with the newly-conscripted manpower.

In the gray predawn, Robin addressed the troops, assuring them that they were on the side of right and that they were fighting for a just cause. "Sir Henry has shown a flagrant disrespect for the law but the law must be obeyed. Without law there is no order and none of us can live in peace and security." From the rustling and murmuring it was clear the men didn't care. Some wanted vengeance and action, others a chance at glory. No doubt a few wanted simply to get on with it, perform their duty, and return home in one piece.

Slogging through the snow covering the clearing, Robin and his men lugged gear to the bank of the brook, loaded their equipment and supplies onto hastily-assembled rafts, and made the crossing. They no sooner unloaded their equipment on the opposite bank than the archers took position outside the city at the point farthest from the castle. They shielded themselves behind portable screens to provide cover fire as other men laid ladders on the ground at various points along the castle's curtain walls, staging them for the escalade. Robin's archers launched flaming arrows over the city walls. From the city's battlements, defenders retaliated with arrows of their own, but the urgency of fighting the fires pulled them from their stations. From his command post Robin couldn't hear the crier sound the alarm but the whining wind keened as if with the wailing of frightened inhabitants.

Robin wondered about those arrows. Among them might there be ones identical to those that had struck him and Sir Maxwell? Robin restrained himself from running into the fray to dig one out of the snow. There would be time later; no shortage of arrows would be loosed today.

Robin's archers had set so many roofs on fire that the blaze quickly engulfed the city. As Sir Howell had predicted, it raged beyond the inhabitants' control and they fled rather than try to fight. Thinking to seek refuge in the castle, they threw open the postern gate and crowded the track to the moat. Subjects bringing supplies to the castle jammed at the closed gate. The fleeing city dwellers pressed into the throng crowding the drawbridge, trying to stay out of the line of fire from Robin's archers and the castle's defenders. Too late, the defenders sought to raise a drawbridge clogged with people, animals, and laden carts. The citizens hammered at the drawbridge chains, detaching them, and pounded on the iron-clad oak portcullis gate, demanding admittance and their lord's protection.

At the rate they're going, Robin thought, we won't need a battering ram to demolish the gate. Henry's own people would break it open. Denying his tenants sanctuary was not the best tactic Henry could have chosen. It wouldn't take too many casualties for loyalties to shift to the king over Henry's betrayal.

"Protect the women and children," Robin ordered. "Get them to safety. Recruit the men for our army."

The riot at the gate drew some of Henry's soldiers from the wall walks. *Good, fewer men to repel the escalade.*

Robin's army stormed the postern gate and flooded into the city. Robin gave the order to get the fires in the city under control. "Get the women and children to shelter."

Other men set to dismantling the stockade before it caught fire; they would put the lumber to good use in constructing the war machines. Archers shot flaming arrows towards the castle's wooden structures and kept the defenders engaged as Robin's army moved supplies into the abandoned city and established a base. Robin posted guards on all the tributary roads to protect arriving reinforcements.

"Begin the escalade," Robin told his commanders. The strategy required coordination to be successful. Only the most nimble soldiers could make any speed up the ladders while weighed down with armor and weapons, but a rapid ascent was critical. From his vantage point on the city's crenelated watchtower, Robin marked the progress of fleet-of-foot soldiers as they raced to the ladders, quickly raised them against the walls, and climbed.

Robin winced at the cries of agony as one of his men was scalded by the hot water poured on him by a defender while another solider made a rapid and painful descent still clinging to the ladder that a defender pushed away from the wall. Some of Robin's archers lay still behind their screens, felled by enemy arrows, blood pooling with the melting snow. Robin took solace in the fact that most of the escalade soldiers made it to the top of the curtain wall, scuffled with and bested the defenders.

On the ground, desperate and angry citizens moved a battering ram into position, driving the huge log with the help and direction of Robin's soldiers. Above, the wall walk guards abandoned their high posts, no doubt called to aid in defending the gate, leaving the way clear for the invaders. So many of Robin's soldiers scaled the ladders it looked like trails of ants climbing the walls.

Anticipating an imminent breach, Robin issued the command to swarm the gate. Of all his fighters, those in the vanguard took the greatest risk. Driven by loyalty or whipped into a fever of blood lust by their captains, they imperiled their own lives to pave a way for the others. If they made it through the neck between the gate and the bailey without having rocks or boiling water poured on them from the gatekeepers, they would be met by defenders ready and waiting for them. The ensuing clash would be no tournament melee. Death would be the penalty for losing this confrontation.

With a resounding crack followed by savage yelps, the Windbrook Castle gate yielded to the battering ram and the invaders swarmed into the opening. What if Zachary were among Windbrook's defenders? Would anyone recognize the prince? Could Deidre keep him safe? Robin ran down from the tower and made for the gate only to find Sir Kenneth and Sir Alan alongside him.

"Your Majesty, the thick of the battle in the bailey is no place for our king," said Sir Alan.

It was no place for any man. Robin could hear the clash of metal on metal, the snap of splintering wood and the more sickening pop of breaking bones, the screams of wounded men. He could smell smoke and burning hides.

"It's too dangerous. We have many knights, many soldiers. We can handle it but we have only one king. Please, Sire, put some distance between you and the hostilities," Sir Kenneth said.

"Zachary," Robin cried. With Sir Alan and Sir Kenneth all but blocking his path, Robin hastened toward the gate. An arrow rang against his helm. Robin looked up to see a lone defender in the watchtower. Another arrow clanked against Robin's armored chest and he flung himself to the ground. The impact shot pain up his wounded arm.

Robin's knights fell alongside him and covered him with their shields. "We will find His Highness."

Robin could barely hear through his helm and over the noise around them.

"Please let us return you to safety, Your Majesty. If we lose our lord, who will lead? Will anyone go on fighting?"

"If Zachary is lost what is there to fight for?" Robin shouted. He had no wish to take another arrow in the arm or any other part of his body but he had knights, guards, and soldiers to protect him. Who but Deidre would protect Zachary? He pushed Sir Kenneth and Sir Alan off and lifted his head. Another defender had joined the archer on the battlement. Crossing the field to reach the drawbridge would be a deadly scramble. "Men, get ready to run."

In a crouch, Robin prepared to spring then froze in place.

CHAPTER TWENTY-FOUR

"What's going on?" he asked.

"Where?"

"There. In the castle watchtower." The bowmen had pulled away from the crenels and arrow loops. The black pennant with Sir Henry's blazon inched down the flagpole. A few breathless moments later, another pennant crept up, a flag of pure white. "He's surrendered? Sir Henry has surrendered?"

This early in the hostilities? It was almost unheard of. Robin was prepared for a protracted battle.

Sir Kenneth and Sir Alan let out whoops, jumped in the air, and slapped each other's gauntleted palms.

"Let's proceed with caution, men," Robin said, although his muscles twitched to run to the castle and learn Zachary's fate.

Sir Kenneth nodded. "It could be a trick to lull us into complacency."

That wasn't likely but it was possible that not every opponent had gotten the word that they had lost the battle. Others might take it upon themselves to retaliate personally.

Watching each other's back, the three did not run but walked fast. Around them, men rushed toward the castle from the city. Not soldiers, they were surgeons speeding to aid the wounded.

The drawbridge was impassable with people trying to get in and people trying to get out.

"Make way for the King," Sir Alan hollered, and he and Sir Kenneth elbowed people aside.

Casualties from both armies clogged the gateway neck. Robin paused to reassure each man. Winners, losers, they were all his subjects.

The gateway opened onto a bailey littered with shattered weapons and broken bodies. Those who were still upright stood dazed and uncertain. Robin leaped onto an overturned cart and yelled for attention. From somewhere in the crowd a bugler blew a ragged fanfare. When most eyes seemed to have turned in Robin's direction he said, "Men, the hostilities are suspended. We have seen the white flag. A truce has been proffered."

Where was Sir Henry? He was nowhere to been seen in the bailey. Robin leaned down and asked Sir Alan, "Where is Sir Henry? Find him. Make sure he doesn't try to escape." Maybe he already had.

Sir Alan nodded, bowed, and went to alert the men to be on the lookout for the errant knight.

Robin continued. "We understand how your lord's perfidy confused your loyalties. We are all citizens of the kingdom of the Chalklands. Our ultimate goal is to bring unity so that we may once again live in peace and harmony."

Robin wasn't blind to the possibility of lingering dissension. There would be discontent among Robin's men who wanted to see Henry's knights punished for the damage and deaths they caused, and wariness among Henry's men who feared the victor's retribution. Robin needed Sir Henry and he needed him now. The sight of the man arrested, bound, and hauled off for judgment would send an important message.

At Robin's feet, an armored man with Sir Henry's blazon on his tabard bowed and said, "Your Majesty, I am Sir Henry's constable. In my lord's ... absence ... it is I who announced the truce in accordance with our lady's wishes."

Absence? So Henry had already fled. And what was this about a lady?
Sir Henry had a wife? Mistresses, maybe, but this was the first
Robin had heard of a wife.

"Would Your Majesty please come with me?"

Before he could answer, Sir Kenneth appeared at the
constable's side. "Sire, we have a ... situation."

Puzzled, Robin jumped down from the cart and followed the
two men. Soldiers and servants trailed behind.

I should feel like a conquering hero, Robin thought. He held
his head higher, squared his shoulders, and took long strides, the
better to set his cloak sweeping but his eyes raked the crowds
seeking Zachary's face.

They crossed the bailey and headed not for the keep as Robin
would have guessed, but towards the rear of the castle grounds,
past the kitchens and gardens, past the stables, kennels, and
stores of winter fuel and grain, and came at last to the livestock
pens. Robin spied women, children, and old men hiding from the
hostilities behind barrels, sacks, and stacks of firewood. The
animals whinnied and lowed.

A small crowd filled the tiny yard in front of the pigsty.
Beyond it, Henry's soldiers guarded the postern gate. The
drawbars had been pulled back, which Robin found curious
given the siege conditions. The heavy oak beams ought to be in
place across the doors to reinforce them against attackers from
the rear.

Two more of Henry's men gripped the arms of a young
woman who, despite her restraints, managed a bow.

"Sire," said Deidre. "I did as Your Majesty commanded."

By her side stood a tall gowned figure with mahogany hair
and a complexion that was even paler than normal. "Your
Majesty," Zachary said in a tremulous voice, and bowed.

"The Lady Dale," said Sir Henry's constable.

The Lady Dale? Lady? Robin opened his mouth but nothing
came out.

On the straw sprawled the prone figure of Sir Henry.

"In light of our lord's condition, we deemed it prudent to
bring a halt to the hostilities," said Zachary.

Your lord? We're your lord.

His knights' question echoed: "If we lose our lord who will lead? Will anyone go on fighting?" they had asked. Apparently not. "Is he dead?" Robin managed to croak.

"I don't know, Your Majesty. He hasn't moved." The constable shrugged.

Onlookers crowded into the small yard and gasped at the sight of Sir Henry lying motionless. The news would spread faster than the fire that had overtaken the city.

Sir Kenneth crouched and turned Sir Henry face up. A dent notched his helm over his forehead. Sir Kenneth looked about. "A tool to remove his helm," he said, and several servants scurried to find one. Robin was certain that when they got it off they would find a severe head wound to match the helm's damage. Sir Kenneth raised the visor of Sir Henry's helm and held his hand under the man's nose. "It doesn't appear that he is breathing. Perhaps he is unconscious and his breath cannot be detected."

"She did it," Zachary said.

Deidre squared her shoulders and tipped up her chin.

The guards holding her seemed to be uncertain as to what to do. Moments earlier they could have easily executed her for assaulting their leader. The declaration of a truce meant she was no longer a murderous enemy but could be declared by the victor as a hero.

"Tell us," Robin said.

"Sir Henry meant to flee," said Deidre.

That explained the postern gate's retracted drawbars.

"I accompanied Sir Henry and Prince Zachary—" She frowned. "Lady Dale, I mean. Sir Henry was loading their belongings into saddle bags. I heard Sir Henry give instructions to the servants, to the guards. They were going to leave. The drawbars were pulled back. They were about to mount their horses, to flee. I—"

"She poleaxed him," Zachary said.

Robin spotted the pollaxe where it leaned against the pigsty. Yes, that would explain the dent in Sir Henry's helm. Used to stun animals in preparation for slaughter, the pollaxe could also be an offensive weapon, its steel head capable of breaching plate armor.

"A weapon of convenience." Deidre pressed her lips together but Robin thought he saw the twitch of a smile. "It wasn't my intention to kill him, Your Majesty," Deidre said. "I just wanted to stop him. Else how could I keep Prince Zachary in my sight as Your Majesty commanded?"

Robin looked at Sir Henry's prostrate form. Deidre had not followed the letter of his command exactly but possibly the intent.

"Did you want to go with him?" he hissed at Zachary.

Zachary took a step back. "No, Sire."

"When you left Bell Castle was it of your own free will?"

"Sire, it's complicated."

No doubt. To nearby servants Robin said, "Bring surgeons here. Determine if Sir Henry still lives and if so what can be done for him." To his soldiers he said, "If he regains consciousness, restrain him." He told Sir Henry's constable, "If he is dead, prepare him for burial. Be certain that your troops are aware that a cease-fire is in force. All hostilities are to stop immediately. Anyone who imperils the truce will be dealt with most harshly." He turned to his own soldiers. "That goes for everyone. Sir Kenneth, locate Sir Alan. You can tell him Sir Henry has been found and he can stop searching for him. Find Sir Howell. Bring them to the watchtower."

To Zachary he said, "Let us go discuss the terms of this truce. Lady Dale."

CHAPTER TWENTY-FIVE

Robin strode away from the stockyard. As he crossed the bailey, Sir Alan came racing up. "Sire, it's being said the Sir Henry is dead."

"If not dead, certainly incapacitated." Robin spied Sir Howell, waved him over, and continued toward the watchtower. From there, Robin could survey the entire battlefield. Soldiers stayed close guarding Robin, and at a discreet distance, his knights and Deidre stood at attention. The two men who had guarded the postern gate stayed at Zachary's side, their uneasy postures conveying uncertainty about who was in command.

"Here are the terms," Robin said. "You will return to Bell Castle. We will name another tenant-in-chief for Windbrook. Reparations will be made out of Sir Henry's treasury."

"That will be difficult," Zachary replied. "There is little in his treasury."

Robin frowned. "That can't be so. Henry was not in arrears."

"That is true. Taxes collected for Your Majesty are secure. Sir Henry was not a cheat."

"Or maybe he just didn't want to draw our ire by failing to pay."

"Why are you so hard on him?"

"Because this isn't the first time that he's defied us. He always seems to have an explanation but he shouldn't have anything to explain. He is a knight of Bell Castle, he is to obey our commands, support the kingdom, not make problems for it. Why are you defending him?"

Zachary shook back the veil of his hennin. "Because he defended us. Henry accepted us for what we are, or at least encouraged us to believe that he did. You, Sire, never gave us a chance."

"That's not so," Robin protested. "We indulged your whimsy for as long as we could." Had he been wrong to object to Zachary's flirtation with life as a woman? Out of a desire to be supportive, to coddle his child he had tried to go along with it, but what was best for Zachary and best for the future of the kingdom would be for his son to cease the madness. It was Robin's duty as a father and a king to speak from the wisdom gained by virtue of his maturity. "We chose that course of action not because we hated you or wanted to punish you, but because we loved you. The life you chose could only end tragically."

"It's our life. It's our choice to make."

"It's not simply your life alone. You are our offspring. You are Prince Zachary, the future of the kingdom."

"We didn't ask to be born. And we didn't ask to be born this way. We are simply trying to make the best of it. We thought Sir Henry was giving us that chance."

"And so you ran away from Bell Castle? You—married him?" Was such a union even legitimate?

"Yes, that is true," said Zachary. "We were married but we were forced into it." He paced, wringing his hands. "We will admit that at first we went with Sir Henry willingly. We were angry about what had transpired at the tournament. We called him our champion then but he has been that for some time. At court we have been shunned and the subject of gossip and ridicule. Sir Henry treated us with respect and kindness. There were days when we thought that we might die of loneliness but for the attention he paid us.

"So when he was badly humiliated at the tournament we had compassion. We went to his pavilion to convey our sympathies. He said that he was leaving immediately, that he would not return, unappreciated as he was by the king. We saw ourselves losing the only friend we had." Zachary blinked away tears.

"Whose idea was it to accompany him?"

"He invited us and we agreed. He said we could come to Windbrook where we would help govern, be respected."

So, Robin thought, Zachary had gone with Sir Henry willingly. The knight could not be charged with kidnapping.

"He said that while he and his men disassembled his pavilion that we should go to the keep and pack whatever it was that we wanted to take with us. 'You may never return either so be certain to take anything of especially sentimental value,' he said. He told us that he would meet us at the keep to help carry away our things."

No doubt it was while Zachary packed that Sir Henry had added the dangerous fuels to the fire then gone to the great hall and told the officer at arms the lie about the prince being at the lists.

"We felt so alone at Bell Castle," Zachary cried. "Conrad was busy all the time with the church, made us feel as though we were somehow wrong. Your Majesty was preoccupied with matters of the kingdom. That's why we started coming to court. We hoped that we could be involved somehow, be of some use. No one overtly mistreated us but we were ignored. Sir Henry had trials of his own. He had to reestablish his reputation, win back everyone's favor. We lent each other a sympathetic ear and found that to be healing. Henry was just grateful that anyone found his friendship of value and we were just happy to have someone spend time with us. Henry never asked probing questions. He accepted what we shared and didn't ask for more. With him we could just be ourselves, talk about anything, everything.

Robin felt the sting of the unvoiced accusation. His treatment of his son had left a vacuum that Sir Henry filled. The man identified Zachary's vulnerability and exploited it and Robin had not only allowed it to happen, he had laid the groundwork for it.

"After a while, our hurts faded and we found other things to talk about. We shared other interests we had and found that we had much in common. We began simply to enjoy spending time together. The companionship became precious. At last we felt like a real person. We could just be ourselves, we didn't always have to explain ourselves, be self-conscious, defend our identity. We trusted Sir Henry. There was no reason not to. Even you, Sire, had given him back his title."

Sir Henry had been accused of treason and stripped of his spurs. When Sir Walter was found to be the true traitor, Robin had restored Sir Henry's title and made him tenant-in-chief of Windbrook.

"At the tournament we simply wanted to be there as a show of support. As Sir Henry continued to excel it was hard not to get caught up in the excitement. Then when he issued the jousting challenge in our honor, we felt so special."

"Speaking of that tournament, he spent freely for it and at it. You say he has no assets."

"It was important to put on a lavish display. He taxed his lieges. Everyone had to contribute."

So Henry had overtaxed his subjects. No wonder they were so eager to smash the castle gate.

"And he had a sponsor."

"Did this sponsor also help to fund the expansion of Windbrook? This was a lord's manor, not a king's castle, yet look at this place. A keep, curtain walls, a fortified city. You say you can speak for its disposition."

Zachary looked offended. He tipped up his chin. "Yes, we can. We told the constable to declare a truce and he complied, didn't he? Hostilities have ceased; you don't see anyone shooting, do you, Your Majesty?"

The battlefield was far from still. Surgeons tended the wounded, servants cleared debris and hauled away the dead, soldiers recovered armor and weapons but Zachary was right. None of Sir Henry's men fired on anyone.

"No." He turned to Zachary. "Who is this sponsor?" Who in the Chalklands had the kind of money and power that would underwrite Henry's ostentatious display at the tournament, help to build a castle, and supply the men to defend it? No one that Robin knew.

A flush colored Zachary's fair face and he looked down. In a faint voice he replied, "King Ulric."

His lungs empty of air, Robin couldn't speak. Shadowed by his helm's tipped up visor, Sir Alan's face grew even darker. Sir Kenneth and Sir Howell gaped and Deidre looked puzzled.

"Who's King Ulric?" Robin heard her ask Sir Kenneth.

The man who had stolen King Bewilliam's wife. His kingdom, his life. Robin's sons. Ulric had banished Conrad to Mathus Abbey and left Zachary at the mercy of gypsies. Robin had gotten a judgment against Ulric and the adulterous Queen Daya, but clearly that hadn't been the end of it. Sir Alan's words came back to him. The knight had called King Ulric a festering ulcer. Ulric had then and still did covet the Chalklands.

Bell Castle. The bonfire. Robin had been thinking that Sir Henry had started it in a fit of rage or perhaps to cover his flight. Had it not been for the swift and capable response of Robin's subjects, it could have easily spread to and decimated the castle. Had King Ulric instigated it as the first strike in a campaign to overthrow King Bewilliam?

Once word that Sir Henry had lost the battle at Windbrook reached Ulric he would surely ride from his distant kingdom of the Palisades to retaliate against its attackers. He might already be on the way. Some of the soldiers at Windbrook might be King Ulric's lieges.

Robin waved his knights to come forward. "You too," he said to Deidre. "And you," he said to Zachary, "stand over there. We don't want you out of our sight." In sight but out of the range of hearing. Robin did not want Zachary privy to this briefing. It sickened him to realize he distrusted his son.

To the knights he said, "We fear for Bell Castle. Our foes may be on their way, may already be there."

"We can't simply abandon Windbrook," said Sir Howell and he was right. Robin regarded the city below, a landscape of smoldering timbers, singed stone, and scorched plots. People and livestock had scattered. Casualties left families without breadwinners and the domain without manpower. Reparations would have to be made or resentment would grow. Were King Ulric to hold out the promise of support, the people of Windbrook would ally with him.

"It's too close to Bell Castle to be left unguarded. King Ulric could establish a base which would give him a great advantage over trying to launch an offensive from the Palisades."

"And what of Bell Castle?" Sir Kenneth asked. "In our absence, King Ulric may strike there."

If he hadn't already. The stray arrows in the woods. Robin had started to think it was one of Sir Henry's men, but what if King Ulric was already in position and the assailant was one of his men? Robin felt chilled as he envisaged approaching Bell Castle's gates to see smashed walls and smoke billowing from the bailey. "We need to fight on both fronts. We will establish a strong defense here. Rally what manpower remains and reorganize them. Be aware that loyalties are divided. Some may still hold allegiance to Sir Henry."

"Putting Sir Henry's head on a pike for all to see would solve that problem," Sir Alan growled.

"He's not dead," Sir Howell said.

"Yet," muttered Sir Alan.

"A minor detail that could easily be remedied," said Deidre.

"Enough," Robin said. "Some of these men may be King Ulric's. This calls for keen vigilance as there's a great risk of treachery from within."

Sir Henry had only just begun marshaling his siege engines; the components for the mangonel lay stacked in the watchtower. "Finish assembling Sir Henry's mangonel and equip it with ammunition so it's ready to be employed to defend Windbrook's castle. Task Windbrook's smiths with replenishing the supply of arrowheads and bolts."

"In short, ready this castle for an attack."

"Precisely." From what Robin had observed at the livestock pens and storage sheds, Sir Henry had stockpiled a generous supply of fuel and foodstuffs. "His preparations against a blockade will serve us well," Robin said. "Begin restoration of the city immediately. The sooner people can return to some semblance of normalcy the better. Round up the animals that escaped and bring back the people who fled. Restore in them confidence in the kingdom of the Chalklands. We must be able to rely on their service."

"Our siege engines haven't even arrived here yet," said Sir Kenneth.

"We can send a rider to divert them and turn them back. We may even intercept them ourselves. We mean to travel to Bell Castle with all speed. Sir Kenneth, you will remain here and take command until you have fulfilled your service obligation. Then we will relieve—"

"Then I will continue to serve until circumstances no longer require me," said Sir Kenneth. He bowed, and out of gratitude Robin returned the homage. Sir Kenneth volunteering to serve beyond his obligation. How could Robin have ever doubted these men?

"Sire, if I may, I would like to remain as well. Perhaps I could be of assistance to Sir Kenneth. I have made some alliances here," Deidre said.

Robin gave her an indulgent smile. "We have another duty in mind. You successfully protected Prince Zachary as we commanded. You will continue to do so as we journey back to Bell Castle."

"I am eager to be of service in whatever way my lord sees fit." Deidre narrowed her eyes and the hint of a smile tugged at her lips. "That is, if I may have my sword back."

"Indeed you may." Robin wanted to call her 'Sir'. She had certainly earned it. By her actions she halted the hostilities and saved countless lives and property but 'Sir Deidre' felt awkward. 'Lady' was the title given to the wife of a knight. It conveyed honor but by association. It said nothing of fighting prowess or heroism. Had there ever been female knights and if so, what were they called? He would have to think of something.

Sir Alan scowled. "This fighting on two fronts. May it not come to that. It will stretch our resources."

"It will stretch King Ulric's as well," said Sir Howell. "And we have an advantage in that one of our bases of operations is our own home."

"Come," Robin said, and headed for the stairs. "To the encampment to prepare for the return to Bell Castle." To Zachary he said, "You too."

"Sire, we could stay here and continue to govern, in your service of course."

Robin halted and ascended the stairs to face Zachary. "We haven't established that you have that authority. You said that this union with Henry was forced. Explain."

Zachary took a deep breath. "We assumed Sir Henry intended a pact, but after we arrived here he said that we would marry. He forbade us to leave, he made us say the words of a marriage ceremony. On pain of death. We had never intended to be a consort. We thought that we would rule as an equal."

Clever move of Sir Henry's. A pact could be broken. An alliance by marriage could not so easily be undone. As Zachary's spouse, Sir Henry would be heir to Bell Castle and the entire kingdom of the Chalkands once King Bewilliam and his sons were dead. Was that the grand plan, that Robin would die in this battle? That Conrad would not survive his mission in the Holy Land? And then what of Zachary? Would Sir Henry assassinate the remaining heir? If Sir Henry did not regain consciousness they might never know.

And what of this marriage? Was such a union even valid? Robin thought of the advocate Terrowin. He was learned in the finer points of domestic law; he would know. A marriage, even one as peculiar as that of Sir Henry and Prince Zachary, couldn't be binding if it was made under duress. Had Zachary been forced into it as he claimed or did he have a scheme of his own? Maybe he intended that neither Sir Henry nor King Bewilliam would survive the battle at Windbrook. "Why would you do this?"

Zachary scowled. "We have ambitions. We told you that. We want to rule. We have made every effort to show that we are capable but we have been rejected. Your Majesty made it clear that we would never rule at Bell Castle."

"Not like this." Robin waggled his finger at Zachary's gown.

Zachary crossed his arms over his chest. "Sir Henry led us to believe that would not be a deterrent."

Robin snorted and stomped down the stairs.

At his army's encampment in the ruined city, Robin briefed his commanders and summoned a scribe. The young man quickly unpacked his compact traveling desk, a storage box with a sloped cover that served as a writing surface, and took Robin's dictation. Robin reviewed the missive and finding it accurate, applied his seal. The communication would be sent to Bell Castle by carrier pigeon, trained to fly for miles to return to its home. The message would arrive well before Robin or even a swift rider to alert Sir Albert of the king's return and warn him about Sir Ulric. With every passing moment, Robin became more certain that his enemy would launch an offensive. The only question was how soon.

*****

The sight of Bell Castle's pennants in the distance would have impelled Robin to drive Hope faster if the horse weren't already galloping at top speed. The tear from Windbrook had been the fastest and most punishing journey Robin could remember. Packing only what they could carry on their backs or in their saddlebags, he and his men had ridden with hardly a break, stopping only when they encountered their own troops to tell them the battle was over. On the move, he and his men made less of a target, Robin thought, and his anxieties about Bell Castle kept him going when he could just as easily have rested. As the castle came into view, what lay before him stopped him in his tracks.

"Halt," he yelled to those behind him.

Hoardings were in place where they hadn't been before. The temporary wooden extensions would serve as added protection for archers positioned behind the arrow loops in the crenels. More soldiers crowded Bell Castle's watchtowers. The defenders faced off against a vanguard of enemy bowmen arrayed on the ground at the base of the curtain wall. Behind the attackers stood a line of cavalry, purple pennants flying from the tips of their lances, and a small horde of foot soldiers. Tents and shelters marked the opponent's encampment. King Ulric was in place and preparing for an offensive. No doubt a surrender demand to Bell Castle was already in Sir Albert's hands.

Sir Howell pulled up alongside Robin, followed by Sir Alan. The three men raised their visors and sat atop their mounts side by side for a moment in stunned silence.

"Was Sir Henry's flight to Windbrook all just a carefully engineered ruse to draw manpower and armaments away from Bell Castle?" said Sir Alan.

"Possibly," said Sir Howell. "Sir Henry might have started that fire and then fled, intending for us to give chase."

Sir Alan spat. "That's very calculating. I don't think he's that smart."

"Maybe he isn't. Maybe it was Ulric's plan. In any case, I doubt Henry meant to pay such a high price."

Could anyone have anticipated being ambushed by a young woman with a pollaxe? Deidre had surprised them all. "None of that matters," said Robin. "What does matter is what we are going to do about it."

Sir Howell broke another moment of tense silence. "All appears to be at a standstill. No one seems to be firing."

"We suspect a truce has been called, that King Ulric has already demanded surrender and awaits a reply or a show of resistance."

"Neither of which Sir Albert would supply without Your Majesty's command."

"If he got our message, he knows of our victory at Windbrook and that we are en route."

"How long can he hold out?"

"Our message warned him of the possibility of attack. He would have laid in supplies. We need to reach out to our vassals, tell them not to make deliveries to the castle now. They'll just be seized by Ulric's men. We should divert those supplies to a secure location for our use. And we need to bolster their defenses." Ulric's men would scour farms just coming into first fruit to provide food for his army. The pigs, sheep, cattle, and goats of Robin's subjects would be meals for Ulric's soldiers. Robin turned his horse to face his men. "All is not as desperate as it may seem. We are in an excellent position here to flank King Ulric's army. Our defenders can engage the vanguard from the safety of the castle while we attack the rear."

"Then converge and crush the center." Sir Howell's grin was almost devilish. "We need to get word to Sir Albert, coordinate our movements."

"It's not as if we can simply go in the front gate. There's no way Ulric would let us through the blockade."

"Perhaps the sally port. Under cover of night. And hope to identify ourselves as Bell Castle's men before someone takes a shot at us."

"That's one way," Robin said, "but we'll try something else first. Ulric thinks Bell Castle is awaiting instructions from the king regarding the surrender demand. We will send an envoy with our answer. Sir Albert will be told not to surrender, of course, and that we are near, armed, and ready. Let's find a covert place to camp. King Ulric will soon get word about what transpired at Windbrook, but it's critical he not know of our presence here yet. Send word back down the road. Our returning troops must approach with caution. We must not reveal our position."

Robin's party set up rough shelters and spent a cold dark night shivering in bed rolls and under horse rugs. Guards kept the wild animals that had been rousted from their habitats at bay. It was nearly dawn before the donkey carts that had trailed them from Windbrook joined them in their bivouac. Robin hastened to send a communication to the castle.

CHAPTER TWENTY-SIX

A rustling and a murmur outside his tent roused Robin from sleep and brought him to full alert. His hand on his sword, he flung aside his blanket and sprang from his pallet.

The flap to Robin's tent was pulled aside. "Sir Maxwell, Your Majesty," the guard announced.

The young man ducked into the tent and bowed.

"Sir Maxwell, how come you to be here?" Robin asked.

Sir Maxwell took a deep breath. "I went out the sally port and snuck past enemy lines."

A trek that had called for a lot of belly-crawling from the looks of Sir Maxwell's tabard.

"I know I speak for all your subjects when I say I am grateful for Your Majesty's safe return from Windbrook, Sire," he said in a rush. "The first message that you sent caused us consternation. That Your Majesty was victorious at Windbrook was great news, of course. The warning that we should expect an attack from King Ulric was a shock as Your Majesty can imagine.

"Sir Albert launched an investigation. Our scouts discovered enemy spies camped in the woods. Sir Albert thought it best to leave them there so that they may pass along reports of our formidable fortifications which he immediately strengthened."

"King Ulric demanded our surrender?"

"Yes, but knowing that Your Majesty had already left Windbrook and was headed here, to buy time Sir Albert sent a very carefully worded reply telling King Ulric that he needed instructions from his sovereign. Now Sir Albert knows of Your Majesty's position and the plan to flank King Ulric. He awaits Your Majesty's order to engage."

"Well done, Sir Maxwell. So the fortifications we observed—?"

"Are there to discourage an attack, not a reaction to one. No one has made a move. Yet. However, we determined that the bowman's attack on Your Majesty was deliberate, albeit unplanned. We think that one of the enemy spies found that the very man he had under surveillance had come within range and took it upon himself to risk an impromptu attack on our king. Fortunately for us it was unsuccessful and unfortunately for him it raised suspicion and instigated an investigation. Other than that one assault on Your Majesty and me, there has been no provocation. We haven't taken action. We thought it prudent not to incite the enemy without your order. Sir Albert commanded that we take a wait-and-see approach. Although we haven't done much waiting. We stockpiled supplies, we've been amassing armaments. We've placed soldiers up front where they can be seen but have furloughed others so they can be called up should they be needed."

"Excellent," Robin said. He briefed Sir Maxwell on the battle at Windbrook. "We left Sir Kenneth in command there. Sir Howell and Sir Alan returned with us. It was a hard ride."

"And how does Prince Zachary fare?"

"It has been ... an ordeal." Robin's doubts about the loyalty of his knights had been resolved but his fears about his son had only been aggravated. He had indeed miscalculated the strength of Zachary's ambitions.

Zachary had balked at being relegated to a tent with Deidre posted outside as guard.

"Planning and waging the battle to come demands all our attention," was Robin's response to his son's protests.

"We can fight," Zachary said. "We want to fight for Bell Castle."

"Like that?" Robin said, scowling at Zachary's "Princess Dale" attire.

Zachary glared back. "Give us some armor then. We have the training."

Arm Zachary and give him free rein? Not a chance. "We need to have confidence that your welfare is capably safeguarded," Robin said, but had also instructed Deidre to inform him of any attempt on the prince's part to escape or conspire.

"Prince Zachary is unharmed. How are you, Sir Maxwell?"

"I am well, Sire, thank you. Completely healed."

Robin wasn't entirely mended, so how could Sir Maxwell be when his wound was more severe? Robin smiled at the young man's bravado.

Sir Maxwell drew himself up straight. "I helped with the investigation into the attack on Your Majesty. I led the soldiers to that spot where we were looking for the gryphon. From there we were able to pick up the trail of the assailant and that led us to the whereabouts of the other spies." Sir Maxwell shook his head. "The one who shot at you, Sire, what a fool he was. If he hadn't done that, we might still be oblivious to their presence. Instead, we will not be taken by surprise when the enemy makes his move. We will be ready and now that Your Majesty has returned we will be ready for anything."

Robin's numbers grew in strength with every passing day as supplies and soldiers arrived from Windbrook. Many men were sent back out to secure the countryside and others charged with conscripting more fighters and laborers. Some returned with reports of skirmishes with King Ulric's men and it was clear that Robin couldn't keep his presence a secret much longer.

"We must prepare to put our plan into play," he said to Sir Howell.

"If we continue to drag out this truce, King Ulric's men will tire. Many will reach the end of their term of service and leave."

"The same could be said of our own soldiers," Robin replied. "As well, the longer this blockade runs, the weaker Bell Castle's defenses will be for want of food and raw materials."

Sir Maxwell snorted. "Bell Castle has no fear of a blockade. There is water from the well and Sir Albert began laying in supplies as soon as we received the warning. He has even reserved a few joints of meat with which to foil the enemy. At the most opportune moment, he will toss them over the wall as if to say that we have so much food, we can afford to throw some away."

Clever. "We will send word to Sir Albert to refuse to surrender," Robin said.

"That will end the truce and provoke Ulric to attack."

"And we will respond. Sir Albert will be instructed to know that we will have his back," said Robin.

He outlined the plan, sealed it, and tucked it into a canister. The keeper of the homing pigeons scooped one from its cage, strapped the canister to the winged messenger's leg, and let it loose. Robin strained his eyes to keep the tiny creature in sight, hoping that his envoy would be mistaken for an ordinary harbinger of spring and not deliberately shot out of the sky before it accomplished its mission. He didn't even consider that it might fall victim to a natural predator until a huge bird swooped down from the castle's watchtower and flew toward the pigeon. Robin held his breath. He watched open-mouthed as the large bird caught the pigeon in its feet, flew straight up above the line of fire, and then dropped the pigeon over the castle wall.

"Your Majesty," Sir Maxwell cried. "Did you see that? The gryphon came to our aid. He escorted our messenger to the castle."

Robin was speechless. *Had a hawk simply lost its small prey, or had the creature that Sir Maxwell claimed was a gryphon helped to deliver a vital message to Bell Castle's defenders?*

*****

Bell Castle's refusal to surrender received a swift reply. With the launch of missiles at the curtain wall, the hostilities officially began.

By day, smoke billowed from forges churning out weapons and from wooden structures set on fire by flaming arrows. The shouts of captains and cries of wounded men were lost under the sounds of wood being sawn and hammered and iron being worked.

Nights were cold and dark. Robin ordered a blackout making the encampment hard to find by enemy soldiers who might attempt a raid. On overcast nights there was little the men could do but huddle in small groups, review the day's battle, nurse their wounds, mourn their lost comrades, and plan strategies for the morrow. At the foot of Bell Castle's walls, the lights of King Ulric's army encampment glowed, but Sir Albert had also established nighttime blackouts, a strategy that kept soldiers on the wall walks and in the watchtowers from being silhouetted by the glow from the bailey. Squads of enemy archers stood idle, their targets difficult to see except at a dangerous close range. From the castle, flaming arrows streaked across the black sky like shooting stars.

By day, Ulric's men began erecting their siege engines. The frames of a belfry tall enough to overlook the curtain walls, a battering ram, a trebuchet, and a mangonel under construction hulked against the horizon like menacing dragons. Safer for the attackers than attempting an escalade with ladders, once the belfry forded the moat, the enclosed siege tower would deliver hundreds of Ulric's soldiers right up to Bell Castle's walls. From that position they could lower a drawbridge from the top of the tower and gain access to the wall walks. When completed, the trebuchet and mangonel would launch projectiles up and over the castle walls. Pots filled with flaming tar would smash on impact and set fire to whatever they hit. The enemy could fling offal and dead animal parts which would lodge in crevices. The rotting material would attract flies, spread disease, and stink, making life in the already embattled castle that much more miserable and dangerous.

A cat was poised at the bank of the moat, the wheeled structure housing soldiers pushing rocks and buckets of soil into the moat in an effort to fill it. When enough water had been displaced, they would pile logs on top of the rocks and create a roadway, enabling Ulric to drive the siege engines close enough to the castle walls to do damage.

With the help of Robin's soldiers, Windbrook's citizens had managed to smash the castle's gate with a log. The battering ram that Ulric fabricated was a far more formidable weapon. Suspended by chains from a framework, a tree trunk chiseled to a point would be sent swinging back and forth, pounding the raised drawbridge until it shattered. From the gatehouse, Bell Castle's defenders could lower a thick pad to deaden the blows, but over time, the battering ram would achieve its goal.

It would be a while yet before Ulric's men got all their siege engines built, but once they did, his destructive power would swell. Ulric's army would be hard to repel.

Robin's men assaulted Ulric's rear echelon, but it was clear that more troops would be needed to crush the enemy's army before it could breach the castle's defenses. Robin assembled his knights, commanders, and captains. "We need reinforcements. With more men and more weapons we will be able to stretch Ulric's resources to the breaking point. He'll have to surrender."

"We've enlisted every able-bodied man for miles around," said Sir Alan. "Our vassals are depleted and showing signs of exhaustion. We're plowing through supplies of food and fuel faster than our subjects can replenish them. I fear that if we tax them any further there will be revolt."

Sir Alan was right to be concerned that the army's demand for resources would leave the countryside stripped. Subjects facing famine could withhold their support, even rebel. Nevertheless, the defense of Bell Castle and its ruler was of paramount importance. If the castle fell and its king was conquered, the defenseless people would be at the mercy of the victor and subject to his whims: enslavement, extermination. Once Robin and his soldiers foiled the attack, order in the Chalklands could be restored, reparations to the subjects could be made, villages rebuilt, and farms replanted but none of that would happen if they didn't prevail. For the ultimate good of the people, for the preservation of the monarch and all he could provide, the king of the Chalklands had to be victorious.

"Then range further." Robin paced before the cadre of leaders. Weariness and worry etched their faces. "Send to Windbrook. If there are no hostilities there, they may be able to spare some men."

"Sire, we've done that," said Sir Howell, so softly as to be almost apologetic. "We've gone to every liege lord, enlisted everyone who can stand. As well, our recruitment expeditions are producing diminishing returns. Increasingly, we encounter Ulric's soldiers on our routes. Our men sometimes don't come back. We're having to send out bigger, more heavily armed parties which pulls manpower away from the battlefield."

"Take heart. There must be a stone that we have left unturned." Robin paced some more, then whirled and faced the men. "We have an ally," said Robin. "At White Castle. In Dulcimer."

Sir Howell put a gloved hand to his jaw and ran an index finger across his lips. "Indeed. Our newest lord and lady. Dulcimer is some distance. A dangerous mission. Our messengers will have to pass many of Ulric's checkpoints."

"We will outfit a small party. And stay off the roads. Yes, it will take longer to get there, but they'll be less likely to be waylaid."

"Your Majesty should go with them. Better for our lord to be safe at White Castle than imperiled here on the battlefield."

The others murmured their agreement.

It was expected that the sovereign would seek refuge at a place of safety, but Robin would have none of it.

"Your Majesty," called Sir Maxwell. "I would like to volunteer. I can go it alone, Sire," said Maxwell. "I am fleet of foot. I would race to Dulcimer, faster than a bird could fly."

Or even a gryphon? "You remember the nobles from White Castle?" Robin asked.

"Yes, Sire. They were Your Majesty's guests at the tournament."

Robin nodded. "You will make your way to White Castle in Dulcimer and beg an audience with the lord and lady. Apprise them of our dilemma and tell them that their support is required. Give them a letter of appeal that we will have signed and sealed. The letter will command the lord to assemble an army to provide reinforcement. By no means must that letter fall into any other hands, especially not the enemy lest word of our imperiled state reach the ears of those who wish to see us ruined. As well, possession of the letter will reveal you to be an emissary from King Bewilliam and will surely result in your imprisonment or death. If there is any chance the letter can be taken by anyone other than the lord of White Castle you must destroy it or you will endanger yourself and the other nobles mentioned in it.

"Lord Ferree's army will be instructed to send word to us here as they near our encampment. There will be a secret code word in the letter so that we will be assured that the messenger is trustworthy.

"We will coordinate our offensives with their arrival. King Ulric will be assailed from all sides. He will be trapped. The only question that will remain is whether he will surrender or be destroyed."

Sir Maxwell looked ready to leave without further delay but Sir Howell cleared his throat.

"What say you, Sir Howell?"

Sir Howell sighed. "I had thought it best to send at least two. Should some mishap befall a lone emissary, should he be captured, the other might still make it."

Robin had to agree. "Two would be better."

"As we said, you should go with him, Your Majesty. We will all be relieved to know that Your Majesty is out of danger."

"We will not abandon our men or Bell Castle. It's out of the question."

"I will go," said Sir Alan. "Sir Maxwell could masquerade as the smith he has been, and I, his father."

Sir Howell nodded. "You look old enough to be Sir Maxwell's father."

Despite the gravity of the situation, Sir Howell's insouciant quip provoked chuckles.

"I could do it, Sire. I will let my beard grow. By the time we run into anybody, I will fit the part." He looked to Sir Howell and they both looked to Robin.

Robin faced Sir Maxwell. "Can you do that? Can you maintain that fiction?"

The young man nodded soberly.

"You will depart under the cover of night. You will have no weapons on your person, no blades at all save blunt knives barely capable of cutting meat. To all appearances you will be a father and his son. You will have some money but not much. Not any more than someone in that position would be expected to have."

"Can we not give them a mount? They would make faster time. It would not seem out of place for smiths to have a donkey at least."

"Perhaps they can procure one once they're underway," said Sir Alan.

"If they can find one," Sir Howell mused. "Between us and Ulric, all the supplies for miles around have been commandeered."

"One way or the other, you will make speed to Dulcimer and get assistance from Lord Ferree and Lady Alice."

Now it was Sir Howell's turn to pace.

"You have more reservations, Sir Howell?"

"As I said, not only are we conscripting any man who can stand but so is King Ulric. If Sir Alan and Sir Maxwell are caught, they run the risk of being drafted into the enemy's army. That is, if they're not made for spies and executed."

Sir Alan said, "We will make ourselves unattractive. I will disguise myself as—as a cripple."

"A crippled blacksmith," said Sir Maxwell. "Sounds like my father. With all due respect."

"That might spare Sir Alan, but what about Sir Maxwell? Youth doesn't seem to be a deterrent; in fact it would be a liability. They might execute the 'aging crippled father' all the better to conscript the robust young son."

The men fell silent. Robin gnawed the inside of his cheek. There had to be a way to make the plan work. Now that he had thought of it he was unwilling to give up on it, especially as he had no other ideas. *Who amongst them had a disability that wouldn't interfere with his ability to travel, yet would make him unattractive as an infantryman?*

Who, indeed?

Deidre.

On the night of the bonfire, the young woman had expressed her desire to be of service. Robin had questioned then if there was a place in an army for a woman, but twice now he had found a way to exploit her gender and he was about to do it again. Robin sent a servant to fetch Deidre and her charge and bring them to the council.

"A crippled old man and his daughter will not be seen as a threat or a source of manpower," he told her. "If in your travels you are even noticed, you will be discounted and left to go your way. "

"I am of course honored to serve in this important mission," she said.

"You'll have to give up your sword," Robin said. "As before, you will have to appear defenseless."

Deidre's lips thinned in a grimace of displeasure but she bowed. "As long as I have only to appear to be defenseless."

"Sir Alan, you needn't grow a beard or play the cripple. We will go to Dulcimer." Zachary stepped forward. "We will accompany Deidre. We can look out for each other. No one would suspect two women of being capable swordsmen, yet Deidre has shown herself to be a skilled combatant and of course we have had extensive training in both offensive and defensive techniques. We would take any would-be assailants by surprise."

That wasn't the only surprise. Zachary's offer was met with stunned silence.

Sir Howell spoke first. "Travel as two women? It might work."

The idea had merit. It would remove Zachary from the perils of the battlefield; it would keep him under Deidre's watchful eye.

Creeping through the countryside trying to evade capture would give him little opportunity to conspire with anyone from Ulric's camp.

"As well, we are acquainted with Lord Ferree and Lady Alice. No sealed secret communications will be needed. We can deliver the appeal in person. If we are disallowed from fighting for Bell Castle ourselves we can at least aid in finding more soldiers who can."

Could Zachary have sincere concerns for Bell Castle? Robin dared to hope that his son's apparent allegiance was genuine. "So be it. Make haste and may fortune shine upon you." Brother Thaddeus and Brother Leo would add "May God be with you," and Robin did too. Zachary and Deidre would need all the help that they could get.

CHAPTER TWENTY-SEVEN

Aid did arrive, first from Windbrook. The leader of the platoon explained that many of his men had already met their obligations, yet on hearing that victory at Bell Castle was imperiled had agreed to serve.

"Sir Henry drained so many of his subjects dry it was as if he meant to squeeze blood from a stone," he said. "He lived well at our expense. If this King Ulric is cut from the same cloth, we do not want to be at the mercy of his rule." That King Bewilliam was willing to pay for service had also been persuasive. Robin would have preferred a more affirmative pledge of allegiance than learning that King Bewilliam was considered the lesser of two evils, but now was not the time to argue.

Reinforcements from Dulcimer and Windham Hill arrived next. With the infusion of fresh fighting men, Robin was able to whittle Ulric's forces. Firing missiles from mangonels atop the watchtower, the forces under Sir Albert's command had managed to keep Ulric's men at bay and damaged the belfry, staged to be wheeled across the rolling road Ulric had built to ford the moat, before it could be put to use. Sir Albert managed to disable the battering ram with a grappling iron lowered from the gatehouse that clasped the ram, preventing it from swinging.

Still, it was too soon to declare that victory was at hand. King Ulric's trebuchet stood nearly complete and ready to strike. The powerful counterweighted catapult could hurl missiles from a position that was out of the range of return fire. It could shower boulders weighing hundreds of pounds against the curtain walls until the stone shattered and the walls broke open. Enemy forces could then gain access to the bailey. It was a course of last resort, so damaging that it left little of the infrastructure for an attacker to possess. Bell Castle would be reduced to rubble. Robin had to bring Ulric to his knees before he could put the trebuchet into operation.

Robin smiled. He had a trebuchet of his own. Carted halfway to Windbrook, it had been intercepted and turned back. Siege engines were used against buildings and walls but Robin would use his war machine to demolish Ulric's. He would heave boulders against it from a distance and reduce it to rubble. King Ulric would never anticipate that strike. Robin ordered soldiers to assembled and position the weapon and load it with ammunition.

*****

A commotion outside his tent roused Robin from the light sleep of a battlefield soldier to full alertness. In firm voices, his guards denied desperate pleas to see the king. The petitioner's voice was high and eerily familiar.

Robin scrambled from his pallet, grabbed his sword, and threw aside the tent's front flap.

His guards towered over another figure, small and lost in the folds of a hooded cloak.

"What seems to be the trouble?" Robin asked.

"This woman insists on seeing the king," one of the guards explained.

"Please, Your Majesty," said the woman. She curtsied low and her cloak's hood muffled her speech. "We have something you need."

A camp follower? Despite the danger of being near the hostilities, Robin's army hadn't lacked for attention from local women seeking to share their favors with the soldiers for a consideration. For the most part they were harmless, and while Robin decried the distraction and disruption in discipline, he knew that soldiers were tense and restive. Better to sport with a camp follower than stray in search of diversion or pick a fight with a fellow soldier to relieve the tension.

He had no need for such relief. "Send her away," he said.

"Don't turn us away, Your Majesty. You will want to hear what we have to say."

The woman threw back her hood.

It was Daya.

A few strands of gray streaked her warm brown hair. Fine wrinkles creased her forehead, the corners of her eyes, and her full lips. He noted the signs of the passage of time and then saw only the woman he had once loved, who had ruled beside him and given him two sons. The years had not been unkind to Robin's former queen but someone had. Her eye and cheek were purpled with bruises.

"What are you doing here?" Robin asked. His enemy's wife. *Was she sent to spy on him or attempt an assassination?* He signaled to his guards to approach.

"We've come to warn you."

"Why would you do that?" Robin asked, still not certain that he shouldn't simply arrest her.

"We fear for our sons."

"They are no longer your sons. Because of your perfidy, our marriage was annulled. They are the sons of King Bewilliam and only King Bewilliam."

"Regardless of what some clergyman said they are the fruit of my womb. They will always be my sons."

Sons that she had left vulnerable to Ulric's machinations. For the pain she had caused him, caused Conrad and Zachary, he should let Daya agonize over the fate of the young men. He wouldn't, but he wouldn't allay her fears either, not yet. She was at the battlefield, Ulric's queen, at the front. She would have vital intelligence about Ulric's strength. Robin would find that out first. "Why this sudden concern for the welfare of Bell Castle? Ulric's not going to win, you know."

"If Your Majesty knew what he had in mind, you wouldn't be so sure of that."

"Of course you would say that. But just for the sake of argument, let's say Ulric is victorious. Surely out of consideration to you he would show Conrad and Zachary mercy."

"They will not survive the attack. No one at Bell Castle will. King Ulric's plan, it's diabolical. He must be stopped."

"And stop him we will."

"You don't understand, Your Majesty. King Ulric intends to use Greek fire against Bell Castle."

Robin had heard of the exotic weapon but had never seen it in operation. The flammable concoction was reputed to adhere to surfaces and ignite on contact. The solution could be applied to arrows and spears to send the substance great distances and then set fire. Sealed glass jars and pots filled with liquid fire could be hurled at opponents, drenching them in flames.

What made it so deadly was that water would not put it out; Greek fire could burn on water. Structures covered with liquid fire would continue to blaze until there was nothing left to burn. Men struck by it could not escape it or extinguish it but would die in agony.

"He will arm the sappers with it."

Robin had seen signs of miners working near Bell Castle's curtain walls. No doubt the plan was to dig under the walls. Once tunnels were dug, sappers would fill them with branches, lard, tar, any kind of flammable fuel. The fire would consume the timbers supporting the tunnel, resulting in a cave-in that would undermine the walls' foundations and cause them to crumble. Robin wasn't overly concerned. Bell Castle had numerous defenses against sappers. The gatehouse had an early detection warning device: a bowl of water. Rippling water alerted guards to the digging taking place underground. They could retaliate by collapsing the tunnel before it got close enough to do any damage. Even if the sappers succeeded in evading detection, they would have to make deep lengthy excavations to bypass the moat.

218

Greek fire escalated the threat. The heat and tenacity of unquenchable conflagration would cause walls to crack and collapse that much more readily.

"King Ulric also means to use the trebuchet to launch quantities of liquid fire over Bell Castle's walls and into the bailey where it will set anything it touches aflame. Every person within range will be showered by it. There will be no defense."

She was right, it was fiendish. Fire from above, fire from below. Bell Castle would be turned into an inferno and all Robin's subjects would be trapped in it. "Then you must tell us where this demon ammunition is stored so that we may confiscate it and neutralize the threat."

Daya wrung her hands. "We've already risked our life to come here. If Ulric finds out, he will surely have his revenge. Your Majesty can see that he will not hesitate to act. If we help, Your Majesty must promise to give us sanctuary."

Yet the prospect of retribution hadn't stopped Daya from breaking faith with her king and husband any more than it had stopped her from deceiving Robin when she was his wife. He cupped her chin in his hand and scrutinized her bruised face. "What did you do to bring on such ill treatment?"

Daya turned her head away and sighed. "His Majesty was angry, is still angry about the judgment handed down at Mathus Abbey."

The judges had found Daya and Ulric guilty of adultery, had excommunicated them, and annulled Daya's marriage to Robin, voiding any of her claims on the fruits of that union, including their sons.

"Ulric wasn't the only one who suffered. We lost a queen, a wife, with that judgment." Trying to rein in his hurt and anger, Robin clenched his fists. "Oh, wait, we had already lost her. She left, of her own accord. Abandoned her throne, her husband, her children."

"You don't understand."

"No, we do not. We can grant you sanctuary but we need to know. Why?" *Why did she break his heart? How did he fail her? What was lacking?*

"Sire!" Sir Howell came racing up. "Sire, I came to rouse you ...." He spied Daya and froze in place, speechless. "Your Highness?"

"What is so urgent, Sir Howell?" Robin growled, furious at the interruption.

Sir Howell cleared his throat. "King Ulric has moved to escalate the hostilities. Men are getting into position near the trebuchet. I believe that once it's daylight, he means to begin the assault on Bell Castle's walls. The fool. He's willing to destroy Bell Castle in order to call it his."

Using a siege engine loaded with unquenchable Greek fire. Howell didn't know about the hellish weapon that Ulric planned to use although he soon would. Robin wheeled and clutched Daya's arm. "You must tell us and tell us now. Where is the ammunition stored?"

The purple bruises stood out against Daya's growing pallor. "In brass tubes. Locked in a vault in a stockade. It's under heavy guard. Your Majesty will never get near it.

Robin paced in a tight circle, helpless with fear and rage, his breath streaming from his nostrils in puffs like smoke from a dragon's. "But you could. You could escort us. Tell Ulric's guards that you have been sent with a troop of men to transport the ammunition closer to the trebuchet."

Daya shook her head. "It's impossible. We are not a combatant. We have no authority to command the men."

"You are the Queen. They will not disobey an order from their King's wife."

Daya was not persuaded. "They would never believe us. The queen sent to the battlefield to deliver a military command?"

"You will have to make them believe you." Clearly you are more than capable of pulling off a convincing deception, he wanted to say.

"Your Majesty is asking us to betray our lord."

It won't be the first time you broke faith with your husband. "It's either that or Bell Castle and everyone in it is lost. You will do this." He turned to Sir Howell. "We are launching a raid on King Ulric's camp. He has a weapon that he must not be allowed to use. Gather a troop of men with a cart to be drawn by Queen Daya's horse. Our approach will be slow and cautious but we will need to make a rapid getaway, all without being detected. Outfit them all, the men, the cart, the horse, with flame-resistant protective gear of the highest caliber. The risk of fire for this mission is extreme. Have servants fill bags of sand as they did to help smother the bonfire. We will need them on our return. Get our siege engine targeted and loaded, ready to fire at our command. As soon as Ulric's trebuchet is demolished, we will launch our final offensive.

"Bring our raiders here without delay. We must accomplish this foray and be back here before light. We go, now."

Daya rode out on the horse she had come in on while Robin and his men walked alongside, but there was no danger of her fleeing. The horse was yoked to a cart and Robin held the reins. Weighed down by heavy protective hides, they traveled a long circuitous route around the rear of Bell Castle. Staying in the shadows, they skirted the offensive forces positioned there. They moved toward the lights of Ulric's encampment, stifling the coughs and sneezes provoked by the fire-retardant vinegar and urine in which the hides had been soaked. Despite the chill of the night air, Robin sweated under the layers of clothing, armor, and leather.

They came around the corner pegged by Bell Castle's siege engine tower. In the dark, Robin could barely discern the outline of the mangonel that had damaged King Ulric's siege tower below. Atop the watchtower, Bell Castle's highest point, perched a menacing shape like a vulture. Or was Sir Maxwell's gryphon guarding Meeyoo's home?

Fearing that they were already running out of time, Robin picked up the pace, leading the party past the backs of archers stationed behind their protective mantlets. Some lay motionless on the ground, others twitched, dozing uneasily. Some focused on the walls before them and paid no attention to the people passing behind them. Those that did confront them recognized the queen astride her horse, bowed, and retook their post.

"There," said Daya. "There it is."

"Where?"

"Near the trebuchet. That stockade."

As huge as the siege engine was, Robin could barely make out its hulking dark shape against a night sky. He strained to see the stockade.

"Lead us towards it. You will tell anyone who asks that we men have been charged with moving the ammunition."

In a strained voice Daya said, "We only hope that King Ulric is not nearby."

Hope and pray, Robin thought. His eyes stung with unshed tears at the thought of the horror Ulric's plan would inflict if not thwarted. Surely there wasn't any part of Ulric's design that God sanctioned. Let me be Your strong arm, Robin said silently. Let me stop Ulric.

Gaining access to the stockade was less trouble than Daya thought it would be. Though they may have thought it curious for the Queen to lead a corps of men, none of the soldiers proffered a challenge. Likely the battle-weary men had little spirit left for anything other than getting through a day's skirmishes.

The strongbox, on the other hand, presented a problem. It was secured with a heavy padlock.

"What do you mean, you don't have a key?" Robin growled at Daya.

"Why would we have a key for something like this?"

Robin sighed. The padlock didn't mean total defeat. He had picked locks before. As a curious lad he had gotten the castle's locksmith to show him the workings of such devices. Robin had even picked a lock in the dark with the most makeshift of tools and didn't doubt that he could do it now, but time was not on their side. Wrestling with the lock might jar the contents and cause them to erupt.

"Load the box into the cart," he said. "Wedge it in and cushion it well so it won't jostle. Cover it with hides."

The men grunted with the weight of the box and the cart's suspension creaked ominously. One of the men pointed to the soldiers nearby. "They'll be expecting us to bring this closer to the trebuchet, not cart it away. How do we get out of here without being stopped?"

Robin looked around for something with which to disguise the dangerous cargo. "There," he said. "Those corpses."

A few feet away, headless bodies lay stacked like cordwood next to a pile of heads to serve as grisly ammunition for the catapults.

"Brilliant, Your Majesty," said Sir Howell.

Only the most stalwart would interfere with a cart filled with dismembered bodies. Even Robin's men were loath to touch them. Quashing their aversion, Robin and the other men draped the cadavers over the top of the strongbox and made as if to haul the dead away for burial.

Robin waved toward the horse. "Your Majesty," he said to Daya, "if you would please, get ready to ride. We make for our camp. We promised you sanctuary in return for your assistance."

"If we flee, Ulric will know where we are bound. He will send pursuers. They may fire on us." She shook her head. "We will stay and face Ulric's anger. It's not likely to be as deadly."

"What about your mount?" Without Daya's horse to pull the cart, they would never make it back before the sun rose and the truth of their raid was discovered.

"Take it. Get that hideous stuff as far from Bell Castle as possible. It will be worth it to us to know that our sons are no longer in danger from it."

Robin hesitated. He still needed to know the answers to the questions that Sir Howell's interruption had prevented him from asking. *Why? Why was his love not good enough?* Instead he found himself saying, "Conrad and Zachary are not at Bell Castle."

The lines in Daya's face softened. She lifted her face, closed her eyes, and clasped her hands as if in prayer. "Thank you."

With a feeling of dread, Robin watched her set off toward the cluster of tents. He then turned to lead his men in the opposite direction. The cart squeaked in protest of its load. The black sky lightened to inky blue and the stars faded as dawn crept up on night. As they lumbered toward camp, Robin wondered if this was how Prometheus felt when he stole fire from the gods:

victorious yet with a growing sense of foreboding of his fearsome new responsibility.

The familiar sights of their own base camp came into view. Before they went further, Robin and his men jettisoned the rotting corpses that had camouflaged their deadly cargo and gave them a hasty burial rather than introduce disease and vermin to the encampment. They hastened to offload the casket of Greek fire and cover it with the sand bags lest something accidentally touch off the flammable substance.

The battle resumed at first light. Robin didn't have to wait long for Ulric's response to the theft of his weapon. Scouts reported that enemy soldiers thronged around their trebuchet. "It is being repositioned, Your Majesty," they said. "We think he means to use it against us instead of Bell Castle."

"He won't get a chance," Robin replied. "Is our siege engine loaded?"

"Yes, Sire."

"Then fire."

Soldiers released the counterweight that kept the heavy beam in ready position. As the counterweight dropped, the beam swung on its pivot toward the target, carrying with it the deep boulder-filled bucket. At the top of its arc, the beam stopped but the bucket continued, slinging the projectiles into the air. The sound of Ulric's trebuchet shattering was louder than any thunderclap and Robin could feel the reverberations of rocks and debris crashing to the ground.

The blizzard of enemy arrows that had begun at dawn abruptly ceased. For a moment, the silence that followed was more deafening than the destruction of Ulric's siege engine had been. Robin broke it with "Charge!" sending waves of infantrymen armed with axes, knives, and clubs to overwhelm Ulric's dazed and disorganized foot soldiers in a deadly melee. Wielding swords, lances, and spears, Robin's cavalry attacked next and struck the decisive blows, while arrows launched from the castle raked the sky.

From atop Ulric's damaged siege tower a white pennant unfurled. Behind him, Robin heard a whoop as another spotted the signal. Then came a cheer and then another. Robin looked about to see men leaping and jabbing the sky with their lances and swords. Others collapsed to the ground, their heads in their hands, overcome with relief.

Ulric had surrendered. Robin had won. He felt not the elation of victory so much as a dizzying sense of release. It was over. For the first time in many weeks he could take a full breath.

One by one his knights and captains appeared at his side awaiting official confirmation of a cease-fire and new instructions.

Deserters fearing reprisals flew from the battlefield in every direction. "Go after them," Robin ordered. His men didn't need to be told twice. Enemy soldiers could not be permitted to infiltrate nearby towns where they might take vengeance against innocent noncombatants. As well, defeated knights were worth money; they would pay for their release.

Could one of the deserters be Ulric himself? The vanquished king had yet to appear to formalize the surrender.

"Let us advance toward the castle with caution," Robin said. Word of the surrender might not have reached every soldier and some might still be battling for their cause. As if to justify his concern, a flight of arrows crossed the sky and a dark shape the size of a boulder typically launched by a mangonel sailed towards them from Ulric's camp. The catapult's limited range delivered the projectile too short to do any damage. A last parting shot. Clearly not all combatants had gotten word of the surrender.

Robin led Hope forward, skirting the bodies of broken men. *No more. Never again.* His knights had been right. Like a fire not completely extinguished, Ulric's enmity had continued to smolder until it burst into flames anew but that was over now. The Chalklands would know peace.

He looked askance at the last boulder flung by Ulric's catapult to discover that it was not a rock but a human head. Robin sighed at the thought that one of his own men may have been used as a missile, a final insult perhaps. And then he reined his horse to a halt. The lifeless eyes that stared up at him did not belong to a fallen soldier but to Daya.

CHAPTER TWENTY-EIGHT

Ulric, this had to be his doing. He must still be in camp, near the mangonel that had flung the grisly projectile. Hearing but not heeding the confused shouts of his men behind him, Robin spurred Hope to charge toward where stood the shattered siege engines. He raced past commanders of enemy units handing swords to Robin's men and soldiers laying weapons on the ground. At his approach, some recognized him as king by virtue of the crown that encircled his helm and bowed. Others stood with arms raised overhead in surrender. Surgeons scurrying to tend to the wounded ducked out of his way.

"Ulric," Robin roared to the men in the encampment. "Where is he?"

Some men shrugged, others cowered in fear, but at last one man pointed in the direction of the damaged siege tower. Like an enclosed staircase on wheels, the roughly rectangular tower stood atop a platform of logs bridging the moat, dangerously close to the castle. The tower stretched as tall as the curtain walls. Archers at the upper levels could shoot straight at their target while other fighters stood at the ready on the lower levels, shielded by the tower's sides. Once the defenders had been eliminated, the tower's gangplank would be lowered giving attackers access to the wall walk.

The hides covering the front and sides of Ulric's tower to protect against fire were scorched and burned away. Bell Castle's mangonel had smashed the pyramidal roof over the tower's topmost level and driven boulders into its side. Robin leaped from his mount, handed the reins to a surprised Bell Castle soldier and with sword drawn, ran into the tower.

Bodies and broken weapons littered the tower's floor. Sunlight and shadow striated the dim and dusty interior. Robin looked about and saw no one, but thought he heard something creaking overhead. Could Ulric indeed be here and if so, why? A siege tower sheltered soldiers poised to attack, but there were really no hiding places. Where did Ulric think he was going? There was nowhere to go but up.

And out. Out the drawbridge. Onto Bell Castle's wall walks which were likely to be undefended if manned at all in light of the truce, then into the castle grounds. And from there, anywhere.

Robin bolted up the rough wooden stairs onto the next floor which appeared deserted. Over the tumult of the battleground around him he heard the rattling of chains, the whining of pulleys, the creaking of wood—the drawbridge being lowered? Panting, he took another flight, then another.

The drawbridge level came into view. At the winch stood a man. Tall and broad-shouldered, covered from head to toe in armor, he was virtually indistinguishable from any of the other soldiers save for the jeweled gold band encircling his helm. Ulric. Behind the slits in his helm's visor, his eyes glittered like obsidian.

"You son of a bitch, you murdered my wife!" Robin shouted. He swung his sword at Ulric's knees. The blow rang against the protective armor plate.

Ulric stumbled back. "She wasn't your wife and she wasn't even ours. She was a traitor." He reached for his sword.

Robin gained the top of the stairs and immediately threw himself to the floor. Hugging his sword, he rolled out of the way of Ulric's attack then sprang to a crouch. With a two-handed grip, he jabbed the point of his sword into the back of Ulric's leg, protected only by chainmail. "You stole my queen and tried to steal my kingdom."

Ulric staggered away, pivoted, and holding his sword high, lunged to pierce Robin's visor. "You left them both for the taking."

Ulric's blade came so close that Robin could almost smell the steel, but he parried with the tip of his sword, pushing Ulric's weapon aside and bringing the edge of his own to Ulric's neck. Ulric twisted away and smacked Robin's arm with his sword. Despite the protection afforded by Robin's shield, the strike sent pain radiating from the deep wound left by the arrow. Robin didn't have time to wonder if Ulric's stroke had been made with full knowledge of Robin's recent injury; Ulric thrust his trunk forward, pinning Robin's hands and sword against his chest. When Ulric leaned back to make another thrust, Robin retreated and felt the ground beneath him flex; Ulric had backed him onto the narrow drawbridge. All around him Robin could see sky. Stories down was the moat, lined with sharpened metal stakes, whittled sticks, and broken crockery, all designed to pierce whoever might attempt to ply its waters.

Ulric advanced, hooked Robin's leg with his own, and pulled. Robin fell on his back with a clang, head and shoulders hanging off the edge of the drawbridge. His shield went flying off into space. The weight of his helm and armor threatened to pull him over the side. His crown slipped from his helm to plummet down. "No!"

"Ha, there goes your crown," Ulric crowed. "You're next. Then Bell Castle and the Chalklands will be mine."

Ulric lifted his foot to shove Robin over the edge. Robin snagged Ulric's ankle with his armored boot and yanked. Ulric lurched to regain his balance. Robin rolled to the side, sprang to a squat, and stood.

One gauntleted hand on the sword's hilt, the other grasping the blade at midpoint, Robin twisted his body, his shoulder angled as if he intended to dash across the drawbridge to the wall walk. The move put Robin's back to his opponent, an irresistible invitation to attack. Ulric rushed ahead to plunge the point of his sword into Robin's torso. Robin pivoted away, extended his arms, and parried Ulric's sword with his own.

From the corner of his eye, Robin saw a huge shape swoop towards them from Bell Castle's watchtower. It streaked across the drawbridge so quickly it was just a dark blur but for one critical moment it distracted Ulric. Robin stabbed Ulric in the side and punched through his armor. Ulric's lunged away and too late discovered he had misjudged his position. He took a couple of faltering steps to recover his footing, failed, and with a roar of pain and fury, went over the drawbridge's side.

Robin's own momentum about to send him stumbling off the drawbridge, he fought to steady himself and edged back to safety. He stood for a moment at the drawbridge's midpoint and lifted his head to the sky. He closed his eyes, took a breath, and listened until the pounding of his heart slowed and the ringing in his ears subsided.

When at last he had collected himself, Robin followed the route that Ulric had planned: the siege tower's drawbridge to Bell Castle's wall walk atop one of the gatehouse's drum towers and down the stairs. Bereft of his crown, few recognized him as king but his tabard marked him as a member of the victor's army and allowed him free passage.

Like Windbrook after the battle, the bailey was littered with the casualties and debris of war and stank of burned wood, tar, and blood. Men stood with bowed heads and hunched backs, leaning on staves and each other, bleeding, bandaged, and hobbled. Every structure was damaged or scarred. The devastation dampened any victor's exhilaration Robin may have felt.

At last he found Sir Albert who bowed to his king and then wrapped him in a grateful embrace. The knight's eyes glistened with unshed tears and Robin felt his own sting.

"Sire, you have seen action. Is Your Majesty injured?"

"No, but Ulric is dead." He patted his helm. "We lost our crown to the moat but we prevailed." He would have to remember to alert the steward to recover the crown when the moat was cleared of corpses and debris. "May we commend you on your service," Robin said. "Brave, stalwart, and creative. Your ploy to deceive the enemy about the futility of a blockade was inspired."

Sir Albert grinned. "Sir Maxwell found you and told you of our ruse."

"He did. And you received our message about the rear flank maneuver."

"I did."

Together they made their way to the great hall. Was it so wrong, Robin wondered, that he hoped Meeyoo would be there in her usual spot? He pictured her looking up from her custom-crafted "throne," creeping into his lap when he finally settled in his seat, and he felt tears well up yet again.

The halls' exterior was damaged and the interior trashed. He could see that in his absence it had been used as a barracks, a dining hall, and a triage for the wounded, but he didn't see Meeyoo. He hoped she had found a safe place to hide away from the violence. "We need to meet with the captain, the knights and lords, the household staff, begin reconstruction."

"Sire, this will need considerable attention before holding audiences here," Sir Albert mused.

"You have a point," Robin said. Suddenly drained, his thoughts drifted to his bedchamber in the keep. Perhaps Meeyoo hid there. "See what can be done to clear this enough to have court here on the morrow. Have a messenger sent to Windbrook. Sir Kenneth should learn that the hostilities here have ended. If all is peaceful and secure there, he should put a commander in charge and report to Bell Castle.

"Release the soldiers who came from Dulcimer and Windham Hill to return to their homes and send word that is it safe for Deidre and Prince Zachary to return." Robin sighed, overcome with fatigue. "Have the steward send our page, a squire, and guards to the keep. We will meet them there presently." He clapped the knight on the shoulder. "Thank you, Sir Albert."

Sir Albert bowed.

Robin left the great hall and made his weary way across the bailey. Servants and soldiers greeted him with bows, victory salutes, and cries of "Long live the king." He should feel like a hero, but it was difficult to be joyful in the face of so much destruction and loss. Robin found himself noting what needed repair and where it stood in the order of importance, but the list became too long. Everyone and everything was of the highest priority. He would do this tour on the morrow with a scribe.

He longed to rest but continued to the smithy. Of all the noncombatants, the smiths were possibly the most heroic, having worked ceaselessly to keep soldiers supplied with weapons.

Smoke poured from the forge's chimney but the compact building was strangely still. Men sat hunched over on the ground or slumped against the wall. At Robin's approach, they struggled to their feet and bowed. Robin bade them return to a well-deserved respite.

He stepped across the threshold into a choking smog of smoke and pulverized metal. He spied Gregory on his stool. Stretched across his worktable, his head rested on folded arms. Beside him sat a tawny gargoyle. As Robin drew near, the gargoyle came to life, rising up on its haunches. Its ears laid back and its fur stood on end. It snarled, showing fearsome fangs, and raked the air with a paw studded with curved claws as pointed as the lances' coronals. Reaching for his sword, Robin cried, "Gregory, look out," and moved to stab the creature.

Gregory snapped to attention. "Sire!" He slid from his stool, bowed, and said to the gargoyle "Down, Boy." He patted the creature's head.

With a low growl, the gargoyle sat and fixed Robin with glowing yellow eyes.

Still on guard Robin cried, "What is that?" *A live gargoyle?* Reason would have it that there were such creatures, giving rise to the sculptured depictions that guarded castle gates, but Robin had never seen one.

Gregory chuckled. "That's our guard cat, Sir Maxwell's Meeyowyow. He looks fierce but once he takes a liking to you he is as sweet as a kitten. He does, however, discourage strangers from pilfering."

Still wary, Robin said, "He's huge." Robin edged closer under Meeyowyow's hooded stare. Gregory stroked the animal's back and it seemed to relax. Its ears straightened and the twitching of its tail slowed. Robin reached out a gauntleted finger and scratched the cat behind its ears. It responded with a purr that was as loud as a distant thunderstorm. This was Meeyoo's son? The cat was unlike any Robin had seen. Sir Maxwell's reports of the animal's unusual behavior now seemed perfectly credible. Had Meeyowyow been sired by a gryphon? Robin was less inclined to argue.

"Please, be seated, Gregory." Robin could do with a seat himself and pulled over another stool.

"Our apologies. Your Majesty finds us all catching our breath. We were told a truce was declared."

"Not just a truce but a victory. The war has ended. You and your men can rest. It will be normal duty from now on. We came to thank you for your service. Our triumph is due in large part to your labors."

"Thank you, sire. I am so proud of my son. He worked harder than anyone. When he wasn't needed by Sir Albert he was here."

"And made it bravely past enemy lines to bring much needed intelligence to us at the rear. We wished to thank him also. If you see him before we do, have him join us and the other knights tomorrow in the great hall. Meanwhile, we do have need of one small item. Another pair of spurs like the ones that you fashioned for us."

"Were they damaged in the joust? Perhaps we can repair them."

"No, they're fine. We simply need an additional pair. Within the next day or two."

Gregory bowed. "You shall have them."

"Thank you." Suddenly eager to be released from his metal shell so that he too could rest, Robin took his leave and set out for the keep. In its remote corner of the castle grounds, the keep's exterior had sustained less damage than the other buildings that stood closer to the gate. Skirting debris and litter, his energy fading with every step, Robin mounted the stairs to the keep's top floor. He trudged down the corridor. Torches as yet unlit left the hallway dim. His footsteps echoed and raised dust and the hallway smelled dank and musty.

He passed rooms his sons had used.

Conrad. It would be ironic if protecting travelers from assassins had proved to be less hazardous than living at Bell Castle these last few months.

And Zachary. Robin hoped he would learn that his son had been well protected at White Castle, but wondered who would return from Dulcimer, Zachary or Dale.

Robin pushed open the door to his bedchamber, a silent tableau of light and shadow in the dusk. It wasn't long ago that he had shared this room, that bed with Daya. Had enjoyed nights of love, of passion here, had planned a future for family and fiefdom. Now she was dead. Had he ever hoped for reconciliation in spite of the judgment, the annulment, there was no chance of that now. Their story had come to an end. That book was closed forever. Robin felt pinched and small. In killing Ulric, he had successfully avenged her hideous murder but that brought him no comfort.

He scanned the room. Had Meeyoo left that indentation in the bedcovers? He saw no sign of her. Robin hoped she had found some place of refuge during the conflict. He could hardly imagine how terrifying it had been for her.

He was about to search all her usual hiding places when there was a knock at the door and a page requested entrance. Robin gratefully submitted to having his armor removed plate by endless plate, all the while keeping an eye out for a furry face that might peep out from under the bed or behind a trunk. The page peeled off Robin's padded undershirt and leggings, stiff with dirt and dried sweat, and wiped away the grime and dried blood. Robin turned his head at the sight of his battered body, cut, scabbed, and mottled with bruises like a piece of fruit from the bottom of the barrel.

Servants brought him food which he was surprised to discover that he didn't want, and ale which he very much did.

There was so much to do but he found it hard to resist the notion of retiring. It would be nightfall soon. Little would be accomplished in the dark. It could wait, he told himself. He dismissed his page and guards to their night posts, crawled into bed, and laid his head on his pillow, his eyes already half-closed.

"Me. You."

Robin felt a weight on his feet and propped himself up on his elbows. A cat sat and blinked at him from the end of the bed. "Meeyoo, where were you? Are you all right?"

Crying "Me, you, me, you," the cat padded from the foot of the bed to his chest and purred.

Robin straightened, pulled Meeyoo close, and let the tears that he had held back all day fall.

CHAPTER TWENTY-NINE

Though situated near the hotly-contested curtain walls, Bell Castle's church had sustained little damage. Robin stood in the middle of the humbly-furnished room. The cheery modest décor had been Conrad's doing and Brother Leo hadn't made many changes. Spring-morning sunlight heightened the warm glow of the nave's yellow-painted walls and pine settles. The earthenware vase of early-season flowers on the altar was poignantly suggestive of spring's optimistic promise.

The preacher emerged from the vestry and spotting Robin, bowed. "We heard of Your Majesty's return from the battlefield and have given thanks that our king and kingdom are safe."

"We as well," said Robin, although he had not stopped at the church to deliver prayers of thanksgiving. "Would you have had news of Brother Thaddeus?"

Brother Leo beamed. "Indeed we have. We are doubly blessed. Brother Thaddeus and the other Guardian Angels successfully saved several parties of pilgrims from ambush."

Say that Conrad emerged from that unscathed.

"What was even more astounding was that several pilgrims chose to abandon their journey and stay with Brother Thaddeus to avail themselves of his teaching. Others made generous donations of money or worldly goods to the Guardian Angels.

The abbot has determined that as good a soldier as Brother Thaddeus is, he can do greater works as a teacher and church leader. He has called Brother Thaddeus home."

Robin felt as though the nave's golden light had flooded his chest. He clasped his hands. "Thank you," he said to the preacher but perhaps also to God. Silently he pledged that when Conrad came home, he would not pressure him about the sovereignty of the kingdom. He had vowed to support Conrad's vocation and he would keep that vow.

Buoyed with optimism Robin fairly floated to the great hall.

The days that followed were an endless parade of servants, captains, knights, and lords, all with critical needs of equal importance, long stressful hours leavened on occasion when Meeyoo would leave her basket to leap into Robin's lap or trot across the great hall floor bearing the tribute of a mouse or bird.

With both Ulric and Daya gone, contention for leadership at the fortress at the Palisades raised the specter of anarchy. Robin sent trusted commanders to bring order and ensure loyalty to the realm's new ruler until he could pay a visit.

As urgent as business was, Robin called a halt to court when the officer at arms announced the arrival of Sir Kenneth. Robin crossed the hall to meet the returning knight halfway. "How come you to be here so quickly? It seems that we only just sent word to you."

"All is secure at Windbrook," Sir Kenneth replied. "We thought that we might be needed at Bell Castle. We left able commanders in charge and hastened here to find the war is over. Your Majesty has won."

"You seem disappointed. Do you regret not having been part of the battle?"

"Disappointed? Not at all, Sire. And while I am ever willing to serve, I have had quite enough of conflict."

"Then why the grim countenance?"

Sir Kenneth sighed. "It is our onerous duty to report that Sir Henry died. He never did recover from his injury."

"Did he say—?"

Sir Kenneth shook his head. "No, Your Majesty. Never woke, never said a word."

"Thank you, Sir Kenneth," Robin bit back any further comment. This was unfortunate news. There was so much that he needed to know that only Sir Henry could reveal. Who had been the real culprit behind the betrayal at Grimstaff Castle, Sir Henry or Sir Walter? Robin had hoped to get the truth from Sir Henry.

A herald announced that Deidre and Prince Zachary were at the gate. "Wait for us here," Robin said to Sir Kenneth. He hastened across the bailey, his page and guards hurrying to stay with him.

Deidre slipped down from a mount with White Castle livery and bowed. Behind her, astride a second horse sat Zachary attired in a gown. Was he Princess Dale or Prince Zachary still wearing women's clothes as part of the safe-travel ruse?

Zachary dismounted and Robin embraced him, choking back any questions about Zachary's dress. The search for moral support for his adopted identity had led Zachary to flee Bell Castle and enter into the treacherous alliance with Sir Henry. Robin would not make the mistake of leveling criticism and leaving his son susceptible again.

"Your mission to Dulcimer was more than successful," he told the pair. "The reinforcements that you recruited were decisive. And we see that you are safe and well."

Deidre nodded. "Yes, Sire. Suffice to say that getting there was an undertaking. Women were not sought by the enemy to serve as soldiers but that's not to say that we didn't have to defend ourselves. There were many with lecherous intent who sought to waylay us."

Robin imagined that Deidre had swiftly discouraged those advances.

"As for the return journey—" she extended an arm to the horses, carts, and retinue—"the lord and lady were most gracious. We made much better time traveling as nobles than we did slinking about as two ragged women on the run."

"They are well, Alice and Ferree? And the daughters, Joy and Jewel?"

Robin thought that Deidre's eyebrow lifted but she said only, "Yes, Sire. They are all well."

"You have done well," Robin said. He sighed. He had hoped someday to be able to tell Deidre that her uncle, Sir Walter, had been blameless, had been wrongly accused of treachery. Now all he could tell her was that Sir Henry had died without ever regaining consciousness.

Deidre pressed her lips together and sighed. "Thank you, Your Majesty, for telling me." Robin wondered if she had misgivings about striking what proved to be a fatal blow.

Zachary too looked pained. Did Zachary still care for his "champion?" Was his glum expression grief over the loss of a friend and ally or guilt and regret over his part in the whole disastrous episode? What did Zachary feel? Would Robin ever know and would he ever understand it?

"What do you plan to do now?" Robin asked Deidre.

She curtsied. "Whatever Your Majesty requires. I am at your service."

"Good. Because we have a problem. Come with us."

He set off for the great hall. Deidre and Zachary followed, their heads swiveling as they took in the scars the battle had left on Bell Castle's bailey.

They crossed the hall and rejoined Sir Kenneth. Robin climbed the dais to the throne but did not sit. He turned to Deidre and Zachary. "Sir Kenneth reports that all is secure at Windbrook. As much work as there is to be done here, Windbrook also needs reviving. Not to mention a new tenant-in-chief." He looked to Zachary. "Unless you have claim to it?"

Zachary shook his head. "As we said, the marriage was forced. Our pact with Sir Henry was founded on lies. We assert no tenure other than as Your Majesty's blood and heir."

His blood and heir. What had Daya said? That regardless of the law, Conrad and Zachary would always be her sons? By the same token, whether he was Zachary or Dale, this person would forever be Robin's flesh and blood.

"In that case, Deidre, for your service in defense of our heir—"

Zachary's eyebrows lifted.

"—we name you tenant-in-chief of Windbrook." Robin allowed himself a smile. "The alliances that you have made at Windbrook will stand you in good stead."

Deidre's eyes went wide and she dropped to one knee. "Thank you, Sire."

She made as if to rise. "Don't stand yet," Robin said. He drew his sword. Agape, Deidre looked in appeal at Zachary and Sir Kenneth who could only shake their heads in bafflement.

"Do you, Deidre, swear always to defend the helpless and be charitable to the poor? To tell only the truth? To be courageous and never give in to fear?"

Deidre's brow wrinkled. "Why, yes, of course, Sire. Haven't I demonstrated that?"

"You have indeed. Do you swear always to be faithful to the Kingdom of the Chalklands?

"May Your Majesty never have reason to doubt my loyalty."

With the flat of his sword's blade, Robin tapped Deidre's right shoulder, then the left. "We dub you Knight. Henceforth, you shall be known as Dame Deidre." He retrieved a small packet from beside his throne, unwrapped it, and presented his newest knight with a pair of rowel spurs.

The blood drained from Deidre's face and she looked like she might faint. For a moment Robin feared that Deidre might fall backwards and tumble down the dais steps but slowly she got to her feet. "Thank you, Sire. I will do my all to prove that Your Majesty's faith in me is well placed."

No doubt the knighting had seemed hasty, almost impromptu, without the usual preparation or pomp. Conrad would surely decry the absence of any religious connection. Like Sir Maxwell, Dame Deidre faced years of training. Nevertheless, Robin was comfortable with his decision.

He studied Zachary's and Sir Kenneth's reactions. Zachary looked pensive while Sir Kenneth at first registered surprise. He then smiled and held out his hand. "Dame Deidre," he said, and bowed. "May I be the first to congratulate you?"

They took their leave, exchanging reports about the challenges that they had faced on their respective fronts. Zachary remained, arms folded across his chest. "You knighted a woman," he said.

"You have a problem with that?"

"Not at all. She earned it, she deserves it, and she will serve the kingdom well." Zachary's grin was sly. "Next Your Majesty will be declaring that a woman can rule."

"We can trumpet that from the highest watchtower," Robin said, "for all the good it would do. It would be up to the woman to prove it, as it will be for Deidre to gain respect for herself." He watched as she strode towards the door, seemingly oblivious to the stunned expressions of the assembly. "We gave her the opportunity, we can give her our support, but we cannot fight her battles for her, battles which despite her best efforts she may not win."

Zachary opened his mouth to speak, then closed it. His brow furrowed, he bowed and withdrew.

Robin pressed on to conclude the day's business. Meeyoo scampering ahead, he set out for the keep intending a light supper and an early bedtime. Meeyoo stopped in the middle of the path, sat, and looked up. Robin followed her line of sight in time to spy what had caught her attention. High above, a huge bird rose up from the watchtower and made lazy circles above them before soaring off toward the woods.

Was it a bird or was it the gryphon, bidding Meeyoo a good night and leaving her in Robin's care? He bent down and scratched the cat behind her ears. Had a gryphon saved him and his party from an attack by wolves and escorted them to Dulcimer? Had the mythical creature aided Robin's army in its battle against Ulric? Robin chuckled. If so, those actions were on Meeyoo's behalf, to get her to Dulcimer so she could be healed, to protect Bell Castle, her home. But what explained the large winged animal that had for a fortuitous moment distracted Ulric on the drawbridge? Had that been the gryphon? By virtue of being Meeyoo's steward had Robin earned the gryphon's favor for himself?

Did he need to see the gryphon to believe in it?

"Come on, Meeyoo," Robin said, patting her on the back and urging her towards the keep. "Tomorrow we'll give a thought to adding an image to our blazon."

CHAPTER THIRTY

Robin shook his head to clear it and looked about. For a few terrifying moments he thought he had gone blind because black was all he could see. He cast his eyes up and saw pinpoints of light—stars in a night sky. Ragged silhouettes came into focus and revealed themselves as pine trees. Finally, he was able to discern pine cones on the needle-strewn ground. Around him he could see only trees—no buildings, no walls, no landmarks. He was in a pine wood, far from home, separated from his men, alone.

How had this happened? Again.

No, it wasn't exactly the same as the last time that he found himself alone in a forest. Then he had the clothes on his back and his cloak but nothing more, no tools, no weapons, no supplies. At least this time he had his sword and for whatever use it would prove to be, his crown.

How came he to be here? Had his men forsaken him as he had been deserted before? Even if they had, how could they have left him without making a sound, without waking him? Although one part of a pine wood looked much like any other part, his immediate surroundings were unfamiliar. He saw no signs of their encampment. There should be tents, campfires, stockpiles, pens. Someone had moved him from there to here and left him, but how and why? Why couldn't he remember?

His head throbbed and his mouth was dry. He had had wine with his evening meal, wine being easier to transport on a march than ale. There had been times in his past when he had too much wine and he knew it left him bloated in the morning with an aching head, but not like this.

The clues that he could discern did nothing to solve the mystery. Other than where he stood, the pine needles around him were fresh. Had a party of men carried him here and abandoned him, the ground cover should have signs of trampling.

Could he have gotten here under his own power by walking in his sleep? Wouldn't one of his men have taken notice and stopped him?

A dawning realization buckled his knees and he sat. He had lost his mind just as he had when he went up against Grimstaff Castle. Then, the shock of what transpired there and what he learned about the people he trusted and loved robbed him of his memory, leaving him to wander, a penniless homeless vagabond, a king without a kingdom, lost. The horror that it had happened again set the skin of his chest stinging and he cried out in anguish.

"Me. You. Me. You."

Robin opened his eyes. Meeyoo sat atop him, mewling and kneading with her front paws. Through the covers, her claws pricked his chest, setting his skin on fire.

He had been dreaming and his cries had alarmed the cat.

His heart still racing from the nightmare, Robin strained to catch the fading images: the pine wood, the desertion, the feeling of despair. Why now, on the heels of major military triumphs, would he be dreaming of utter helplessness?

Except, he hadn't been helpless. In the nightmare, he had his sword and his crown, but this vision told him that he needed to act so as never to have nightmares about Grimstaff Castle again. And this time, the dream told him, it would be different.

*****

Days became weeks and Bell Castle emerged from the rubble. A visit to Windbrook proved that progress was being made there as well. Reports indicated that the people of the Palisades appeared to accept the joining of their kingdom to that of the Chalklands.

There had, however, been no response to the claims Robin had made to settle an old score which left him only one alternative.

At the head of the long table, Robin greeted each knight when he arrived and bade him be seated although when Dame Deidre arrived, they all got to their feet again and bowed. "Please," she said. "I am here as a knight. Don't feel you have to show me any courtesy that you would not show each other."

"In that case," Sir Alan said, and finished his sentence with a proffered hand shake.

"Now that you are all in attendance," Robin said, "doubtless you are wondering why we are convening in the war room when we are at peace."

"Now that you mention it, Sire ... ," said Sir Howell.

Robin smiled. "There is a debt that is owed us. A sizeable sum. We have sent a demand for reimbursement. With interest for it having been long denied us and for the offense committed against us. It would go far towards the restoration of Bell Castle as well as Windbrook. We could spread enough wealth around to cement the loyalty of the kingdom of the Palisades as well as fund a feast to inaugurate our enlarged kingdom."

The knights murmured and nodded in approval.

"The debt and wrongdoing are something of which four of you gentlemen reminded us months ago in court. Before the Saint Valentine's Tournament.

Sir Albert frowned. "Sire? I don't recall ...."

Sir Alan and Sir Howell looked each other a question and Sir Kenneth shook his head. Sir Maxwell and Dame Deidre exchanged shrugs.

"Our demands have been rebuffed. The offender refuses to comply. At this point, calling in this obligation would require the use of force. We'd need a small army." Robin hung his head and shook it. "If only everyone had not already fulfilled his service obligation." Robin sighed heavily. "We suppose it will have to wait until we have returned to full military strength."

"A large debt, Sire?"

Robin nodded.

"This was our idea?" Sir Alan said.

"Yes, Sir Alan. You, Sir Howell, Sir Albert, and Sir Kenneth."

"We should then match our words with action, should we not?"

"Begging Your Majesty's pardon, but if I recall correctly the redress that we demanded back then was for Ulric's crime. That has been satisfied. What debt is this of which you now speak?" Sir Howell asked, his expression expectant.

"The one owed us by King Reynold of Grimstaff Castle. He cheated us and what's worse, we suspect that he conspired with Sir Henry, treason for which Sir Walter paid the price. We mean to put this right, but we can do this only with your help. What say you?"

The male knights looked at each other and nodded.

Dame Deidre slammed the table with her small fist. "When do we leave?"

Robin had vacillated about including Deidre in this campaign. Robin wasn't the only one who had been wronged; so had Deidre's uncle. The young woman definitely had an axe to grind, not to mention bury in King Reynold's head. Could Robin depend on her to follow his command or in seeking vengeance would she take matters into her own hands?

He needed to know. They all did.

It was one thing to have the knights' enthusiastic support and quite another to amass a sufficient army. Few able-bodied men remained in the kingdom who hadn't fulfilled their service obligation. The knights withdrew, pledging to muster all possible personnel. Sir Alan remained behind.

"Problem, Sir Alan?" Robin asked.

"Sire," said Sir Alan, "I have an idea that will lead King Reynold to overestimate our numbers and compel him to satisfy our demands without greatly increasing the manpower requirement."

"Let's hear it," Robin said.

Sir Alan sucked at his lip, then spoke. "This will sound hare-brained—" Sir Alan's breathlessness, glowing eyes, and avid expression said he thought it was nothing of the sort.

"Out with it, Sir Alan."

The knight described his plan. Robin had to admit that it bordered on lunacy but if Sir Alan was willing to try, so was he.

Sir Alan departed to recruit men for his unusual platoon and to requisition supplies. Several days passed before the knight announced that he was ready to reveal his strategy.

"The troops are stationed behind the barracks and ready for your review, Sire," he said.

Robin followed Sir Alan to the yard behind the barracks where a small troop was arrayed, equipped with an assortment of weapons the likes of which Robin had never seen.

Sir Alan faced the cadre of men, raised his arms and then lowered them.

Positioned behind casks, barrels, and metal drums all covered with tightly-stretched hides, men struck them rhythmically with shortened arrow shafts. To Robin it sounded a bit like thunder or perhaps the pounding of many feet on a distant road. Behind the makeshift drums, other men struck metal disks, creating a clanging like the rattle of swords. Men clattered the wooden shafts together which sounded like hand-to-hand combat. Other men with whistles produced the noise of arrows zipping through the air.

"Your Majesty, step into the bailey if you will," Sir Alan hollered over the tumult. "Tell me what you hear."

Robin hastened to stand out of sight but not out of hearing of Sir Alan's unusual orchestra. Without the visual reference, Robin would swear that some legion was on the march, somewhere swordfights were being waged, and he fully expected an arrow to come whizzing overhead.

It was saber-rattling taken literally.

He rejoined Sir Alan and drew him away where they could talk without yelling. "I am astounded, Sir Alan. When you described it, I never imagined it would be this effective."

Sir Alan beamed. "It will sound to King Reynold like a major army is approaching. For fear of being attacked, he will accede to Your Majesty's wishes."

If this worked, it would transform warmongering forever.

"He'll be duped into believing that we have far superior numbers than we actually do."

"Far superior fire power as well," Robin said, another idea forming. Sir Alan wasn't the only one who could intimidate through subterfuge.

"How's that, Your Majesty?"

"We have Ulric's supply of Greek fire."

Sir Alan looked stunned. "Surely Your Majesty wouldn't inflict on someone else the abomination that Ulric intended for us."

"Of course not. We can be ruthless if circumstances call for it but we are not inhumane." Robin grinned. "But Reynold doesn't know that."

*****

Robin recalled his first journey to the pine-tree forest of King Reynold's realm as a long and tiring one. The return trip had been even longer. Betrayed by all whom he had trusted, Robin had fled Grimstaff Castle, forgot who he was, and wandered, a lost king without a kingdom. He unlocked his memories only by reliving the ordeal.

As they marched toward Grimstaff Castle, Robin worried that revisiting the scene of the betrayal that had turned his life upside down would give rise to the same madness. He hoped that his dream of some nights ago was not a premonition.

The morning fog, sodden ground, and overflowing creeks of spring belabored their trek. King Reynold's domain was one of deep valleys and rolling hills that got taller and more jagged the closer Robin's army came to its destination. Peaks nearly black with evergreens and shrouded with gray mist and white clouds strafed dark forbidding skies. On a mountainside ahead, rising higher than the tallest trees stood the white stone towers of Grimstaff Castle, topped with slate and lead roofs. The formidable structure looked as impregnable as the side of the mountain out of which it appeared to be carved.

"We will encamp here," Robin said when they had the castle in sight.

Robin did not plan to send an emissary to announce his arrival. Reynold had been given plenty of notice of Robin's demands. Now the King of the Chalklands would himself appear at the castle's gates and collect his due.

"Sir Alan, you will remain here with your 'army.' When we reach the gate, have your men 'drum up' some noise to alert the gatekeeper that we are not to be trifled with. Once we have delivered our demands to the king, we will send word if Reynold has satisfied us. If he continues to refuse, we will give you the high sign. At that point, mount the offensive as planned."

Accompanied by the other knights, Robin set off for the castle. Wary Grimstaff guards met Robin's party at the gate.

"This is King Bewilliam of the Chalklands ... and the Palisades," Sir Maxwell said. "He would have an audience with your king."

The gatekeeper took the measure of Robin and his armored men bristling with swords and lances who sat tall astride war horses outfitted in the finest livery.

"His Majesty is not expecting you."

"He should be," Robin said.

The gatekeeper coughed.

"If King Reynold is not in residence, we will negotiate with your commander. Bring him at once."

The gatekeeper scanned Robin's men. A distant rumble drew his glance beyond them to the edge of the pine wood. Robin thought the gatekeeper might have spotted the vanguard of Robin's army because his eyes widened. The woods thundered and clanged, suggesting that the line of soldiers that was visible was but the leading edge of a huge army. Robin grinned and the gatekeeper's face paled. "Wait here, Your Majesty."

Sir Maxwell leaned in close and whispered. "I think we have them worried. Look, Your Majesty—more soldiers."

Maxwell pointed to the wall walks above. Soldiers swarmed to their defensive positions.

Accompanied by guards, King Reynold himself emerged from the wicket gate in the castle's huge oak door and strode down the gatehouse neck. His pale complexion was almost pasty against his dark hair, thick brows, and sharply pointed beard. His dark green cloak, tabard, and leggings were just as severe.

Robin thought he should dismount and greet the king properly. Instead he kept his seat and enjoyed staring down in menacing silence at the man who had cheated and betrayed him.

King Reynold finally broke the uncomfortable interval. "King Bewilliam. Of the Chalklands."

"And the Palisades," Robin added.

King Reynold's eyebrows twitched as he registered the information.

Robin dismounted and made a dutiful bow. "As we delineated in our demand, we have come to collect our crown and our sword which, due to our hasty departure when we were last in Your Majesty's kingdom, we left without. Frankly we are surprised that Your Majesty did not make an effort to return them long before now. In light of this negligence we reiterate the claim we made in our missive."

"Crown and sword?" King Reynold stammered.

"Surely your servants discovered them still in the bedchamber that we had occupied."

King Reynold shrugged. "We determined by your action that you had chosen to forfeit them." King Reynold took a step back and his guards drew close. "You went missing, Your Majesty. We held a banquet in your honor. You never appeared nor did any of your men." King Reynold held out his hands in a gesture of helplessness. "We knew not what had become of you but we could only assume that you had been called away on a more important matter. It is due only to our magnanimity that we did not take offense at Your Majesty's snub of the homage we sought to give."

"We didn't rebuff your tribute; we fled for our life having learned that Your Majesty plotted against us. With Sir Henry."

King Reynold grew even paler at the mention of the traitor's name which Robin took as an admission of guilt. Grimstaff Castle's king quickly regained his composure. "It does not speak well for his liege lord if a knight's loyalty could be so easily turned. No wonder Your Majesty chose not to accept the honor we sought to pay."

"Honor is not all Your Majesty should pay us. There is the matter of the fee for the dragon slaying."

Reynold tipped up his chin and shook his head. "A dragon? We have no dragons here."

"Indeed you do not because we killed it for you. For a handsome commission. Which we were never paid." Robin pointed up at the triple skull that hung on the castle wall, more menacing than even the most artfully crafted gargoyle. "How came you by that?"

Reynold shrugged and said, "Magic. How regrettable that Your Majesty came all this way but now you must go." He turned on his heels.

"Magic?" Robin said. The dark arts made Robin fearful as little else could. He hoped King Reynold would be equally intimidated. "We'll show you magic." Robin pulled his sword, turned to his men, and nodded. They all lifted their standards high in the air in a prearranged signal. The woods boomed, rattled, and clanked. Reynold spun about.

Fearing attack, Reynold's guards closed ranks to protect their king. Above, captains shouted instructions to the soldiers to be ready to fire.

One well-aimed arrow sailed towards the castle. It landed in the moat just in front of the gatehouse. Reynold guffawed. "Is that the best your archers can do?" His laughter died when flames sprouted on the surface of the moat. "What? The water is burning? How can that be?"

"Magic." With his sword Robin signaled for two more arrows. They joined the first, igniting on impact and creating a floating bonfire.

"Guards," Reynold roared. Men with buckets raced out from the gatehouse, scooped water from the moat, and hurled it on the flames which served only to spread the cloying flammable liquid. The puddle of fire widened.

"Put it out," Reynold hollered, but the more water that his men poured on the fire the wider it got.

"It can't be quenched," cried his soldier.

Robin cackled. "Magic."

Reynold sputtered. "What have you wrought? You are the sorcerer we took you for. How else could you have survived despite the impediments we put in your way?"

Ah hah, at last. An admission of guilt.

"We demand that you reverse this evil spell immediately."

"We can," Robin replied. "We have magic powder that can counteract it." At his signal, one of his soldiers hastened to bring Robin a bucket of sand wrapped in an ornate cloth embroidered with fanciful symbols. Robin closed his eyes and murmured some random syllables as if reciting an incantation. Then he threw handfuls of sand on the fire putting out some but not all of the flames. "We can extinguish the rest if Your Majesty will give us satisfaction. If not, we will turn your moat into a flaming river and set the entire castle on fire."

CHAPTER THIRTY-ONE

It took several fanfares for the herald to get the attention of the guests in Bell Castle's great hall, but at last the tumult died down enough that Robin thought it likely he would be heard. He welcomed and thanked his guests. "Tonight we celebrate the heroism and sacrifices made on behalf of the kingdom. Tonight we usher in a bright future, a new era of peace and prosperity."

Robin felt a celebration banquet was essential to recognize his vassals' service and to restore the people's confidence in the kingdom. The Chalklands' subjects and resources had been taxed to the limit to support the battles at Bell Castle and Windbrook, and even the Palisades had been stripped bare by Ulric's efforts to supply his army. The ransom that Robin had coerced from King Reynold, however, had gone far to replenish the royal treasury. Reparations had been made and mercenaries paid.

"It is fitting that we celebrate on this day, the feast of Saint George, a man of valor," Robin said. "A soldier so highly regarded by his Roman emperor that he was named military tribune, Saint George nevertheless gave his life rather than betray his belief in God.

"Like Saint George, every one of our fighting men from infantryman to commander to knight proved to be a gallant fighter. And like Saint George, some of them gave their life because they believed in what they were fighting for. All of us in the kingdom are beneficiaries of that loyalty."

The guests turned to each other and bowed, curtsied, shook hands, knocked fists, and clapped each other on the back.

"Like a tumor, King Ulric's greed grew silently and like a tumor it would have grown until it overtook us. That tumor has been excised. Now we can apply our energies to healing the wound it left. We know that it is not easy to embrace as brothers men we have faced on the battlefield, but we must put aside our enmities. To nurture a grudge would be like picking at a scab. The wound will never heal. We should know." Robin pulled back his sleeve to show the scar the arrow had left. It had been difficult to resist scratching as the new skin knit together.

Those close enough to hear and see Robin's demonstration chuckled.

"The people of the Palisades are part of the Kingdom of the Chalklands now. Thus we wish not only to thank our faithful lords and all the soldiers of the Chalklands for their service, but to welcome liege lords from the Palisades. We look forward to what we can accomplish together."

He looked to where men who had been Ulric's vassals congregated in one corner and was pleased to see some of his subjects approach them, hands held out in greeting. The former adversaries had all accepted his invitation to the feast, each eager no doubt to ply his petition to be tenant-in-chief of the Fortress at the Palisades. There was no question one was needed and Robin was hard-pressed to decide whom to name. All his knights had their own domains and even Dame Deidre had Windbrook to manage.

Brother Leo delivered the invocation and then presented another hero, Brother Thaddeus, so newly arrived from his own perilous service in faraway lands that Robin had been able to do little more than embrace his son in tearful welcome.

Conrad kept his remarks brief, telling the assembly that he was blessed to have had the opportunity to use his skills on behalf of those who wished only to worship. "They journeyed far in search of a spiritual experience but you can achieve an equally rich communion with our Lord without ever leaving the Chalklands. Now that we are home, we are eager to do whatever we can to guide you and support you as you strive to draw close to God."

Conrad's words were received with a momentary respectful and thoughtful silence.

Poets, troubadours, and raconteurs then launched the entertainment, performing original works that Robin had commissioned to laud acts of heroism and sacrifice as well as classics to inspire brotherhood and fealty.

From his seat at the king's table, Robin regarded the great hall and felt not the swelling pride of the victor but rather something more like serenity as if a major endeavor had been brought to a pleasing conclusion. He looked about and wondered from whence came that sensation of closure. The work of restoring Bell Castle and unifying the kingdom had hardly begun. True, he was once again home and reunited with both his sons, but the matter of succession was still an open question. Perhaps it was having obtained redress from his enemies that gave rise to the sense of satisfaction. Robin grinned at the thought of his old sword and crown recovered from King Reynold, now displayed with pride in the gallery overlooking the hall.

Seated at his side, Conrad appeared changed by his time with the Guardian Angels. Rarely jolly or playful even as a child he had been cerebral, lost in his own thoughts much of the time. Now he seemed more grounded, as if tempered by the experience.

"We are pleased that you have returned to Bell Castle," Robin told him, "and we believe so is your flock."

"Flock." Conrad's mouth twitched in a small smile. "We hadn't thought of them as such."

"Clearly the abbot sees you as a leader."

"Not the sort of leadership role that Your Majesty intended for us."

Robin shrugged. "So be it."

Conrad nodded. "Thank you." He looked about the great hall. "It was quite appropriate to dedicate this celebration to

Saint George," he said. "We imagine that he is a favorite of yours, being a fellow dragon slayer."

"He was?" This was news to Robin. He had meant only to encourage his soldiers with the example of a man so highly regarded for his fighting skills that a heathen ruler elevated him to a position of great responsibility and glory.

"Apparently, or so it's told along the pilgrims' route. It is said that there was a well in an ancient pagan city guarded by a dragon. To get water, the people had to lure the dragon away. Usually a sheep would work as bait but one day there were no sheep to be found. The people needed water and so they decided to offer up a maiden, a princess. Saint George happened upon this travesty. Calling on God to protect him, he killed the dragon and the princess was spared. The people were so impressed that they too turned to God."

Conrad's expression was serious and Robin tried not to grin, though he found the tale delightful.

"The dragon, of course, was Satan," Conrad said.

"Yes, yes, of course," Robin murmured but Bell Castle's great hall had vanished. Once again he was flailing through a wood in a distant land, racing to rescue not a princess but an empress who was threatened by a dragon.

"Not a dragon, a wyvern," Empress Alexandra had later insisted, as if that distinction would have made a difference had Robin not arrived in time to slay the beast.

"Your Majesty finds that amusing?" Conrad said.

"No, not at all," Robin stammered. He would have to excuse himself before he broke out in uncontrollable smiles at the recollection of his sojourn at the empress's Sea Gate Fortress. Why was he thinking about that now?

A group of guests eager to hear firsthand tales of battles fought and won in distant lands tugged Conrad away, freeing Robin to return to his recollections. He picked at the delicacies filling the table before him, but his mind's eye saw the fresh fish and fruit from another banquet, one that had been held in his honor, though his accomplishment then paled in comparison with his recent victories. He could almost smell the salt of Sea

Gate's ocean air, feel the humid breeze on his neck, and hear Alexandra's laughter.

Lady Alice's daughter Joy approached the table. She congratulated Robin on his military successes then lingered as if waiting for something, to be asked to sit or to dance, perhaps. Reluctant to break the enchantment of his reminiscences, Robin simply smiled. With a crestfallen expression, Joy curtsied and departed.

Robin hastened to return to his memories of Sea Gate Fortress.

"Your Majesty?"

Startled from his reverie, Robin looked up. "It would appear from your grin that you are enjoying the feast, Sire," said Lady Alice.

Robin rose. "We are. And you and yours?"

"Very much." Alice looked toward the dance floor.

Joy appeared to have recovered from any disappointment she may have felt at Robin's lack of interest. Apparently another guest had captured her attention. Robin spied her dancing with Terrowin, the advocate, and found that highly appropriate.

"Please, join us," he said to Lady Alice. "Were it not for the reinforcements that you and Lord Ferree sent we might not be having this celebration."

Lady Alice curtsied and took the seat that Robin offered. "I doubt that. You would have found another way to succeed, my lord. However we are honored to have Your Majesty think that we were instrumental in the victory."

"And we are grateful that you could safeguard Prince Zachary."

Lady Alice looked across the room where Princess Dale, not Prince Zachary, and Jewel were engaged in conversation with other guests. "Princess Dale, you mean, Sire?"

Apparently so. Since his return from Dulcimer, Zachary had continued to dress in women's clothing. He dutifully came to court. Zachary's complaint that he was shunned and ridiculed haunted Robin and he tried to involve him in the proceedings, but Robin's vassals and counselors avoided the prince in female garb. Robin found Zachary's advice and observations insightful and regretted that during the audiences he was never consulted. Knowing how important it was to Zachary, Robin tried to get his advisors to seek Zachary's opinions, to little avail. It was as Robin had warned Zachary: a female who wished to rule had to overcome much distrust and resentment from those who felt it simply wasn't a woman's place.

Robin wondered how Empress Alexandra had managed to counter that opposition to achieve the success that she enjoyed. A woman alone, she ruled an extensive realm. Was there something he could learn from her example that would be useful to Zachary?

At the moment, Bell Castle's great hall was filled with merriment and gaiety but not long ago it had been at the heart of fierce battle. Zachary's ambitions and his commitment to his Princess Dale identity had almost turned the tide in favor of Robin's foe. Zachary's issues were Robin's and he could ignore them only at the price of his hard-won victory.

"Your Majesty recalls that when we were here for the Saint Valentine's Tournament, Dale and Jewel quickly forged a friendship."

Robin recalled he had been curious as to just what was going on between the two, even imagining some deadly conspiracy.

"During the sojourn with us at White Castle, that friendship grew. They are quite fond of each other." Lady Alice smiled.

Had a sorcerer stolen Robin's voice he could not have been struck more mute. Robin didn't know what to make of it. Were his son and Lady Alice's daughter close in the way of a man and woman? When Prince Zachary and Jewel met at the tournament, he had hoped for just such a coupling, had envisioned it resulting in an heir, but a relationship between Princess Dale and Jewel? To what would that give birth? "How do you feel about that?"

Though Lady Alice smiled, her eyes spoke of worry. "She is our daughter whom we love. Whom we will always love. Were she to prove to be immoral or evil we would disapprove of course, but we would never stop caring and hoping for the best for her.

"She is also Jewel, a grown woman. We could try to tell her what to do. Forbid her from disobeying. Lock her in a tower like the wealthy pagan did his daughter, Saint Barbara, for all the good that did him."

It hadn't done Robin much good either, to restrict Princess Dale to a bedchamber in the keep.

"Better, perhaps, to simply accept it even if we can't fully understand it, especially if there is nothing we can do to change it." Lady Alice shrugged. "At least then we can continue as a family."

From the dance floor, Lord Ferree beckoned his wife to join him and with a curtsy, Lady Alice excused herself.

Alone again at the king's table, Robin toyed with the serving pieces at his place: a spoon, a knife, and something he called a bread saw. It was a utensil he had created during his time laboring in a forge. His bread saws had proven useful and popular, but Sea Gate Fortress had nothing like them. Diners there had to shred their bread into ragged pieces with their fingers instead of making neat even slices with his small tooth-edged knives. Had he access to a forge then, he would have made a supply of them for the empress and her guests.

He had also wanted to make a pair of eyeglasses for Alexandra's cartographer. James was a brilliant man but always misplaced his reading stones. During Robin's time as a smith's apprentice, he engineered a frame that would hold the magnifying stones before the eyes, hooking around the earlobes rather than sitting on and pinching the bridge of the nose. It would make a fine gift for James who had helped a lost king to find the Chalklands.

As if lifted away from the hall by a sudden guest of wind, Robin felt carried off on another wave of memories.

Days as a deckhand on a cargo ship. The work had been hard and nearly ceaseless but there were idle moments when he delighted in the unique experience of being on the ocean. The limitless expanse of sky and sea was intimidating yet liberating. The constant movement of wind and water reminded him that the Earth was a live thing. The ocean's strange fish and fowl were like magical creatures come to life.

At the island fortress of Sea Gate, people made their home right up against the sea. The people there lived out their lives much as did those in the Chalklands: attending to their responsibilities, caring for those who depended on them, dealing with misfortunes, and reveling in moments of joy. Yet life at Sea Gate Fortress was also touched with charm. Ocean breezes wafted through the windows and set draperies fluttering. In quiet moments there he could hear the cry of sea birds and the crash of the surf. The moist salt-scented air made fabrics always soft, limp, and cool to the touch, almost damp. It put a curl in his hair and the hair of the woman who ruled over that domain. Alexandra, the Empress of Sea Gate Fortress. Robin could picture her now striding barefoot along the shore, her hair streaming from her head, her skirts swirling around her ankles like waves.

The empress had asked him to stay, to serve by her side as consort. She sought to expand her empire with his help but then he had no money, no resources to offer, only dreams and ambitions. He had turned his back on Sea Gate Fortress and set out to find his lost kingdom in the Chalklands. Had he been asked "why?" he could not have said. Perhaps on some level he understood that had he stayed at Sea Gate it would be as a paler version of his true self, one that would grow fainter with each passing day until he was simply a shadow trailing Alexandra, the Empress.

He pictured himself passing through the fortress gates now not as Robin, a damaged and ruined man, but as King Bewilliam astride the noblest of Bell Castle's destriers, attired in his finest robes, and wearing his most ornate crown. Accompanied by soldiers and servants, he would arrive with carts laden with gifts of gold, jewelry, furs, and fine fabrics. Yes, he would bring his impressive credentials, riches, and power. Just the thought of it made Robin sit taller.

He imagined the expression on Alexandra's face, how her eyes would widen in admiration, her lips part with surprise and delight.

Or would they? He recalled the days and nights spent at Sea Gate Fortress. He wasn't a king then, just a penniless vagabond, yet somehow he had earned her respect, trust, even her affection not by winning battles, not by virtue of pedigree or possessions, but simply by being himself.

How would she greet him if he appeared not as Robin but as King Bewilliam?

There was only one way to find out.

ABOUT THE AUTHOR

Devorah Fox is the author of *The Lost King, The King's Ransom,* and *The King's Redress* in *The Bewildering Adventures of King Bewilliam* literary fantasy series and co-author with Jed Donellie of the contemporary thriller, *Naked Came the Sharks.* Publisher and editor of the *BUMPERTOBUMPER®* books for commercial motor vehicle drivers, she is developer of the *Easy CDL* test prep apps for the iPhone and iPad. Born in Brooklyn, New York, she now lives in The Barefoot Palace in Port Aransas on the Texas Gulf Coast where she writes the "Dee-Scoveries" blog at http://devorahfox.com.

Connect online:
Email: devorahfox@aol.com
Facebook: https://facebook.com/DevorahFoxAuthor
Twitter: @devorah_fox
Smashwords:
https://www.smashwords.com/profile/view/mbapub.

www.ingramcontent.com/pod-product-compliance
Lightning Source LLC
Chambersburg PA
CBHW072210170626
46813CB00003B/875